The bloggers PIECES

www.transworldbooks.co.uk

By Cassia Leo

The Shattered Hearts series
RELENTLESS
PIECES OF YOU
BRING ME HOME

PIECES OF YOU

Shattered Hearts Book 2

Cassia Leo

CORGI BOOKS

TRANSWORLD PUBLISHERS
61–63 Uxbridge Road, London W5 5SA
www.transworldbooks.co.uk

Transworld is part of the Penguin Random House group of companies
whose addresses can be found at global.penguinrandomhouse.com

Penguin
Random House
UK

First published in Great Britain in 2013
by Transworld Digital
an imprint of Transworld Publishers
Corgi edition published 2015

A CIP catalogue record for this book
is available from the British Library.

ISBN 9780552170734

Typeset in 12/15pt Adobe Caslon by Kestrel Data, Exeter, Devon.

Penguin Random House is committed to a sustainable future for
our business, our readers and our planet. This book is made from
Forest Stewardship Council® certified paper.

MIX
Paper from
responsible sources
FSC® C018179

Printed and bound in Great Britain by Clays Ltd, St Ives plc

3 5 7 9 10 8 6 4 2

Table of Contents

Chapter One

Chris

The smell of sweaty bodies wafts toward the stage on a steamy puff of air as I pull out the last licks on 'Relentless'. The crowd goes wild. The girls in the front row, their eyes wild, clawing at the stage trying to reach my feet. I stare at them, mesmerized. All I can think is that Claire used to want me like that. At one time, Claire would have crawled across a desert for me.

Tristan shakes my arm to break my trance. I force a smile for the crowd. Take a bow and say my goodbyes to the good people of Charlotte, North Carolina.

We hop into Tristan's car after the show and head to Cary to christen his new house with some debauchery. I'm not in the mood to hang out tonight, but I'm also not in the mood to be alone. And I can't call Claire. It's almost midnight on a Thursday. She'll be asleep or studying.

And she has a boyfriend.

I chuckle out loud at this thought Tristan looks at me as he drives down I-85. 'What the fuck are you laughing at?'

'Nothing.'

'You're cracking up, man. You need to get your head out of Claire's ass and have some fun tonight.'

'What I need is to stop taking advice from you.'

The past year without Claire is almost a blur. Just a mess of images, going from one show to the next, one hotel to the next. one drink to the next, one girl to the next. I don't remember much of it.

What I do remember is being utterly and completely miserable. It's just not fucking fair. I set off to Los Angeles to live the dream and I lose the love of my life, my dog dies, and now I've lost my daughter. Worst fucking year of my life. This isn't at all what I pictured when I decided to take that record deal.

When I let Claire convince me to take that record deal.

I never wanted to leave Claire. I knew it wouldn't end well. But I've always been a complete sucker for her. I've always done everything with the intent of making her happy.

For a year, I've replayed our last conversation a million times in my head.

'Stop calling me. Please.'

'Claire.'

'Stop saying my name. I have to go.'

Then dead silence. For a whole year.

But I did just as she asked. I stopped calling. And I stopped saying her name. For a couple of months. Until I couldn't do it any more and I called her, only to find her phone was disconnected and she wasn't talking to my mom any more. Just like that. She was gone.

It made no sense to me then, but now I know why she did it. *Fuck.* As much as it hurts and pisses me off, I even understand it.

Tristan changes lanes to head for the 421 interchange, but I quickly protest.

'Stay on I-85. You'll get there faster.'

He shakes his head because he knows I'm just torturing myself. If we say on I-85 we'll have to drive through Chapel Hill. I'll see all the street names I haven't seen in more than a year. Places where Claire and I shared a million memories during her freshman year at UNC.

One thing I can say for Tristan, he'ds good at keeping quiet when it's necessary. Seventy silent minutes later, we pull into the curved driveway of Tristan's mini-mansion in Cary. Even with Tristan speeding down I-85, Jake and Rachel beat us here. Rachel drives like a crazy person.

'Well, look who woke up and decided to join us,' Rachel remarks as I climb the steps to the front door. Her eyes are wide and her mouth hangs open, a bad zombie-like imitation of me at the end of the show tonight.

'Fuck off. Don't make me do my impression of Psycho Rachel.'

She rolls her eyes at me as if she's not afraid, but this shuts her up. She doesn't want anyone to remember the crazy way she behaved last year when she and Jake broke up for a few months. It's difficult not to go a little crazy when you realize you've lost the one thing you're living for.

Thirty minutes later, the house is crawling with at least forty people, most of whom I've never seen in my life. Tristan and I switch roles for the night and I take his usual spot on the corner of the sofa, sipping a Miller Lite, while he serves drinks and chats up his audience from the breakfast bar in the kitchen. Every time I look up, I catch some girl I've never met staring at me. It's only a matter of time before one of them approaches me to tries to sit next to me and spark up a conversation.

As expected, a skinny blonde with a red bandana tied around her head as headband and cutoff jean shorts sits next to me. Her red lipstick has left a perfect half-moon mark on the martini glass she's clutching in her left hand. She smiles at me, but I don't return the smile. Instead, I look out across the living room and dining area to the kitchen where Tristan is pouring some vodka into a shot glass.

'Are you okay?' the girl asks in a voice that reminds me a little of my mom's. A soft, southern lilt that you can tell she's trying to hide.

I glance at her again and she's wearing a look of great concern that makes me a little sick to my stomach. 'I'm fine. Thanks.'

Tristan downs the shot he just poured and slams the shot glass down on the counter. I take a long swig of beer, as if this will help me keep up.

'You rocked the show tonight,' the blonde continues. 'I'm Charlie.'

I nod, but I can't bring myself to say, *Nice to meet you.* It would just be too phony. And I really want this girl to get the hint. She's not hooking up with me tonight, or ever.

'Do you live here with Tristan?' she asks. 'I'll bet you two have a lot of fun here. Even if it is pretty quiet.'

I turn to look at her and she smiles now that she has my full attention. 'Charlie?'

'Yes?'

'I'd really like it if you could leave me alone right now.'

She narrows her eyes at me. 'I was just trying to talk to you. You don't have to be a prick about it.'

'I believe I was pretty polite. But I can be rude if you'd like.'

She rolls her eyes as she stands up and heads for the breakfast bar. I almost breathe a sigh of relief before another girl heads in my direction, as if she was just waiting for Charlie to leave so she could pounce on me. I let out a sigh of exasperation instead.

'Was that your girlfriend?' asks the girl with the dark hair that falls in waves over her fake boobs.

'No, my girlfriend isn't here tonight,' I reply.

She looks stricken. 'Oh, you're with that Dakota girl, right?'

11

I grit my teeth at the mention of Dakota Simpson; the Disney star I fucked twice ande almost had to get a restraining order to get her to stop calling me and showing up at my concerts.

'No, I'm not with her.'

'Oh. I head she's all coked-up anyway.'

She's not, but I don't bother correcting her. I don't need to defend Dakota from untrue rumors. That's a sure way to perpetuate the rumors about us being together.

The girl with the boobs looks around awkwardly as she realizes she's getting nowhere with me. 'Well, nice meeting you.'

She shoots up from the sofa and heads toward the backyard patio where she came from. I feel a twinge of guilt for shooting down these girls, but I'm not interested in any easy fuck tonight.

I pull my phone out of my pocket and open up the picture I have set as my new background wallpaper. My heart aches just looking at it. I take another long pull on my beer, then I place the empty bottle on the coffee table.

Abigail is lying peacefully on a fluffy, cream-coloured blanket; an angel I never knew I had until three weeks ago. I clench my teeth to hold back the flood of emotions I'm feeling: the rage from being kept in the dark; the pain from loosing everything important to me; and the fear that I may never get it back.

Fuck that. I'm getting Claire back if it's the last fucking thing I do.

Chapter Two

Adam

I step onto the small stage constructed in the sand and, though I can't stop grinning, the only thing on my mind is Claire and how I wish she were here to see this. Hank Langley hands me the third-place trophy and pulls me into a sloppy one-armed hug. Hank is the promoter for the competition. We've stayed in touch since I quit surfing and he's the only reason I made it onto the roster for this event.

As soon as we arrive at the hotel, the mini-bar is ransacked and champagne is ordered from room service. I grab my phone from my backpack and sneak off to the bathroom to call Claire.

I open the bathroom door and Paul Leyva is boning some chick on the counter. The same Paul Leyva who was ranked fourth in the world on the ASP world rankings last year. The chick makes eye contact with me and I slam the door shut before I make my way into the hotel corridor. The scroll pattern on the carpet makes me think of the curtains in my dad's study. He doesn't know where I am this weekend. If he knew I'm competing again he'd tell me to give it up. Twenty-two is too old to start competing again. What he doesn't know is that I'm doing this as much for Claire as I am for myself.

I sink down onto the carpet next to the ice machine and dial her number. She picks up halfway through the first ring.

'Hey.'

Her voice is soft yet eager and fills me with relief.

'Hey, baby. What are you doing?'

I hear a rustling on the other end and I imagine she's putting down a book or a pile of notes.

'Studying. I have a statistics test on Monday. Where are you?'

'I'm at the hotel. We just got back. I came in third.'

She pauses for a moment. 'I'm so proud of you. I knew you'd do well.'

'I'll be there in six days. You can congratulate me then.'

There are so many things I want to ask her. She told me last night that her ex would be dropping off some more pictures today. I want to know everything, but I don't want to pry. I don't want to push her away, but the long pause on the other end concerns me.

'I don't know if I can wait six days,' she finally says.

'I wish I was there with you to rub your sore muscles and fall asleep in your arms.'

'I wish you were here, too. I miss the fuck out of you. Are you lying down?'

She giggles because she thinks I'm trying to initiate phone sex.

'I just want to picture you,' I insist. 'I'm in the middle of the hotel corridor. I'm not going to jerk off out here.'

'Yes, I'm lying down.'

'What are you wearing?'

'I'm wearing the Sugar shirt you bought for me.'

'Is that it?'

'And my panties.'

'Take them off.' She pauses, but I hear her breathing quicken. 'Please.' The movement on the other end gets me excited. 'Claire?'

'Adam?'

'When was the last time I touched you?'

'Six days ago.'

'When was the last time you touched yourself?'

She giggles again and I wait for her to get over her embarrassment and answer. 'When you called me this morning.'

I don't know why I torture myself this way when there's a roomful of girls down the hall who'd get on their knees for me in a heartbeat. Maybe I just need to prove to myself that I've changed.

'I love you, Claire.'

'I know.'

'You know I would never hurt you.'

'I know. Are you okay?'

I want to tell her how much it scares me that she's been seeing Chris while we're apart. I want to tell her how much it kills me that he can show up at her dorm or outside her classroom anytime he likes. But she doesn't want to hear that shit.

'Yeah, I'm just tired. I'll let you go so you can get your homework done, but I want you to think of me tonight . . . when you touch yourself.'

'I wouldn't think of anyone else.'

'I can't hide anything from you, can I?'

'Adam, I love you. I'll wait six days or six years. Whatever it takes. Nothing and no one else matters.'

This isn't true. There is one other person who matters as much, or more, to Claire than I do. And I can't even be upset about it because that's exactly as it should be. But that doesn't change the fact that being her number two worries the hell out of me.

'Tuck yourself in tight. Goodnight, baby.'

'Goodnight.'

I lean forward to slide the phone into the back pocket of my shorts then sit back against the wall and stare at the framed picture of a floral still life on the wall in front of me. If I go back to the room, I'll probably get so drunk or high I won't remember what I did in the morning. But I can't stay out here. Maybe I should just take a taxi to the airport and catch the next flight to Raleigh to surprise Claire.

Fuck that. That's a desperate move. I'm not desperate.

I trudge back to the room, resigned to lay off the booze and keep my head clear so I don't fuck up. When I walk through the door, I'm smacked in the face with the aroma of some good smoke. I step inside the hazy hotel room and spot Yuri Takahashi, number twenty-six in the world and one of my best friends, sitting at a table near the window toking it up, smoke curling from the small pipe in his hand.

A hand clasps the back of my neck and I can tell by the size and the way it grips me softly that it's not one of the guys. I turn around and the girl I just saw getting boned by Paul is giving me a *come-fuck-me* look. Her dark hair is tousled and her black eye makeup is smeared across her left temple. I'm surprised I notice these details since she's standing before me topless, wearing only a short skirt.

'Not gonna happen,' I say, pushing her hand off my neck.

She curls her lip in disgust. 'What? Are you gay?'

I shake my head as I turn my back on her and make my way toward Yuri.

'Hey, it's the fucking comeback kid,' Yuri says when he sees me.

He grins broadly as he passes me a freshly packed bowl and a lighter. I think of Claire and I almost hand it back to him, but I need to hide inside myself tonight. I bring the pipe to my lips and suck in as I hold the lighter's flame to the bowl. It's been more than a week

17

since I've toked so the hot smoke burns my throat and stings my lungs. I hold in the smoke as I pass the pipe back to Yuri.

He shakes his head. 'That's your bowl, bro. Finish it.'

I let the smoke out of my lungs and finish off the bowl. I hand the pipe to Yuri and he taps the ash out into an ashtray before he packs it again. The music coming from the iPod clock radio on the nightstand gets inside my head. I lean back in my chair and close my eyes as I lose myself in the music.

The sounds of giggles and whispers can barely be heard over the song. I don't know what's going on until I feel someone's hand in my crotch. I open my eyes and the topless girl is back and she's trying to undo the button on my shorts.

I push her hands away and she laughs. She's fucked up. So am I. But I'm not stupid.

I stand up and she reaches for my shorts again. 'Fuck off,' I mutter as I step around her and make my way out into the corridor again.

I stand there for a minute, unsure of what the fuck I'm doing. I'm fucked up and my mind keeps circling back to the same thoughts over and over again. I think of texting Claire, but she needs to study. Then I think of going back inside, but I'm too stoned to deal with the temptation. I need to get out of this hotel. Fuck the backpack. I have my wallet and my phone. That's all I need.

I make it down to the lobby and jump into the first taxi I find outside the hotel. 'Orlando International.'

The cabbie looks at me and I wonder if I look as stoned as I feel. Something about my appearance makes him skeptical and he appears about ready to kick me out of the cab, but he relents and pulls away from the hotel entrance.

I don't know what the fuck I'm doing. I'm running; that's what I'm doing. I don't trust myself.

The taxi pulls onto the highway and I realize I also left my trophy in the hotel room. I can call the front desk and ask them to ship it to me tomorrow, if it's still there.

When we reach the airport, I'm a bit more sober – at least, I think I am. I hand the driver a wad of cash and make my way to the first airline check-in counter I find. The girl behind the counter looks bored as she chats with a burly guy in a security uniform. I glance at her nametag: Wanda.

'Can I help you, sir?' Wanda asks.

I blink a few times thinking this might sober me up a little more. 'When's the next flight to Raleigh?'

Chapter Three

Claire

I never wanted to be like my mother. And for a brief moment in time I thought I had escaped that fate. But life has a lovely way of reminding you that you are no better than anyone else – even a dead heroin addict.

It wasn't until three weeks ago I finally understood that being like my mother isn't such a bad thing. She may have brutally removed herself from my life when I was only seven years old, but she left behind the foundation for me to have a better life than her own. She taught me how to keep myself safe, which really came in handy as I was shuffled from one foster home to the next for eight years after her death. And, of course, there's the enormous trust fund she left me – though I have no interest in ever claiming a dime of that money.

So I guess things could be worse, but it's hard to

imagine how as I lie here on the twin bed in my dorm doing statistics homework on a Saturday evening while my boyfriend is surfing in Florida. Of course, judging by the tone of the conversation we just had, it doesn't seem like Adam is really enjoying his trip. Just remembering his words and the sound of his voice makes my stomach stir.

I'll be there in six days. You can congratulate me then.

His voice was husky with exhaustion and it only makes me miss him more. I want to be there with him in Florida. Instead, I'm stuck in my dorm playing catch-up. This is the price I pay for taking my sophomore year off from UNC.

I glance at the alarm clock on the nightstand between my and Senia's beds. She should be back from hanging out with Eddie in a couple of hours. The sight of the stack of photos on the nightstand makes my chest ache.

Chris came over this morning to drop off some pictures of Abigail on his way to the airport. He could have emailed them to me, but he insisted on bringing the actual photos in case I wanted to put them in a frame or an album. That's bullshit. He's trying to get under my skin. He wants me to feel comfortable around him again.

When he left, I laid the photos facedown on the nightstand so I wouldn't feel that longing every time I glance at my alarm clock and see my daughter's face. But seeing the pictures turned facedown is just as jarring. It fills me with a stinging guilt that I'm certain has become part of my DNA by now.

Against my better judgment, I lift the stack of photos off the nightstand and lie back on my pillow. The first picture is of Abigail – I don't even know her last name yet – lying on someone's bed and smiling at something above her; something out of frame. I can't help but refer to her as Abigail Knight in my mind. She's a piece of Chris, and one look at her soft blonde hair and pouty lips and it's apparent that she's a piece of me. But neither of those pieces belongs to us.

The process of an open adoption is much less complicated than I thought it would be. The only thing that needs to be hashed out is the actual agreement. Abigail's adoptive parents have verbally agreed to send us pictures and emails occasionally. We get to know her. They're just not sure whether they want Abigail to know us.

The second photo is a close-up and she has Chris's dark eyes. I trace the curve of her eyelid and I can see the way it turns down slightly at the corner, just like Chris's.

My phone buzzes as it vibrates on the nightstand. I lay the photos on the nightstand and pick up the phone, hoping it's Adam with a joke text to pull me out of this funk. It's Chris.

Chris: Just landed in London. I got a voicemail from Tasha. They want to meet us on Tuesday. I'll be back by then.

22

Tasha Singer is the lawyer Chris hired to handle the adoption. I think it's funny that her last name is Singer. Chris thinks I'll find her name less funny when I finally meet her. He claims she's the hottest thirty-two-year-old he's ever met. He thinks this stuff makes me jealous, but it doesn't.

I love Chris. Nothing will ever change that. But it's not the same love we shared a year ago. It's the kind of love shared between friends who know each other's deepest secrets. The kind of love shared between friends who've forgiven each other's worst sins.

Me: Okay. I have class from 7–2. Will be in my dorm by 3.

Chris: I'll pick you up outside your class at 2.

Me: Fine.

Chris: Don't take that tone with me. Don't forget I still remember all your most ticklish spots.

Me: Stop being a jerk. And stop texting me. I'm trying to study.

Chris: Goodnight, Claire-bear.

I don't respond. Why would I respond to that? He's baiting me.

I finish my homework and start reading the text for my Family and Society class. This has got to be the worst class I can possibly be taking right now, but it's pretty much required if I have any hope of being a superstar social worker.

23

I open *Public and Private Families* by Andrew Cherlin and I've only read three pages when the dormitory door flies open and Senia charges inside, her dark waves flying. She tosses her purse onto the desk and collapses facedown onto her bed. Her skirt flies up and her panties are showing, but she doesn't seem to care as she buries her face in the pillow.

'What's wrong?' I ask as I set down the textbook and sit up.

'Ugh!' she groans. 'I'm so stupid!'

Even though the pillow muffles her voice, I can still hear the strangled sound in her scream. She's crying.

I get up from my bed and take a seat on the edge of her mattress. I rub her back and she mashes her face even harder into the pillow.

'What happened?'

She shakes her head then flips over onto her back. 'He's been fucking someone else, that's what happened.'

'Eddie?'

'Don't say his name. He disgusts me.'

Senia and Eddie have been together for almost seven months now, but I never would have suspected Eddie for a cheater. He's always been insanely jealous and possessive. I always assumed Senia would be the one to dump Eddie once she got bored of his clinginess.

'How do you know he's been . . . ?'

'I found the fucking text messages. They're already exchanging *I love yous*!'

24

She covers her face with her hands and my heart breaks for her. Senia has never cried over a guy in all the time I've known her. Even when she was a shy freshman two years ago, she kept her head about her when it came to relationships. I've always admired her ability to compartmentalize her emotional life. Her relationships never affect her studies and school never affects her social life. I'm the one who quit school when my personal life became too much for me to handle. She's always kept it together. It's not like her to fall apart like this.

Then I think of what she just said. 'What text messages?'

'I was trying to look up times for that new Jack Black movie and a text came in. I can't even tell you what it said. It's gross. He's a fucking pig.'

My mind instantly flashes to the text Chris just sent me. *Goodnight, Claire-bear.* Or the one about him knowing my ticklish spots. Would Adam flip out if he saw those?

I spring up from the mattress and grab my phone off my bed. It takes a while to scroll all the way to the bottom of the list of texts I've been exchanging with Chris, mostly about adoption stuff, but there are some texts from him that could be construed as flirty.

'What are you doing?' Senia mutters.

'Trying not to be a fucking pig.'

'Are you cheating on Adam?'

'What? Hell, no. I just want to make sure there's

25

nothing remotely incriminating on my phone. Chris is trying to get under my skin.'

Senia sits up and cocks one of her perfect eyebrows. 'Are you really that afraid of Adam's jealousy?'

'I'm not afraid. I'm trying to avoid misunderstandings.'

She shakes her head before she lies back down on her stomach with her head at the foot of the bed. 'I need to get drunk tonight.'

I look up from the screen of my iPhone, which I will probably have to trade in soon because I can't afford the data plan without my job at the café.

'I'll be your designated driver.'

'We don't have to drive. We can take a cab. Please drink with me tonight.' I stare at her for a moment until her shoulders slump. 'I was only kidding. You can drive.'

We decide to go to an Irish pub near campus. Eddie never wanted to take Senia to this pub, so we're certain we won't run into him here. She's lucky she and Eddie don't have any classes together this year, especially considering they're both chemistry majors.

Not sharing any classes together was a major selling point when Senia was considering whether to take their relationship to the next level after the first few dates. But Eddie's intensity was also a huge turn-on for her. He matched her intensity and wits, ounce for ounce. I was so certain that Eddie and Senia would

26

one day get married. They fought a lot, but it seemed he couldn't get enough of her feisty attitude or five-foot-ten Amazonian body.

But appearances can be deceiving.

We enter the pub and I'm hit with the stench of beer and testosterone. Social Distortion is blaring and people are yelling to be heard over the music and each other. Apparently, the hostesses don't work Saturday nights. People just come in and sit or stand wherever they choose. The booths and tables are all full. There's a small area near the back of the pub, about the size of my twin bed, where people are thrashing to the music. It's way too bright in here for this place to have a night-club feel, but the atmosphere is total chaos.

I've been to plenty of clubs and parties with Senia, but I have a bad feeling about this place.

Senia leans over the bar to order her first drink – a gin and tonic with a lime twist – and I roll my eyes as some neck-beard ogles her ass. Senia has never had a problem attracting guys. Her model-perfect features and athletic body that she spends hours sculpting at the gym are really just bonuses. She oozes sexuality while I probably ooze 'too much subtextuality.'

With her drink in hand, her eyes scan the crowded bar. 'Eddie said this pub was on the corner of Drunk and Loser. I'd say it's on the corner of Getting Over and Your Ex.'

'I think your jokes are becoming as bad as Adam's.'

'That's impossible. Adam's cheese-level is off the

27

charts.' She grimaces as if she's in pain. 'You have such a cool boyfriend. Why did I get the cheating douche-nozzle? Do I deserve this?'

Oh, no. She hasn't even taken her first sip and I already sense a drunken meltdown coming.

'Don't even think like that. You always said there was something a little off about Eddie. Remember the time he asked you to do *that thing* in the shower?'

I can't even say it aloud. It's too gross.

'All guys have at least one weird fetish,' she says, looking a bit hurt that I've insulted Eddie.

I want to tell her that Adam doesn't have any weird fetishes that I know of, but it seems I'm going to be standing on the corner of Eddie is a Douche-nozzle and Eddie is a God tonight. I lean my back against the bar and consider ordering a water, when a hand waving in the distance catches my attention. It's Tristan, Chris's bass player, best friend, and an even bigger douche-nozzle than Eddie. He's sitting at a booth with his arm around a blonde who looks somewhat familiar, like I've had her in a class or something.

'Is that Tristan?' Senia asks.

Tristan tried to hook up with Senia at a Memorial Day barbecue last year. Tristan, who can drink more than anyone I know without getting drunk, didn't hesitate to challenge Senia to a game of Quarters. And they almost had sloppy sex on the bathroom counter until Senia threw up on his shoulder.

'Let's go say hi,' Senia says as she grabs my arm and hauls me through the crowd.

As we approach, Tristan's gray eyes are locked on my face. Tristan has always made me uncomfortable. When Chris and I were together, I would often catch him staring at me when Chris wasn't around. The problem with Tristan is that he doesn't stare at girls when he wants to fuck them. He's only been in one serious relationship since I've known him. When we were seventeen, Ashley and Tristan were together for over a year until she crushed his heart. I used to catch him staring at her the way I've often caught him staring at me. Chris once noticed it and nearly beat the shit out of him. I guess Chris isn't around tonight.

'Hello, Claire,' Tristan says in a smooth voice that's just barely tinged with a New England accent from the first twelve years of his life spent in Maine. He removes his arm from around the blonde's shoulders and runs his hand through his light-brown shoulder-length hair before he turns to Senia. 'I remember you. How many of those have you had tonight?' he asks, glancing at the drink in Senia's hand.

'First one, but I'm willing to let you buy me another,' Senia responds.

The blonde glares at Senia and the bad feeling I had about this bar just keeps growing.

'Hey, Tristan, why don't you introduce us to your friends?' I say.

Tristan cocks an eyebrow as he stares at me and I try not to make a rude comment. As hot as Tristan is, I've never seen him as anything more than Chris's friend, someone that I have to put up with.

'Claire, this is Julie,' he says, nodding at the blonde on his left. 'And these two sexy beasts are Ben and Abby.'

My eyes widen at the mention of the name Abby. It's a common name, but just hearing it makes me long for Abigail even more.

Ben is sweet looking but sort of scrawny with messy brown bedhead hair and Abby is beautiful with her understated makeup and glossy brown curls pulled up into a perfectly tousled ponytail. They both smile and nod their heads.

Tristan asks Julie to scoot over so I can sit next to him, but I quickly take the seat next to Ben and Abby so Senia can sit next to Tristan. Tristan casts a knowing glare in my direction and I roll my eyes so he knows I'm not impressed. Chris and I may not be together, but that doesn't mean I'm going to jump on Tristan's bandwagon.

'Chris didn't want to come out with us tonight,' Tristan says, a slightly bitter tone in his voice as if I'm responsible. 'He had other *plans*.'

I know Chris is in London, but I'll play along. He's trying to make me jealous, like I care if Chris is out with another girl.

'That's too bad. Sounds as if he went *solo* tonight,' I reply. I'm not sure if Tristan has gotten over Chris going solo last year, but judging by the unimpressed look on his face, I hit a nerve.

He quickly recovers and smiles at me, the same smile he uses on stage to make the girls swoon. Chris has his own smile he uses on stage. He calls it his 'crowd smile.' Chris's crowd smile is a warm grin that tugs the left side of his mouth up just a bit further than the right. Tristan's version is a bit more subtle, but just as sexy.

I manage to ignore his stares and taunts for the next hour as everyone on his side of the booth gets shit-faced drunk. Ben, Abby, and I watch in a combination of amusement and horror as Tristan alternates between sloppily making out with Julie and whispering in Senia's ear. Senia smiles in response and slides out of the booth.

It's time for me to intervene.

I grab her wrist as Tristan slides out of the booth after her. 'You cannot go anywhere with him.'

'Chill out. He's just escorting me to the restroom.'

'I can do that,' I say as I slide out of the booth.

Senia throws me a look like I'm being a total buzz-kill. I don't want to let her go anywhere with Tristan. The last thing she needs right now is another heart-break. But maybe she just needs to get this out of her system. Having meaningless sex after a breakup seems to be a ritual we've all come to accept as normal.

I sit back down and Julie's head is resting on top of the table. She's passed out. I would sit next to her so that Abby and Ben aren't squished together, but I'm

31

afraid of what will happen if she wakes up and finds Tristan gone.

About fifteen minutes later, Tristan returns without Senia. He slides into the booth as if nothing happened.

'Where's Senia?'

'Is that her name?' Tristan replies, looking completely bored. 'She's still in the restroom.'

'You're such an asshole,' I mutter as I leave and barrel through the crowd toward the restroom sign in the corner.

I make it to the door with the gold handle and shove it open. Four girls are standing in front of the mirror washing their hands and fixing their makeup and all the stalls are occupied.

'Senia?'

'What?' she calls back, and I can tell she's crying.

I knock on the door of the stall and she fumbles with the latch before it opens. She's sitting on the toilet, fully-clothed, with a giant wad of toilet paper in her hands. Almost all her makeup is gone and caked on the toilet paper as tears stream continuously down her face.

I lock the door behind me and kneel down in front of her. 'What happened? Did Tristan do something to you?'

She laughs then blows her nose. 'I was so ready to do it,' she slurs, 'but I just kept thinking, "That's not how Eddie would kiss me. That's not how Eddie would touch me." Then I started crying and he left. Totally pathetic.'

'It's not pathetic,' I say as I grab a clean bunch of toilet paper off the roll and exchange it for the filthy wad in her hands. 'You and Eddie loved each other. Even if he did turn out to be a royal asshole, I know he loved you in his own way. It's okay to feel lost right now, but you're beautiful and smart and you *will* find someone else. And not Tristan, who's an even bigger asshole than Eddie.'

'Ugh. He is. But I must admit that he has a bigger . . . *bass* than Eddie.'

'See? You're still cracking jokes. You're gonna be *just* fine.'

She chuckles as she wipes off the rest of her eye makeup then looks up at me. 'He said something horrible to me.'

'Who said something horrible?'

'Tristan. He said, "I guess you'll do."'

'He said that to you?' I stand up, ready to storm out of the stall and give that douche a piece of my mind, but Senia grabs my arm.

'No, you can't say anything.'

'Why?'

She grimaces as she replies, 'I think he was talking about you.'

'I don't get it.'

'It doesn't matter. Let's get out of here before I make an even bigger fool of myself.'

Chapter Four

Chris

This is my second time in London, and I never travel with a bodyguard overseas, but I think that policy is about to change.

As soon as I step out of the cab in front of the hotel on Warwick, I'm swarmed by five girls who are waiting for me at 7:30 a.m. Tristan and Jake didn't come with me to play this gig. I booked this London show for one reason and it has nothing to do with the current tour or my UK fans.

I sign autographs for them while a girl with teased hair and too much eye shadow gently squeezes my bicep. Why do girls wear so much fucking makeup? I wonder if she put all that shit on her face before she came here thinking it would impress me. Another girl with auburn hair gazes at me with a dazed expression as I sign a picture of me she obviously ripped out of a magazine. I hand the picture back to her and she smiles.

'I love you so much,' she says in a breathy English accent. '"Relentless" is my favorite song of all time.'

This shit gets old. How do you pretend to be excited to hear the same phrase you've heard a million times before? I'm a musician, not a fucking actor.

'Thanks. It's really close to my heart, too. Have a great day, ladies.'

I take off quickly before they can start jabbering. I make it to the room and pull my phone out of my pocket before I collapse onto the bed. The curtains are pulled tight so the room is nice and dark even though the morning sun is shining bright outside. I glance at my screen and scroll through the six new texts I've received since I left the airport. Nothing from Claire.

If she wants me to stop texting her that's exactly what I'll do. And not because I know it will drive her nuts. I'll do it because I'm willing to do pretty much anything to get her back.

But also because it'll drive her nuts.

I text Tasha to let her know that Claire is okay with Tuesday for the meeting then ignore Tasha's smiley response as I dial the number of a local tattoo artist I met during my last visit to London. Arthur is the only reason I'm here, so I'm super stoked when he picks up on the third ring.

'Chris "Fucking" Knight. Why the fuck are you calling me at this bloody hour?'

'Hey, Art. You think you can squeeze me in today? Just a quickie. A name.'

Claire doesn't know I covered up the tattoo of her name I got on my shoulder blade three years ago. I can't do much about that, but I can do something else even better. Not sure how or when I'll get to show her this new one, but I'll find a way.

'It's Sunday, mate. The shop's closed. Stop by at eleven.'

I should take a quick nap, but I'm too wired from the flight and the excitement of some new ink. I open the photo app on my phone and scroll to the bottom of the list of folders. I touch the folder labeled 'CB.'

The first photo is of Claire and me sitting on a piano bench. She's smiling as I kiss her forehead. This was taken at a show in Toronto; one of the last shows she attended with me before we broke up. The next picture is of her sleeping on the sofa at our house. Her mouth is hanging open and she's clutching the throw pillow in her fist. I close my eyes and lay the phone next to me on the bed because I'm finally starting to feel tired.

Maybe I'm just exhausted from everything that's happened the past three weeks. I had resigned myself to a life without Claire. I was certain she wanted nothing more to do with me. But nothing she says to me now can erase that kiss.

I felt it in the curve of her mouth, the way we fit together, the way she leaned into me, seeking me. She still loves me and, despite the fact that she majorly fucked me over, she's still the one and only future I'm certain of. Claire and I were made for each other. I'm determined to make her remember that.

Chapter Five

Adam

The flight is uncomfortable, but I'm sober by the time the plane hits cruising altitude. Just knowing that I'm going to be home soon, and that I had enough sense not to book that flight to Raleigh, fills me with relief. By the time I pull my truck out of the lot at Wilmington International, I'm feeling one hundred percent back to normal.

I always knew Claire would be my downfall.

The twenty-minute drive home is spent in silence. I realize now why Claire always hated listening to the radio whenever we were together. Now I'm the one avoiding the radio, but I left my iPod in my backpack in the hotel room so I have to suffer in silence.

It's ridiculous how much I hate Chris's music now. Just remembering how I bought his album and watched his videos fills me with shame. It's alternative with a rock-blues edge, but it's all washed out by pop vocals.

At least, that's what the article I read about him in *Entertainment Weekly* said.

I smile a little as I remember that *Entertainment Weekly* review.

When I enter my apartment I'm hit with the scent of that fucking coconut-scented oil Claire put in a dish on my coffee table. It's six in the morning. I have just enough time to take an hour-long nap before I check on Cora and head to Shell Island to teach the Sunday session. I take a five-minute shower then lie down in bed with my phone to shoot Claire a text.

Me: Knock, knock.

Claire: Who's there?

Me: Me . . . in five days unless I can get this fucking time machine to work.

Claire: Guess what I'm doing?

Me: Lying naked in bed?

Claire: Close. I'm changing into my pajamas. I just got home. Senia broke up with Eddie and made me go out with her. It did not go well.

I trust Claire, but it seems like the universe is pounding the hundred-mile wedge between us deeper into the earth every day.

Me: Is she okay? Are you okay?

Claire: She's passed out. I didn't drink, but I'm about to pass out too.

Me: Sleep tight, babydoll.
Claire: I'll call you when I wake up.

I wake up from my nap and head over to Cora's apartment feeling much more relaxed now that I know I'll be hitting the breaks soon. I knock on her door and it takes her almost ten minutes to answer. Though Claire and I both have keys to Cora's apartment, we try not to barge in unless it's obvious Cora can't make it to the door.

The door swings open and she's already walking away toward her recliner. 'Tina's coming over today. She's rescheduling all her patients this week; something about a birthday party on Tuesday. I think she's lying.'

'Tina's always lying,' I say as I shut the door and make my way into the kitchen to check on the things Tina, Cora's caregiver, never checks on; the things Claire taught me to check on when we first met. 'Do you have anyone coming to look at the apartment this week?'

The apartment below me has only been empty for three weeks, but I'm going to have to sneak some extra funds into my rent check if Cora doesn't find a new tenant soon. I can't let her go broke just because Claire went back to school. After all, even though I'm pretty miserable over it, I am the one who encouraged her to go. I have to accept responsibility for the emptiness of Claire's old apartment, and the void it's left in Cora's bank account as the landlady of this building. Of course, paying double the rent will cut into my savings, but I can do it for a few months – for Cora and Claire.

Everything is in order in the kitchen, but when I enter the living room Cora is already leaning back in the recliner with her eyes closed. For a moment I fear the worst.

'Cora?'

She waves me off. 'Go home, honey. I'm not up for any fun and games today. All I can handle right now is a long senior-citizen siesta. Tina will be here soon. Go do your water tricks.'

'You sure? I can hang out if you need some company. My class doesn't start for ninety minutes.'

'Get out of here before I sick Bigfoot on you.'

Cora's been more tired than usual lately. Tina says it's normal for someone her age to have bouts of lethargy. I don't like to think of Cora as any age, but I suppose there are certain truths one has to come to terms with when you reach the age of eighty-six. I haven't told Claire. As far as she knows, Cora's as spunky as ever. She doesn't need anything else to worry about.

I make it to Shell Island an hour before class so I immediately jog out across the sand, surfboard under my arm, to get a feel for the surf. The water is choppy – it's hurricane season – but I paddle out and chill on my board for a while as I watch the waves break on the shore.

The water ebbs beneath me and I think of Claire's

crazy meditation habit. It's not much different from my need to surf. I can't function if I've gone too long without immersing myself in the ocean, without feeling the power of the water pushing me. Surfing is a healthy addiction, like meditating.

Today I quit smoking. For good.

I leave everything in the water today. I should save something for my students, but they're such beginners I don't need much energy to teach them how to stand on a board in the sand. I start a new group of students today, even though I won't be around next week to continue. Jason will pick up where I leave off. The first day is always the easiest.

I shake the ocean out of my hair as I come out of the water. A couple of girls in bikinis are standing next to Jason, my boss and the lead surf instructor at the academy. The girls smile and the shorter one whispers something in the other one's ear as they watch me approach.

'What's up, bro?' I say to Jason with a nod of my head.

Jason is thirty and still single so I'm used to the young female students fawning over both of us, but I'm not in the mood for it today.

'I thought you weren't coming in today,' Jason says. 'I already asked Nayla to take this class. She's on her way.'

'I'll text her to tell her I'm here.'

'This is Nadia and Brittany. They're sisters and

they're part of the new class. We're just waiting for Fred and Paige, the couple that came in last week.'

'Cool,' I reply without looking at the girls.

A long, awkward fifteen minutes pass before we decide that Fred and Paige are too late. We'll have to start without them.

The first ten minutes of the lesson are always spent introducing the academy and myself and talking about what we're going to be doing for our first lesson. When I'm done with my spiel both girls put their hand up like they're in a fucking classroom. They can't be much older than eighteen, if they're even that old.

'You don't have to raise your hands.'

The taller one, Nadia, speaks first. 'We already took surf lessons in Carolina Beach last summer. Can we skip the stuff in the sand?'

Jason has just left us to go teach an intermediate class further down the beach. He doesn't like me to skip the basics, even when a student insists, but I'm not exactly opposed to skipping the positioning and pop-up section of the lesson. I always have to put my hands on someone's arms or legs to get them positioned correctly and I don't feel comfortable touching these girls without Jason around.

'Yeah, we can skip that. Grab your boards and we'll paddle out.'

Brittany can't seem to get her short arm around the board and she keeps looking up at me innocently as if I should be helping her.

'Just carry it on your head,' I say as I set off toward the water.

Once we're all out in the water, Brittany climbs onto her board with ease, but Nadia keeps slipping off. I watch her try for a couple of minutes as the pair of them giggle every time she slides off.

'Oh, my God! I'm such a dork!' Nadia shrieks and they both laugh again.

I slide off my board and into the water to help her. I come up next to her and get a firm hold on her board to hold it steady as she attempts to climb on again. She knocks me on the side of the head with her hip as she climbs on and I lose my grip on the board. She screams as she slides into the water again and the board flips on top of both of our heads.

'Fuck!' I shout as I push the board off.

'Sorry!' she shrieks. 'I didn't mean to hit you. This is so embarrassing. It's like my first day at Duke all over again.'

I glance at her quickly to satisfy my curiosity and I guess she could pass for nineteen or twenty. I flip her board over and get a firm grip on it again.

I nod toward the board for her to get on. 'How long have you gone to Duke?'

I only graduated from Duke three months ago, not that I would remember her, but we may know some of the same people.

She's careful not to bump me with her hip this time

as she climbs onto the board. 'I just started a week ago. Excuse my language, but it's fucking terrifying.'

I laugh as I climb onto my board. 'Yeah, I remember my freshman year.'

We make it through the rest of the lesson without anymore falling or accidental touching. I'm trusting myself more by the hour.

'I won't be in town next weekend so you'll be taking your next lesson with Jason or Nayla. They're both better instructors than I am, so you'll be in good hands,' I say as we make it back to the sand.

They both look disappointed as they pull on their swim dresses over their bikinis.

'Will you be here the next week? We can wait.'

Nadia's the one who asks, but they're both staring at me waiting for my response.

'No, I won't be here the following weekend either. I visit my girlfriend every weekend at UNC.'

Nadia's face scrunches up for a split second like she's been physically punched in the face, but she quickly covers it up by pretending to squint at the sun as she pulls her dark, wet hair into a ponytail.

'That's cool. Then I guess we'll see you around.'

I feel a little bad as they turn to walk away. 'Hey!' They turn around with hopeful expressions. 'Want to hear a joke?'

Brittany cocks an eyebrow, but Nadia's lips curl into a slow smile as she nods.

'Knock, knock.'

They turn to each other and exchange a can-you-believe-this-guy look.

'Who's there?' Nadia replies.

'Police.'

'Police who?'

'Police come back next week to continue your lessons.'

After a brief moment of silence that I'm pretty sure is mixed with a bit of confusion, they burst out laughing.

My job is done.

I lift my towel off the sand as they walk away and slip my phone out of the folds. One voicemail from Claire. I play the message and smile at the sound of her voice.

'I got four hours of sleep and now I have to study again, but I wanted to call you to tell you how much I love you and how glad I am that I can trust you. Call me later.'

Putting together this voicemail with what she said earlier about Senia and Eddie breaking up, I'm guessing Eddie must have cheated on Senia. I'll have to surprise Claire with something nice the next time I see her to make sure I stay in the 'good boyfriend' category. I grin as I hang the towel around my neck. I know the perfect gift for Claire.

Chapter Six

Claire

Tuesday's appointment with Tasha Singer and Abigail's parents comes too fast, but I know that as soon as this day is over the rest of the week will go by much too slow as I anticipate finally seeing Adam after nearly two weeks apart. My body aches for him. I miss everything about Adam. I even miss the way he stands, his shoulders straight as he looks down his nose at me with that intense glare in his green eyes.

Mr Collins concludes the lecture on Bayes' Rule and my stomach gurgles – not with hunger – as I stuff my netbook and *Probability* by Jim Pitman into my backpack. I finish the last few gulps of water in my bottle and tuck the empty bottle next to my books before I heave my backpack over my shoulder.

My nerves are zinging with the anticipation of today's meeting as I descend the steps in the lecture hall, holding my breath as I squeeze past a girl wearing too much Chanel perfume. As I make it into the corridor, the thumping of my heartbeat in my ears drowns out the sounds of students clamoring around me to get out of the lecture hall. I see Chris leaning up against the wall next to an announcement board and just the sight of him calms me a little.

He's wearing sunglasses and his head is tucked down as he thumb-types on his phone. I can't help but feel a twinge of jealousy as I wonder who he's texting, if he's even texting anyone. He could be looking up driving directions for all I know.

It's actually more likely that he's just trying to keep his head down to keep from being recognized, and he seems to be doing a good job. He's wearing a long-sleeved T-shirt that covers his tattoos and perfectly distressed designer jeans. He looks up when I'm a few feet away, as though he can sense me. His lips curl into a smile and I have to remind myself of all the ways we've hurt each other so I don't melt in the middle of the corridor.

'Hey, babe.'

'Don't call me babe.'

'Hey, baby.' I storm past him and he chuckles as he catches up to me. 'I'm just teasing you. Give me your backpack.'

'I can carry my backpack. I do it every day without you and I've managed not to keel over yet.'

'Have it your way, sis.'

'Ew. Don't call me that either.'

He slips his phone out of the back pocket of his jeans where he just tucked it away a few seconds ago. I can't help but glance at the screen and I see the notification that he has two new text messages. I stare straight ahead to avoid bumping into anything as we descend the steps out of Phillips Hall toward Cameron Avenue.

'Where did you park?' I ask, trying not to sound too annoyed that he has his face buried in a text conversation.

He finishes typing and sends the message before he looks up and glances around. 'Oh, fuck. We need to turn around. I parked behind the annex.'

By the time we make it to the parking lot, he's already received and responded to three more text messages and attempted to make small talk about my statistics class. I don't think I can be any more annoyed with him until I see the motorcycle with two helmets hanging from the locked seat compartment.

'You expect me to go to an important meeting like this with helmet hair?'

'We have two hours before the meeting. We're going home to get my car first and you can freshen up over there.'

Home. It's such a small detail amongst everything he just said, but it means so much.

'Why didn't you just come in your car? Why do we have to make an extra stop?' I ask as he unlocks the seat compartment and pulls the helmet strap off the hook. If Adam were to find out that Chris picked me up today on his motorcycle, he would hate Chris even more.

He hands me the helmet and I'm grateful he hasn't tried to put it on me.

'Because I can't bring my car here. It's too fucking obvious and I'm trying not to get noticed.'

I tighten the straps on my backpack before I take the white helmet from him. It's the helmet he bought me two years ago. It still has the sparkly pink Roxy heart sticker on the back. I tighten the strap under my chin and he can't resist double-checking that it's tight enough. I step back so he can't touch me with his hot fingertips, calloused from years of strumming those steel guitar strings.

He smiles as he shakes his head. 'Just trying to keep you safe.'

He secures his helmet and climbs onto the bike. Just looking at him on the bike brings back so many memories. Good memories. I bite my lip as I climb on behind him and slide my arms high around his waist so they're almost over his chest. He grabs my hands and slides them lower.

'Sorry, but I'm going to suffocate if you hold onto me like that.'

'Just go.'

This isn't his old bike. His old bike was blue. This bike is silver and looks as if it cost more than my entire UNC tuition. He pumps the throttle and I feel the vibration of the engine murmuring between my legs. I squeeze my eyes shut and loosen my arms a little as I try to block out the memory of the time we had sex on his blue bike.

He rolls slowly out of the parking space and I tighten my arms around him. I know Chris and he loves to scare me whenever I'm riding with him. As expected, he accelerates quickly as soon as we hit the highway and my stomach flips as the inertia pulls me back. He leans forward and I have to lean with him as I hug him tightly, my heart pounding as I try not to lose my grip.

Thirty minutes later, we're home. I step off the bike and pull off my helmet then punch him in the arm.

'Did you have to go so fast?'

'Ow!' he cries as he hangs his helmet on the bike then rubs his arm. 'Yes, I did. You want to have time to get prettied up before we go, don't you?'

'Is this your subtle way of telling me I look like shit?'

'Claire, it's impossible for you to look like shit. Come on. My mom's dying to see you.'

I stand still for a moment as I emotionally prepare myself to see Jackie Knight. Chris takes a few steps then looks back at me.

'Are you coming?'

'Does your mom know?'

Does she know what a horrible person I am? I want to ask. *Does she know I kept the worst kind of secret a person could keep from you?*

Chris's sparkling features are dulled by this question. He takes a few steps toward me and looks me in the eye. 'As much as I would love to tell my mom, just to have someone to talk to about it since you don't want to, no, I haven't told her. And I won't tell her until this is all figured out. As far as she knows, we're just going out to lunch today.'

'You can't let her think we're getting back together.'

'That's what you're worried about?'

'No, I just don't want to feel double the wrath.'

This makes one corner of his mouth quirk up in a tiny half-smile, but it disappears quickly. 'Claire, let's just drop one bomb at a time. If she wants to think that us having lunch means we're getting back together then let's not shatter her heart any more than it already is.'

He's referring to the fact that I didn't contact Jackie for almost a year after I found out I was pregnant. I couldn't face her while I was pregnant with her grand-child. Then I couldn't face her knowing I'd given up her grandchild for adoption. I'm beginning to wonder if I should even go to this meeting with Abigail's adop-tive parents today. What kind of parent would allow their child to be anywhere near me? I might sell them to the highest bidder or get bored and leave them at the McDonald's Playland.

'Hey, don't start getting down on yourself,' he says as he grabs my face to force me to look at him. 'We both fucked up. I should have been there for you, but I was too busy feeling sorry for myself and thinking I could replace you.'

I pull his hands off my face as I turn away. I can't look him in the eye and talk about this at the same time or I'll fall apart.

'Please stop being so understanding.'

I walk up the paved brick pathway leading to the front door of the only real home I've ever had; the home I shared with Chris and Jackie for three years until I moved into the dorms at UNC two years ago. Jackie and Chris both insist that this is still my home, but something feels different. Like I broke this home and I shouldn't be welcome here.

Chris rushes past me to get to the door first. He unlocks the deadbolt and my chest tightens. He looks over his shoulder and flashes me a soft smile before he pushes the door open.

'Welcome home.'

The smell hits me first; the scent of the lavender-bamboo scented candles Jackie buys in bulk because she's certain they're going to discontinue them one of these days. I step inside and it looks different. Chris must have paid for some renovations. Dark hardwood floors have replaced the beige carpet. The wallpaper is gone and the walls have all been painted soft neutral colors. Most of the furniture has been replaced and the house now looks like the inside of a Pottery Barn catalog, comfy and classic.

I want to cry. Jackie has worked so hard all her life, first as the oldest child in her family then as a single mom to Chris. But she always made room in her heart

53

and her home for her foster children. She deserves this and I'm so happy that Chris has been able to give her the home she deserves.

The water is running in the kitchen and I follow Chris toward the sound. As soon as we step into the kitchen the water shuts off and Jackie looks over her shoulder straight at me. She looks exactly the same as I remember.

Her dark hair is cut short and stylish, but I notice a few red highlights. Her makeup is impeccable, as usual, and she's wearing a classy gray cardigan and jeans that hug her round hips. Jackie was always stylish and always took the time to make herself pretty, even when she had foster kids climbing the walls.

For a moment we're both frozen, stuck in a kaleidoscope of memories and unspoken words. Then the first tear trickles down her cheek and I go to her. She opens her arms and I throw my arms around her waist and bury my face in her shoulder.

'Oh, honey. You're home,' she murmurs into my ear as she smooths down my hair.

I tighten my arms around on her and breathe in her soft, floral scent. I don't want to let go.

Chapter Seven

Chris

Watching Claire and my mom comforting each other fills me with the worst kind of longing for the way things used to be. Claire should have spent the last year here, not bouncing around from the dorm to Senia's house then to that apartment. She needed us and because of my stupid pride she suffered alone.

They finally release their grip on each other and my mom brushes the tears away from Claire's face. Claire's eyes are red as hell, the way they get when she's crying uncontrollably. I've seen that look on her too many times.

'I'm so sorry I didn't come sooner,' she says.

'That's water under the bridge. The important thing is that you came back and that you never, ever do that to me again.'

This gets a small, congested chuckle and a smile

out of Claire, but the pain she's hiding from my mom quickly returns to her dainty features.

'All right, that's enough,' I say. 'Claire has to freshen up so we can get going.'

'Oh, poo. You just got here,' my mom complains as she glares at me across the kitchen. 'You can't leave yet. You two can hang out later. Let me have some time with my girl.'

Claire looks at me and I can't help but gaze at her for a moment. I love that Claire has never been good at hiding her emotions. It took almost a year after she arrived at our house for her to allow herself to be vulnerable in front of anyone. But once I tore down those walls I fell irrevocably in love with her. She's so hard on herself, but I've never met anyone more loving than Claire.

I know she gave up Abigail for both of us. I have no doubt that she believed she was making the right decision. But I can't reconcile the girl I fell in love with – the same girl who made me wait more than two years to have sex with her – with this girl who fell in love with a guy she's known less than two months. Is this guy better than I am or did I just leave her heart wide open for him to get inside?

'Stop staring at her, Chris,' my mom says and I'm snapped out of my thoughts.

Claire looks down at the floor. She knows I'm thinking about something we can't discuss openly in front of my mom.

'Sorry, Mom, but we have to go soon. Claire has to get back to the dorm so she can study. I'll bring her by another time. I promise.'

The disappointment on my mom's face kills me. She nods, looking a bit defeated, then turns to Claire and grabs her hands.

'In case I don't see you anytime soon—'

'I'll be back. I—'

'Shh! I don't want you to promise me you'll be back soon. I know you've got classes and lots of studying and parties and all that college nonsense. I just want you to promise me you'll come home for Christmas. It just wasn't any fun without you last year. Right, Chris?'

Fuck. Knowing Claire, she's going to think I put my mom up to this.

'Mom, Claire probably already has plans for Christmas. Let's not put any more pressure on her.'

'Oh, come on. You were miserable without Claire here last Christmas.' She turns to Claire in full gossip-mode. 'You should have seen him. He was a mess, brooding in the bedroom with his guitar for days.'

'Come on. She doesn't want to hear that shit.'

Claire wipes the tears from her cheeks as she stares at me. She's not thinking about how pathetic I am. She's thinking of how sorry she is for not being here last Christmas. I want to tell her that she has nothing to feel guilty about, but I can't speak openly about any of that stuff here.

She finally turns away to face my mom. 'I'll be home for Christmas if I have to crawl here.'

I try not to let this statement get my hopes up, but right now I'm just insanely grateful that my mom seems to be more convincing than I am. They embrace again and I give them a moment before I break up the love-fest.

'All right, all right. You guys can cuddle some more later. Claire and I have to get going.'

I place my hand on the small of Claire's back, something I've done a million times, but this time I expect her to push my hand away or shoot me a severe look. She doesn't do either. She allows me to lead her out of the kitchen and up the stairs to her old room where she can fix her hair and makeup. I open the bedroom door and wait as she stands at the threshold for a moment.

I take a few steps inside and turn around. 'We didn't change anything. It didn't feel right since it's still your room.'

She steps inside and gazes around. Her twin bed is still covered in the lilac comforter and white pillows. Her shelves are still stacked with dozens of fantasy novels. I haven't even upgraded the ancient desktop computer on her desk. Everything is the same.

'Maybe I shouldn't have come here,' she whispers.

'Just brush your hair and we'll get out of here.'

She takes a few tentative steps toward the white desk and sits down in the rolling desk chair. She slowly pulls open the top drawer on the right and pulls out a purple brush. I can't help but feel nostalgic as I watch her run the brush through her soft, blonde hair.

I can't stop myself as I spin her chair around and place my hands on her knees as I kneel before her. 'I know that everything seems awkward and fucked up right now, but this is your home. Whether or not we're together. Don't let that Christmas shit make things weird. You know my mom is just being pushy.'

'It's not awkward or fucked up and I think that's what's getting to me. I expected it to be weird, but it's not. It's just . . . home.'

She looks me in the eye as she says this so I know she's telling me the truth. I want to kiss her so fucking bad that my whole body aches for it, but I can't. Claire is not the cheating type and I don't want to be the source of any more of her misplaced guilt.

'Hey, I know you've seen me play a million times, but I'm doing this jam session with Neil Hardaway at a blues club in Durham a week from Saturday. It's the final stop on this "Home Sweet Home" tour Xander set up for me. I know you have a boyfriend, but it's fucking Neil Hardaway. You know this is a dream of mine and I'd love to share it with you.'

The pained expression on her face tells me she's about to let me down. 'I can't. I'll be with Adam that Saturday. I'm sorry.'

Just hearing his fucking name come out of her mouth, the same lips I've kissed for hours, makes me want to punch something. I take a breath to calm myself because this isn't like me. Only Claire can get me this worked up.

'Don't apologize,' I say as I let go of her knees and stand up. 'Come on. We gotta get going.'

We make it downstairs into the hallway where I open the door to the attached garage and flip the light switch. The stale smell of gasoline and rubber is stagnant in the late summer warmth. She enters ahead of me and immediately walks toward the Porsche.

'Where's Mr Miyagi?' she asks, referring to our old Shiba Inu.

Mr Miyagi got to go to Japan with me in April before he passed, but he was almost thirteen years old. He lived a long life.

'He's gone.'

Claire looks like she's about to cry.

'Don't cry. Please. You're gonna make me cry. I'm just starting to get over it.'

She bites her lip, trying to hold it together. 'I should have been with him.'

'He died in May. I was with him. He went peacefully. I even took him to the dog park that morning. He just laid there real quiet, but he was smiling.'

She covers her face. 'Oh, no,' she whimpers as she shakes her head.

I want to pull her into my arms, but I'm afraid she'll push me away. I give her a moment to compose herself. Finally, she pulls her hands away from her face and looks at me with pure hurt in her eyes.

'We have to get going.'

She glances around the garage at my car and my mom's Volvo for a moment before she steps down and makes her way toward my car. 'You got a Porsche?' she asks incredulously as she gazes at the shiny, black hood. 'Could you be any more flashy?'

'Hey, I don't spend money on a lot of shit. I don't even have an apartment in Raleigh. Let me have my cars and my bikes.' I make my way to the driver's side of my mom's Volvo. 'We're taking the Volvo. I have to at least pretend to be responsible.'

She tears her gaze away from the Porsche and we both climb into the Volvo. We sit for a moment in silence as I slide the key into the ignition and adjust the radio station.

'Pretend to be responsible?' she says. 'But you *are* responsible, Chris. You don't have to pretend to be anything. I'm the one who should be worried about looking irresponsible.'

I open my mouth to refute this when my phone vibrates in my pocket. 'Hold that thought.' I slip the phone out of my pocket and see Tasha's name. 'Hello?'

'Chris, I've got bad news.'

I let out a deep sigh because I already know what she's going to say.

'They backed out?'

'Yeah, but this is normal. It's the way these things go. They're good people, as far as I can tell, but she got cold feet. I guess she's a big fan of your music and she got a little nervous about meeting you. Then her husband got freaked out about the whole rock star thing.'

'Fuck!'

'Hey, it's just a setback. We'll give them a few days to cool off then I'll call and try to set up another meeting. Don't get discouraged.'

'What happened?' Claire whispers.

'Thanks, Tasha.'

As soon as I say her name, Claire's face falls. I tuck the phone into my pocket and we sit in silence for a moment. I don't know how much more heartache Claire and I can take. All I know is that this was not the homecoming I had planned for today.

'Hey, did I show you this tattoo?' I say as I pull up the sleeve on my right arm and show her the shattered heart tattoo I got on New Year's Day.

It's just a two-inch red heart broken into a bunch of pieces, but some of the shards are colored black and spell out the one word I think of when I think of Claire: home. She gazes at my arm for a moment before she looks up at me.

'This is really hard for me, too,' she says. She doesn't have to say anything more.

Chapter Eight

Adam

I pull into the parking lot at Spencer Hall and, as usual, there's no parking on a Friday night. I pull back out and find a parking space in the lot on Franklin. I'm walking past the Chapel of the Cross, just a few hundred feet from the dorm, when my phone vibrates in my pocket. It's my dad.

'Yes, sir.'

'Your mom needs you to come into the office tomorrow to help her with the Blackwell close-out. She's having a problem reconciling the change order log. You need to be there by two.'

'I can't. I'm not coming home until Sunday. I'll go in early on Monday to look at it.'

'No, you'll be there tomorrow. The auditor is coming on Monday morning and this shit needs to be done by then. Your mom has a church thing on Sunday, so it has to be tomorrow.'

My dad knows I can't refuse now. Religion is a topic we no longer discuss ever since I stopped going to church when I was seventeen – after Myles' death. I don't know if I believe in God anymore. The universe seems to be too random and unforgiving a place to be part of any grand design. But a part of me wants to believe. I want to believe that there was a reason Myles fell to his death. I want to believe there's a reason I fell in love with Claire. I want to believe there's a reason for me to keep driving one hundred miles every weekend for a girl who doesn't believe she's worth it.

'I'll be there at five. That's the earliest I can make it.'

I hang up before my father can respond. I always thought it was strange how people in movies never seem to say goodbye to each other before they hang up the phone. Now I do it all the time with my dad. There's an abruptness to our conversations, a sense of urgency that drives the words out of us until the second we hang up. All our phone conversations sound clipped and often, on my part, flippant. I can't help it. He makes me feel like a fucking teenager.

If he didn't hold such a big secret over me, I'd have quit years ago. I'm going to have to come clean to Claire tonight. This may be our last weekend together before my dad sends me to Hawaii to close the deal on the Barking Sands Training Center construction project.

I reach the front entrance at Spencer Hall and get lucky when a scrawny guy in a UNC hoodie comes out the door. I resist the urge to punch him for reminding me of Chris Knight. Being on this campus always puts me on edge. I keep expecting someone to magically know I just graduated from Duke – or 'Puke', as they like to call it.

'Thanks,' I mutter as he holds the door for me.

I make my way up to the third floor to room 330B, ignoring the four girls who smile at me on the way up. But I can't help but smile as I approach the door. Twelve days is too fucking long to go without Claire.

I knock on the door and hear a short scream followed by giggles coming from the inside of the dorm. I shake my head as I wait for someone to answer. The door opens and Senia is standing there, all five feet ten inches of her, with her perfectly penciled eyebrow cocked.

She nods toward the interior of the room. 'Hurry up before she finishes getting dressed.'

I laugh as I step inside and see Claire hastily pulling a gray T-shirt over her pink bra. Her back is to me, but just the sight of her calms me.

Senia claps me on the arm. 'I'll leave you two to your plans. I'm going downstairs to hang with Isabel for a while.'

Isabel is the girl Claire switched dorms with so she could share a dorm with Senia this semester. I've never met her, but Claire claims she's a huge slut with a heart of gold.

The door closes as Senia leaves and Claire finally turns around. She smiles hugely as she runs to me. She jumps and I catch her around the waist as she crushes her lips to mine. I slide my tongue into her mouth to taste her and she whimpers. I kiss her slowly, savoring the sensation of her warm lips on mine.

'I love you,' I whisper as I move down to kiss the smooth skin on her jaw. 'I've missed you so fucking much.'

Her skin tastes clean as I kiss her neck, but I'm getting a hint of something else, something sweet.

'Why do you taste like that?' I whisper in her ear before I take her earlobe between my teeth.

She lets out a soft sigh before she answers. 'Senia bought me some cotton-candy-flavored body powder.'

I set her down on the floor and look her in the eye. 'Did you put it *all over* your body?' She slaps my arm and I laugh. 'What? I just want to know if I'm gonna have to go on a low-carb diet when I leave here.'

She rolls her eyes as she strolls to the desk to grab her phone. 'You're always on a low-carb diet anyway.'

'It's not a low-carb diet, it's a training diet. And I'd go off my diet to feast on you any day.'

She tucks her phone into the back pocket of her jeans and glances around the room. 'Do you want anything from the vending machine? I'm gonna go grab a bottle of water.'

'Yeah, get me a Gatorade or Powerade. Whatever they have.'

She shakes her head at me before she leaves. I would offer to go with her, but I had actually planned to ask her to get me something from the vending machine so I can be alone in her room for a moment. I quickly pull her gift out of my back pocket and stare at the slim, midnight-blue box for a moment before I place it on top of the stack of textbooks on the desk. I sit in the desk chair and pull my phone out to text Yuri while I wait for Claire.

Me: Hey. I have to be back in Wilmington tomorrow afternoon. Can we meet up tomorrow around noon?

Yuri always texts back right away. He's one of my oldest surfing buddies who I've known since we went to high school together in Carolina Beach. He offered to meet me in Raleigh on Sunday to give me the trophy and backpack I left in the hotel room, but now I'll have to text him to let him know we have to meet up a day earlier.

Yuri: That's cool. I'm bringing my girl cuz she's not leaving till Sunday morning. A long road trip will give her a reason to give me a road job.
Me: Cool. Tell Lena to save me some of that juice for later.
Yuri: Dude, I've got gallons of it on reserve for you.

I tuck the phone back into my pocket as Claire walks in with three bottles of Gatorade and one bottle of water. I shoot up from the chair to help her. She closes the door and locks it as I set the bottles on top of the desk next to the stack of textbooks. She approaches the desk and completely overlooks the box as she grabs her bottle of water. She unscrews the top and guzzles half the bottle in one long swig.

'Why did you only get one bottle of water and three bottles of Gatorade?'

'Because I can go back down and get water any time, but you have to stay in here all weekend. I heard some girls talking about you in the lounge, plotting to get their hands on you.'

'Really? So are you saying you don't trust me to go to the vending machine by myself or you don't trust those girls?'

I grin as I sit down in the desk chair again and pull her onto my lap. I swing her legs over mine and she wraps her arms around my neck.

'I wouldn't trust those girls around you for a single second.'

She leans in to kiss me and I turn my face.

'Don't you want to put down that bottle of water?'

She reaches over to put the bottle of water on the desk and she finally sees the box. Narrowing her eyes, she looks back and forth between the box and me.

'What is that?'

'A small token of my affection. It's not a big deal. Just open it.'

She looks nervous. 'You're scaring me. What is it?'

'Open it and you'll find out.'

She grabs the box and my heart pounds as she slowly lifts the lid.

Chapter Nine

Claire

The silver locket gleams in the lamplight and for a moment I'm stunned into silence as I trace my finger over the letter 'A' engraved in the surface.

'The 'A' is for Abigail, not Adam,' he clarifies, and his voice wavers with nerves.

'I know,' I whisper as I pull the necklace out of the box.

I open the heart-shaped locket and find a picture of me on the left. The right side is empty.

'I left it empty so you could put a picture of her in there.'

I close my fist tightly around the locket and wrap my arms around Adam's neck. 'Thank you.' I clench my teeth together to hold back the tears. 'Thank you so much. I love it.'

He pulls me closer and I tighten my grip on him as I press the side of my face into his solid shoulder.

'Are you okay?' he asks, but I don't respond.

I can't tell him that I've been trying to avoid looking at Abigail's picture ever since her parents backed out of our meeting. He knows how upset I was when it happened on Tuesday, but he doesn't know how horribly I'm coping with it. I stuffed all my pictures of her into the manila envelope Chris gave me four weeks ago, then I asked Senia to hide the envelope.

The pain starts at the base of my ribs and spreads like fire into my chest and throat until I have no hope of answering his question.

'Claire? What's wrong?' He tries to pull away so he can look at my face, but I hold tightly, too afraid that I'm going to ruin this moment.

He brought me a beautiful gift and I can't even accept it without becoming a wreck.

'I'm sorry. It's beautiful. I swear I love it,' I whisper as I clutch my fist so tightly the clasp on the necklace digs into my palm. 'But I can't wear it. I'm sorry. I put all her pictures away.'

His shoulders slump and I finally let go of him so I can look at his face. 'Why didn't you tell me? Man, I feel like such a dick now.'

'No, don't feel bad. This is beautiful and I do hope to wear it someday. It's just too much right now . . . not knowing if I'm ever going to see her.'

He pulls my arms off his shoulders and opens my fist. 'I'll hold onto it if it's too painful for you.'

'No!' I cry as I clench my fingers around the locket.

'No, I want to hold onto it. I really do love it; I just want to put it away for a little while. Is that okay?'

'Baby, you could throw it in the fire and that would be okay. Whatever makes you feel better.'

I heave a deep sigh of relief and kiss his cheek. 'I love you.'

He chuckles as my lips skim his jaw and land on his neck. 'I'm so happy to be here with you.'

I lick his neck and he moans softly. His hands slide under my shirt as I press my lips to the sensitive area behind his ear. I drop the locket onto the desk and grab fistfuls of his hair as I pull his mouth to mine. His lips are so soft and warm.

'I've been dreaming about this all week,' I murmur into his mouth.

His hand slides under my knees and he scoops me up in his arms. My stomach flips as he stands from the chair and carries me to my bed. He sets me down gently, our lips never losing contact as I reach for the waistband of his jeans and pull him down on top of me. Just feeling the weight of him on top of me sends me over the edge and my body trembles with my need for him.

'Are you okay?' he whispers as he kisses my neck and I nod hastily. 'Good, 'cause I'm about to wreck you.'

I giggle nervously as he spreads my legs open. 'Go easy on me. It's been two weeks.'

He groans and I lift my hips as he grinds into me.

'Please take this off,' I beg as I yank his shirt up.

He chuckles as he pulls his shirt over his head and gazes down at me with that sexy smile that I've missed so much. His body is so perfectly smooth and sculpted from all the training. I reach up and lightly trace my finger over the tattoo on his chest, the compass filled with waves, and he grabs my hand. He kisses the inside of my wrist then lays my hand down at my side. His hand slides sideways over my belly then under my lower back. He lifts me up so my back is arched and plants a soft kiss just above my belly button. The smile in his eyes as he looks up at me makes my chest heave with anticipation.

His fingers whisper over my skin and I sigh as they land on the button of my jeans. He takes his time undoing the button and I feel my body growing hungrier and more impatient by the second.

'What do you want me to do to you?' he asks as he drags the zipper down and lays a soft kiss on my abdomen.

I hate when he asks me this. I get so flustered when I talk about this stuff.

I reach down and run my fingers through his hair as I look him in the eye. 'I want you to make me . . . scream your name.'

I whisper the last three words and he laughs softly. 'You're so fucking adorable. Do you need a joke to relax?'

He grabs the waistband of my jeans and I lift my

hips so he can slide them down, taking my panties with them. 'Yes, please.'

'This one's going to be dirty,' he says as he tosses my jeans and panties onto the floor and kisses my hipbone. 'First, take off your shirt. I want to look at you.'

I tear off my shirt and slip out of my bra then lie back as he sits up on his knees to look at me. It's a testament to how comfortable I feel with Adam that I don't even flinch at the fact that the lights are on. Adam has never made me feel anything other than completely beautiful.

His eyes take in every inch of me, his gaze skimming over every valley and curve before landing squarely on my face. 'I'll save the joke for later.'

He slides two fingers inside me and I close my eyes as I hold my breath. His fingers slide in and out of me as his thumb massages my clit.

'Oh, my God,' I breathe as I roll my hips against the motion of his hand.

'Look at me.' I shake my head as the pleasure builds inside me and he laughs. 'Come on, baby. I want to see your eyes.'

I open my eyes and he smiles as he slides his fingers out of me right before I come.

'That's not fair,' I protest.

He ignores my grumbling as he lies on top of me and kisses me hard. I'm breathless, lost under the weight of his body and the power of his kiss. His hands roam over my waist and he takes my breast in his hand.

'I'm always fair,' he whispers in my ear then he moves down, laying a soft trail of kisses straight down the middle of my torso until he reaches my center.

I gasp as soon as his tongue touches me. 'Adam.' He lets out a soft grunt in reply. 'Don't stop.' I try not to writhe away from him as the warmth builds inside me, spreading out from my core in furious waves. 'Adam!'

'Say it louder,' he says, and the sensation of his breath and the vibration of his voice send chills through me.

As the orgasm reverberates through my body, a cry of euphoria explodes from my lips. 'Adam!'

I hear a soft chuckle as he finishes me off with another lick and a soft kiss. My body trembles as he kisses each of my breasts then sits up. He takes off his jeans and I attempt to recover as he slides a condom on.

'Sweeter than sugar,' he says, as he lies on top of me, resting his elbows on either side of my head, and kisses me.

I rake my nails softly over his ribs and he twitches between my legs. He kisses me slowly, taking his time, drawing out the moment until I finally grab fistfuls of his hair and pull his face back. I don't say anything. He knows what I want as soon as he sees the hunger in my eyes.

He eases himself into me and I wrap my legs around his hips to coax him farther inside. I draw in a sharp breath as he hits my core and a spark of pain ignites the fire inside me.

His eyes are locked on mine, his brow furrowed

as he watches every change in my face while moving rhythmically in and out of me. 'Are you okay?' I nod and he kisses my forehead. 'I love you, Claire.'

'I love you, Adam.'

He presses his lips to mine and I know, from that one look and the way he's kissing me so tenderly, that there's something he's not telling me.

Chapter Ten

Adam

Waking up in Claire's bed is always disorienting. I sleep like the dead in my own bed, but sharing a twin bed with Claire while Senia is lying eight feet away from us is not my idea of the perfect sleeping arrangements. Especially when all I have to do is smell Claire and I get turned on.

I sweep her hair to the side and kiss the back of her neck to wake her up. She stirs against me then pauses when she feels me stiff against her backside. I scoot back a little so she doesn't think I'm trying to make any suggestions. She turns around to face me and I kiss her forehead.

'Good morning, babydoll.'

She curls her leg over my hip and tucks her head under my chin. 'Good morning. What are we doing today? I don't have to study until six or seven, so we have all day.'

I lightly drag my fingertips up and down the silky skin on her thigh as I try to think of a way to break the news to her. 'Baby, I have bad news. I can't stay the entire weekend anymore.'

She jerks her head up and hits the underside of my chin forcing my teeth to clamp down hard. 'Sorry,' she says as she rubs my chin. 'What do you mean you can't stay? When are you leaving?'

I pull her hand away from my chin and kiss her delicate fingers. She stares at me with those beautiful blue eyes and the disappointment in her face makes me want to tell my dad to go to hell with his last-minute demands, but I can't.

'I'm leaving around noon. I have to help my mom with some closeout documents for a project.'

She sighs as she unfurls herself from me to lie on her back as she stares at the ceiling. 'This sucks. I thought we were going to spend the whole weekend together. Now I'll have to go to that Chi Omega brunch at the gallery tomorrow with Senia.'

'I can hear you,' Senia mutters from the other side of the room.

'So looking forward to it,' Claire shouts back.

I slip my hand under her tank top and she smiles as my fingers crawl over her skin. I take her breast in my hand and squeeze. She finally turns to look at me.

'Why didn't you tell me this last night?'

'Because I wanted to enjoy what could possibly be our last night together for a couple of months.' She glares at me, unsatisfied with my incomplete response. 'We have a conference call with the C.O. at Barking Sands on Thursday. They're going to tell us if we got the project. I'm almost one hundred percent certain we got it.'

'You're going to Hawaii? Why don't you look more upset?'

'I *am* upset. I'm very fucking upset, but this trip is a long-term investment.' I slide my hand down and under the waistband of her panties. I love that she lets me do this with Senia just a few feet away. 'I've already entered a competition over there and I told my dad that this would be the last project I work on for the company before I quit.'

'And he agreed to that?'

I nod as my fingers search for her spot. I know I've found it when she lets out a small gasp. I stroke her gently and her eyes close as her mouth falls open in a silent cry.

'Once this trip is over, I'm free. I already have another job lined up with an architectural firm in Raleigh.' I slide my finger inside her and I can tell she's holding her breath. 'I'll be back before Thanksgiving. Then we can be together.' I slide my finger out and use her wetness to caress her. 'Every day.'

Her hips writhe against my hand and I move my fingers in time with the rhythm of her thrusts. I smile as she squeezes her eyes and mouth tightly shut to suppress her cries. Finally, her body quivers and curls into me as she climaxes. I tease her a little more, just to torture her, then she opens her eyes as I pull my hand out of her panties.

'Two months,' she says in a breathy voice as she looks up at me. 'I can hardly handle two hours. This is cruel.'

I slowly slide my finger into my mouth because I have to taste her. 'You taste like a fucking cream pie,' I whisper in her ear.

She giggles as she curls herself around me again. 'Who's going to check on Cora while you're gone?'

'I'm going to threaten Tina into doing all the shit she slacks off on.'

'You can't threaten her.'

'I'm only kidding. I'm gonna bribe her.'

She smiles and I tilt her face up to kiss her. I want her to know that I feel the same way about leaving. I want her not just to remember me; I want her to *feel* me when I'm gone. She molds her body to mine and I grab the back of her neck to hold her steady as I roll her on top of me.

'Ew . . . I can see you guys,' Senia complains as she jumps out of bed.

Claire sits up so she's straddling my stomach as she watches Senia pull on some shorts and a hooded T-shirt. Senia pulls the hood over her head, probably to hide her messy bedhead hair, then slides her feet into some sneakers.

'Where are you going?' Claire asks, but I stay quiet.

I'm looking forward to having Claire all to myself for a few hours before I leave.

'I'm going to Starbucks then to hang out with Isabel. I'll be back later. You guys just . . . *enjoy* each other while you can.'

She slams the door on her way out and Claire stares at the door for a moment in a daze. She looks down at me and I can see she's upset.

'It's Eddie. I think seeing us together is too much for her right now. I feel horrible. Should I go after her?'

I try not to look disappointed as I reply, 'You should, if you think it will make both of you feel better.'

She stares at me for a moment as she contemplates her options. It feels like everything and everyone is conspiring to get between Claire and me, and it's really starting to piss me the fuck off. But I try not to let her see this.

I want to believe that Claire and I will survive our time apart. And I know that it shouldn't matter whether I leave now or in three hours, but our relationship already seems to be hanging by a thread. This is really bad timing to go on a long trip, but this is my way out of the family company. And I *need* to get out. I can't work a hundred miles away from Claire for the next two to three years.

'I'll talk to her later,' she says as she lies on top of me.

I grab her face and kiss her hard, the kind of kiss she

won't forget for a long time. I kiss her until I'm certain she'll suffocate if she doesn't come up for air. I pull her face back to look at her and she's crying.

'Why? Why do you have to leave?'

'Because sometimes you have to suffer without the things you want now so you can have everything you need later.'

I brush the tears from her face with my thumbs and she closes her eyes as she leans into my hand. This is too fucking hard.

We spend two hours lying in bed, talking and studying each other like curious animals, exploring every curve and crevice and savoring every blissful sensation. The whole time, the unspoken question of whether we can make it through this is heavy between us, like an invisible shield separating us, protecting us from getting close enough to get hurt. This is exactly how I wanted to spend my last day with Claire and it's also not at all how I wanted to spend it.

We stand just inside the door of her dorm as I get ready to leave. Her arms are wrapped around my waist and I stroke her hair as we gaze at each other in silence. The ache in my chest turns into a throbbing dread that something is going to happen with Chris while I'm gone. I trust Claire, but I don't trust him for a second.

'I love you, Claire. I want you to know that I won't do anything to jeopardize what we have. And I trust you, but I also want you to know that if anything does happen while I'm gone, I won't hesitate to hop on a plane and come back here to fight for what's mine. I can't lose you.'

'You're not going to lose me. You're still my favorite olive.'

I smile for the first time in hours and I know there's only one thing left to do.

'Knock, knock.'

She rolls her eyes. 'Who's there?'

'Sherwood.'

'Sherwood, who?'

'Sherwood like to stay, but I have to get going now.'

She shakes her head. 'I love you so much.'

I wrap my arms around her waist and lift her off the ground to give her one last kiss. I trace my tongue over her top lip then take her bottom lip into my mouth and suck gently. She moans and just the sound makes me want to take her back to bed so I pull my head back before we get carried away.

'I'll try to stop by next Friday on the way to the airport, but just in case I can't, I want you to know that you are all I'll be thinking about when I'm on that plane. And every day that I'm away from you will be worse than the day before. But I will come back and everything will fall into place. That's my promise to you.' I kiss her forehead before I set her down on the floor. 'You have my whole heart.'

'Are you going straight to the office now?'

'I have to make a stop in Raleigh to meet Yuri. He's

bringing my trophy. I'd ask you to come, but I won't be able to bring you back.'

She squints her eyes as she contemplates this. 'Can I come? I can take my car.'

I stare at her for a moment before I answer. 'Nothing would make me happier. You're gonna love Yuri. His jokes are even better than mine.'

'That's not saying much,' she says as she moves to the closet and yanks some jeans and a T-shirt off the hangers.

'Hey, you love my jokes. I see how you look at me with those googly eyes every time I deliver a punch line.'

'You're right. I love you *because* of your sad jokes, not in spite of them.'

I sneak up behind her as she slides her feet into some flip-flops and wrap my arms around her waist. 'I promise I'll text you plenty of sad jokes when I'm in Hawaii, like this one. Why did Adam accept the apple from Eve?'

She spins around in my arms so she's facing me. 'Why?'

'Because he couldn't eat her cherry.'

Her top lip curls up in disgust. 'So terrible and now I feel bad for Adam and Eve.'

'Don't feel bad. Adam eventually found Steve and they lived happily ever after.'

'That's much better. Gotta have the happily ever after.'

I kiss the corner of her mouth then grab her hand to leave. I don't say what's on my mind. She doesn't need to know how much I doubt that we'll get our happily ever after.

Chapter Eleven

Claire

The drive to Raleigh is nerve-racking. Four weeks ago, I would have pulled over to the side of the road and meditated for a while to calm my nerves, but I'm trying to limit the meditation to once in the morning and once at night. I'm not a fucking monk. I need to get a grip on my life without having to check out every few minutes at the first sign of emotional turmoil. It's not as if I think meditation is unhealthy, but it was most certainly unhealthy the way I used it to block out the world. If Adam can quit smoking pot cold turkey, I can limit my meditation fix to twice a day. I have to learn to be present, to feel the emotions instead of stuffing them down beneath a veneer of false serenity.

I pull into a parking space on Wilmington Street about a block away from the Busy Bee Café where Adam and I are meeting Yuri and his girlfriend. When I step out of my car – Senia's old Ford Focus that she gave me the day I moved into the dorm – Adam is walking along the sidewalk toward me. Just watching him, the way he walks with that easy confidence that comes so natural to him, I know that the next two months are going to be hell.

We walk along the sidewalk together in silence, but I can't help but smile as the girls who pass us in the opposite direction ogle him. From the corner of my eye, I can see him look at me then he gives my hand a gentle squeeze.

'What are you smiling about? Are you happy to be getting rid of me?'

'Just happy to have you.'

He kisses my temple as he reaches for the door at the Busy Bee. I step inside and I'm treated to the most amazing smells, like garlic fries and tacos. I instantly start salivating as the hostess asks how many are in our party.

'We're looking for our friends,' Adam says and the hostess smiles at him. 'A little guy that looks like a darker, sexier version of Keanu Reeves.'

If the girl weren't wearing a pound of blush, I'm sure I could see her cheeks flush red. Adam doesn't understand the effect he has on girls. It's both adorable and infuriating.

'I think they're in the back.' She pulls a couple of menus from the rack and nods toward the dining area. 'I'll take you there.'

She leads us to a table in the back of the dining

room and Yuri's eyes open wide with excitement at the sight of us. He and Adam engage in a quick, slap-on-the-back guy-hug then Yuri moves in to hug me. I'm surprised by this gesture and I end up giving him an awkward pat on the arm when he releases me.

'Claire, I've heard so much about you,' Yuri proclaims excitedly. 'This is Lena, the servant of my loins.' Lena punches him in the arm and he laughs. 'I mean, the goddess of my universe.'

Lena looks like a female version of Yuri. They have the same golden tanned skin that seems to glisten even in the dim restaurant lighting. They also have the same dark, almond-shaped eyes that glimmer with mischief.

Lena holds out her hand to me as I take a seat. 'Nice to meet you, Claire. Don't pay any attention to him. He's compensating, if you know what I mean.'

I try not to laugh as I shake her hand, but the what-the-fuck look on Yuri's face kills me. The hostess rolls her eyes as she leaves our menus on the table in front of Adam and mutters something about our server then quickly leaves.

'We've been here five seconds and you've already offended the hostess. You two should be ashamed of yourselves,' Adam says as he passes me a menu. 'What are you all drinking?'

Lena holds up her frosty glass. 'We're both drinking the cream ale. It's fucking delicious.'

'Not as delicious as my homemade cream ale,' Yuri mutters before he takes a few huge gulps from his glass.

'Dude, can you show a little respect for Adam's guest?' Lena snipes at him before she turns to me. 'So what are you studying at UNC?'

'Sociology. I'm a year behind so I'm doubling up on my units this year to try to catch up.'

'Double units? What are you doing here with these losers?' Lena says with a playful smile.

'Speaking of losers,' Adam interjects, 'did you bring the trophy?'

'It's in my trunk with all the rest of my junk,' Yuri replies.

The waitress takes our drink orders and we both get an iced tea. I don't say anything, but I'm glad Adam isn't drinking today. He orders some tacos and I order a bacon cheeseburger, which puts a smile on Yuri's face.

'I like a girl who isn't afraid to eat a juicy burger.'

'Don't talk to my girl that way,' Adam says, and I can't tell if he's kidding, but Yuri's raised eyebrows tell me he probably isn't.

I've only hung out with two of Adam's friends before and I admit I was a bit inebriated from the champagne cocktails on my twenty-first birthday. I don't remember him making any possessive comments that night, but I've always known about his temper. And he did admit to me that the reason he was on probation and forced to attend anger management classes was because he beat the shit out of the guy he caught his ex-girlfriend cheating on him with six months ago.

I brush off the comment and we make it through the

rest of the meal without further incidents, until Adam asks what happened with the job interview I went to on Thursday afternoon.

'They called me back yesterday,' I say as I push my plate away and reach for my glass of water. I take a nice, long drink as I attempt to stall.

I can feel Adam's gaze on the side of my head, but I really don't want to tell him what happened when the manager at EspressOasis, the café in the campus food court, called me yesterday.

'What happened?' he persists.

I drain the last few drops of water from the glass before I answer. 'They can't work with my schedule.'

'What about weekends?'

'I told them I couldn't work weekends.'

'Because of me?'

'It doesn't matter. I can find something else that will allow me to work weekends now that I know you're going to be gone.'

'Why don't you just call them back and tell them you can work weekends now?'

'Because they already gave the weekend position to someone else.'

The silence at the table and the way Adam is looking at me with those green eyes full of regret makes me nervous. Thankfully, he doesn't say anything else about the job – until he walks me to my car.

We walk side by side as we stroll down Wilmington Street holding hands. He pulls my hand up and lays a soft kiss on my knuckles. I smile and let out a sigh. This is it.

We reach my car and he grabs my purse out of my hand to lay it on top of the car. Then he traps me against the car with one hand on either side of my head as I lean back against the driver's side window.

His gaze penetrates me, burns through me as he searches my eyes for something. 'Do you need money?'

'What? No, I don't need money.'

Shit. He can smell the poor on me. The truth is I'm probably going to have to cancel my cell phone service if I don't find a weekend job soon.

'Don't lie to me, Claire. If you need help I want to be the one to do it.'

That's what this is about. He doesn't want me to accept help from Chris.

'Adam, I'll be fine.' I grab the front of his shirt and pull him toward me so our lips are almost touching. 'But I promise if I find myself in a bind that you will be the first person I call. You are my hero, after all.'

I kiss him hard, partially to distract him from the conversation, but mostly to imprint the sensation of my lips in his memory. I'm not stupid. I know Adam will have girls – hot girls in bikinis – chasing after him in Hawaii. Yes, it scares the shit out of me. Possibly more than Chris scares him. Just the thought of Adam with another girl makes me want to wrap my arms and legs around him and never let go, or drop everything and go with him.

I don't want to stop kissing him, but he starts to chuckle so I finally loosen my grip on his shirt and he breaks the kiss.

'I'm not going to war. I'm going to Hawaii.'

'That's not funny. I'm really scared.'

'Why? You don't think I'm going to cheat on you, do you?'

'No, but it's not you I'm worried about.' I stare at the wrinkles in the front of his T-shirt where my fingers were just clenched tightly, grasping for my lifeline. 'Adam, I don't think I've made it clear enough. I was drowning when I met you. I was barely breathing until you saved me. I'm afraid of what will happen to me without you here.'

The muscles in his jaw twitch as he clenches his teeth to hold back whatever emotion he's feeling. I don't want him to hold back. This is our last day together. I want to see everything he's feeling.

'Talk to me,' I beg.

He blinks his eyes a few times before he wraps his arms around my shoulders. He kisses the top of my head as he squeezes me tightly. I bury my face in his chest and he finally speaks.

'I will never let anything happen to you as long as you're mine. You know that, don't you?'

I nod as I close my eyes and breathe in his scent and his warmth. 'I know.'

'But I want you to know that if you ever feel like you need me to come back – for any reason – I'll hop on the next plane. I'll do whatever it takes to make sure you never drown again.' He grabs my face and forces me to look him in the eye. 'You put some kind of love spell on me with your wicked dance moves and now I need you like Paula Deen needs butter, or insulin, or whatever.' I laugh and he kisses the tip of my nose. 'I'm going to miss the fuck out of you, but I promise this is going to be worth it. Do you believe me?'

I grab his hands to pull them away from my face and he looks disappointed. 'I believe you, but I'm still scared.'

He reaches into his back pocket and pulls out his wallet. He slips a wad of cash out and attempts to hand it to me.

'I don't want that.'

'I know you don't want it, but you need it.'

He tries to force the money into my hand. I wrench my hand away then stuff both my hands behind my back.

'I'm not taking it.'

'Please take it, Claire. It would make me feel better if I knew I didn't have to worry about you, at least not for another few weeks while you look for a job. I'll send you more later.'

'I'm dead serious. I don't want your money.'

'Why? You can take a fucking car from Senia, but you can't take a few hundred bucks from me?'

'It's not the same.'

'Why? Because it's me? Would you take it if it were Chris?'

'Please don't start with that.'

Adam has only made one other negative comment about Chris, three weeks ago when we got in a fight over the fact that Chris texted me while Adam and I were hanging out in my dorm – well, we were doing a little more than hanging out. That's why I erased all of Chris's texts from my phone when Senia told me what happened between her and Eddie. Adam and I have been straddling the line between crazy in love and Crazy Town ever since everything blew up at Chris's concert five weeks ago. I'm not surprised that the stress of this impending separation has brought on another Chris accusation, but I'm also not in the mood for it.

He shakes his head as he takes a step back and my heart stops as a van swerves to avoid hitting him.

'What the fuck are you doing?'

He steps forward again and glares down at me. 'All right. I'm just going to come right out and say this because I need to say it before I leave.'

I hold my breath as I wait for whatever he's about to get off his chest.

'I don't like that you're spending so much time with him. I don't trust him.'

I can't believe he's doing this now. Actually, I can't believe he's doing this at all. He knows the only reason I've seen Chris three times in the last five weeks is for the purpose of the open adoption. Is he actually trying to make me feel guilty for that?

'Are you saying you don't want me to see Chris anymore, ever?'

'No,' he insists, but the millisecond flash of hope I see in his eyes at this suggestion tells me that's exactly what he wants. 'I know you have to see him for the adoption stuff, but him showing up at your dorm to drop off pictures or outside your class to pick you up . . . Why can't you drive your own car there? I don't fucking get it.'

I lean back against the car and gaze at the reflection of the blue sky on the side of the *Raleigh Times* highrise building across the street. 'I didn't know you felt this way.'

'How could you not know?'

The incredulous look on his face makes me furious. 'Because I don't read minds.'

'Jesus Christ, Claire, I know you've only been in one other relationship, but this is fucking common sense.'

'Are you saying I lack common sense?'

'Don't do that. You know what I mean.' He closes his eyes and shakes his head. 'Let's not do this today. I'm sorry I brought it up.'

He searches my face for a sign of agreement, but I'm fuming inside. I don't even want to look at him.

'I shouldn't have come here. Everything was fine before we left the dorm.'

He grabs the sides of my waist as his legs straddle mine and I can tell he's getting ready to kiss me.

'Stop.'

'Really?'

'Yes.'

He lets go of my waist and steps sideways so he's no longer straddling my legs. 'Whatever you say, Claire.' He pauses for a moment and I know this argument has gone too far. 'Maybe we should just take a break.'

I let out a soft chuckle. 'I can't believe you.'

'You can't believe *me*? You can't even *look* at me.'

I turn and look him straight in the eye. 'I don't want to take a break, but I also don't want to feel like I can't hang out with one of my best friends because you're afraid of something that's never going to happen. Chris and I are over. I thought I made that perfectly clear.'

A blue hatchback pulls up next to us and Lena is in the passenger seat. She's smiling until she sees the serious expressions on our faces. Yuri leans over her and shoves the trophy and his backpack through the open passenger-side window.

'Dude, we got tired of waiting for you in the car,' he says as Adam grabs the trophy.

Adam sticks his hand through the window to do a little secret handshake with Yuri.

'Thanks, man. I'll see you on Koki Beach.'

'I'll be there, bro,' Yuri says before he takes off down Wilmington.

Koki Beach. They had this all planned out, but I just found out about it this morning.

'All right,' he begins. 'You do what you have to do and I'll do the same. I know you would never do anything to hurt me, *intentionally*. And I hope you know I won't do anything to hurt you, even unintentionally. You have my word on that.'

I'm so annoyed that I can't even be more annoyed by that *intentionally* remark. 'You already hurt me by keeping this from me until this morning, even if it was *unintentional*. You're no angel, Adam, so please stop making me out to be the devil in this relationship.'

He sets the trophy on the pavement at his feet and it's so tall it almost reaches his hip. Third place in his first competition. This is not the first time he's going to leave me.

'You're right,' he replies. 'I apologize. I never should have said that. And I can't keep you from having a relationship with Chris. Whatever works for you two works for me, as long as it doesn't infringe upon my boyfriend duties, if you know what I mean.'

I smile reluctantly and he seizes the opportunity to grab my hand and plant a soft kiss on my palm. I step forward and throw my arms around his neck. He lifts me up and pins me against the car as I wrap my legs around his waist.

We hug like this for a few minutes in silence as I try unsuccessfully to fight the tears.

'You're the best thing that ever happened to me,' he

97

whispers in my ear. 'I'll break all the rules to keep you.'

He leans his forehead against mine and my mouth stretches into the biggest, uncontrollable grin I've worn in a long time.

'I love that smile,' he murmurs as he leans in to kiss me.

Our lips haven't touched yet when a car pulls up so close behind Adam that my heart stutters in my chest.

'Claire Nixon,' a voice calls out as Adam turns around to see who it is.

I see the black Porsche and I'm about ready to kill Chris, until I see Tristan sitting in the driver's seat. Chris is on the passenger side calling my name.

'What the fuck!' Adam and I both shout at the same time.

'You almost hit him!' I shriek.

Tristan laughs, but Chris at least attempts to hold in his laughter. Before I can even process what's happening, Adam is wrenching open the passenger-side door and Chris's eyes are locked on him as he steps out of the car and pushes Adam back.

Adam is only a couple of inches taller than Chris at six-foot-two-inches, but he's solid as stone from years of surfing and training. I'm actually afraid for both Chris and Adam right now. Adam is still on probation for another six months. If he gets cited for anything, even something as minor as being a public nuisance, he'll probably go straight to jail.

Adam lunges forward and swings at Chris's face.

The sound of his fist connecting with Chris's jaw makes my stomach lurch. Chris falls backward toward the seat just as Tristan scrambles around the back of the Porsche and rushes Adam.

'Stop it!' I shout as Tristan and Adam roll around on the asphalt, fists and curse words flying in all directions.

Chris stands up from the passenger seat, rubbing his jaw, and I push him back before he can join in. 'Get your fucking friend off of him!' I shriek.

He glares at me. 'You should keep your boyfriend on a fucking leash!'

I step toward them to attempt to break it up, but Chris grabs my arm and pulls me back. He struggles for a few seconds to get a grip on Tristan's arms, but he finally yanks him off and I immediately grab Adam as he gets to his feet.

'Get out of here before the cops come!' I whisper-shout at him. 'Hurry up!'

His lip is bleeding and there's a bloody scuff from where his cheek must have scraped the asphalt. I want to reach up and wipe the blood from his mouth, but a small part of me is afraid that if I try to touch him right now he'll hit me. His chest is heaving and his hands are still balled up in fists as he glares at Tristan and Chris over my shoulder.

'Go!' I shout to break him out of his rage-trance.

Finally, he looks down at me, and the guilty look on his face kills me. 'Fuck! I'm sorry.'

He kisses my forehead before he grabs his trophy and takes off running toward where his car is parked down the street. I spin around and Tristan is laughing as he uses the front of his T-shirt to sop up the blood pouring out of his nostrils.

'You think that's funny? What are you, twelve?' I push him as hard as I can and he falls back against the Porsche.

He continues to laugh as he makes his way around the back of the Porsche to the driver's side.

I round on Chris. 'I never would have expected this from you.'

'I'm the one who stopped it!' he barks.

'After you started it!'

'I wasn't driving the fucking car.'

I shake my head in disgust as I turn around and grab my purse off the top of my car. I'm shaking with rage as I pull my keys out of the purse and deactivate my car alarm. I look over my shoulder at Chris before I get inside.

'Don't ever bring that asshole around me again.'

I take a few deep breaths as I drive down Wilmington. My phone rings as soon as I turn the corner.

'Adam? Where are you?'

'I just wanted to let you know that I'm fine and I'm really fucking sorry. I don't know what got into me.'

Adam's temper has always been simmering just below the surface. I've known this almost from the moment I met him. I've seen him trying so hard to keep it under control since all this stuff started happening with Chris. But I'd be lying if I said it doesn't frighten me.

'Claire?'

'You really scared me.'

The silence that follows is charged with all the implications behind these words. Is it what Adam *did* that scared me? Or is it *him* that had me so frightened I felt as if my heart was going to leap out of my chest? I've never seen him like that.

Yes, it was *him* that scared me.

'Man, I fucked up. I messed up our last day together.'

'Just call me when you get home tonight,' I say as I pull my car onto the highway.

'I will. And I am really, really fucking sorry. I shouldn't have done that.'

'I know. I'm just glad you're all right.'

Chapter Twelve

Chris

The harsh sound of the hotel phone ringing startles me awake. My hand fumbles over the cool surface of the bedside table until I find the phone and pick up the receiver.

'Housekeeping. When can we come to clean your room?'

A crack of sunlight shining through the curtains hits my face as I open my eyes, sending a sharp pain slicing through the left side of my head. I blink a few times until the spots disappear and glance at the alarm clock on the table: 1:17 p.m.

'Never,' I mutter into the phone and hang up.

I turn over in the bed and my arm hits someone next to me. *Fuck*. I almost don't want to look.

I haven't gotten drunk enough to have a hangover in months, but all this shit with Claire and Abigail is bringing up feelings I thought I'd long since buried. It seems all the women in my life are determined to make my life more difficult.

Claire hasn't returned any of my calls or texts since the incident in Raleigh. I even sent her an arrangement of her favorite flowers – daisies – with an apology note, but she's still ignoring me. I texted her last night before the show to tell her I have some news on the adoption, certain that this would elicit a response, but she still hasn't responded.

I turn my head to glimpse my bed buddy and find Tristan Pollock, my bass guitarist and best friend since seventh grade, knocked out with his hair covering most of his face. Tristan and I had a falling-out when I took the solo deal last year, but we quickly made up when I insisted on having him play bass on the West Coast tour we did in the spring. Now, all the old resentments are gone and I'm relieved to be waking up next to him.

I turn my head again to get a look at the other bed in the hotel room and I glimpse the back of Rachel's head. Rachel and Jake, my drummer, have been together longer than Claire and I have known each other. She goes to every show with Jake. If I didn't know her I would think it was because she was possessive as fuck. But the truth is that after seven years together, they still can't get enough of each other. They're inseparable – the way Claire and I used to be.

I grab my phone off the nightstand and check to see if there are any new messages. I scroll through the nine new texts I've received, but none of them are from

Claire. I stare at the text I sent her last night and shake my head.

Me: Tasha gave me some new info. Come to my jam session on Saturday, I'll fill you in. I want to apologize for being the world's biggest douchebag.

I sit up in bed and my head immediately starts pounding to the beat of my heart. It's the same beat I've used to write a million songs about Claire, and this is where it's gotten me. I should just fucking quit already. I could get used to playing local clubs to pay the bills. I'd even get a regular job if that's what it took to get Claire back.

I sling my legs over the side of the bed and the first thing I want to do is text her. I went more than twelve months without sending her a single text and now it's the first and last thing I want to do every day. It's funny that when the one person you live for is ripped out of your life you can still find a way to convince yourself it's for the best and that you will eventually get over it.

What a joke.

Xander, my manager, set up the show we played last night in D.C. as part of this surprise tour we've been on for the past five weeks and I'm starting to get really fucking annoyed. Last night's show on the mall was insane and way more packed than I expected. I don't remember how or when I got back to the hotel room, but I do remember feeling like my life, not just my vision, was spinning out of control.

I stand up and make my way to the restroom, but Jake calls my name before I make it there.

'What?' I call back.

'I have to go first. I'm gonna puke.'

He tumbles off the bed and rushes past me into the bathroom. I barely catch a glimpse of his dark scruffy hair and man-beard before he slams the door closed behind him. The door doesn't do a good job of drowning out the sounds of his retching.

'God, what a fuckin' lightweight.' Rachel's voice is raspy. She's probably parched as hell from whatever the fuck we did last night.

I haven't lost time from too much alcohol in ages. It's a scary feeling, not knowing what – or who – you did the night before. It appears as if I didn't do anything or anyone I'd regret, but I have enough regrets accumulated from all the things I have and haven't done this past year. Waking up next to Tristan today can't erase all the shit that's happened since I left Claire.

I take a seat at the desk in the hotel room and grab the pen and pad of paper bearing the hotel logo. It's a habit. Anytime I see a pen and paper I have to write something, lyrics or notes, or nonsense. I write what comes to mind and I've come up with the beginnings of some good songs that way. I pull the cap off the pen with my teeth, press the pen to the paper, and write.

Dear Claire,

Remember the time you caught me changing in my bedroom before we got together? Remember that embarrassment? That longing? I feel it every fucking day. Leaving you was the stupidest mistake I've ever made.

I tear the sheet of paper off the pad and I'm about to crumple it up when Rachel snatches it out of my hand.

'Don't fuck with me right now. I've got the mother of all hangovers.'

She ignores me as she reads the note to herself then hands it back to me. 'You're an idiot. You can write a fucking song and a note, but you can't actually *do* anything.'

'Of course I can't do anything. She has a fucking boyfriend.'

'Do you expect her to just magically want to get back together with you? Earth to Chris, girls *want* to be pursued. Playing hard to get only works in new relationships. You've known Claire too long for those games to work on her.'

I roll my eyes as I lean back in the desk chair. 'You don't understand. Claire thinks she's in love with this guy. If I try to, as you say, *pursue* her, she'll think I'm trying to fuck things up for her.'

Rachel shakes her head as she leans against the dresser and pulls her hair up into a ponytail. 'You're right. I don't fucking understand. How could she throw that away? You guys were perfect for each other. Give me her new number and I'll talk some sense into her.'

'Hell no. I don't need you fucking things up any more.'

'Hey, she used to be my friend. Don't be selfish. Give me her fucking number.'

Jake finally comes out of the bathroom and I can smell the vomit on him as he passes between Rachel and me on his way to the bed. Rachel scrunches up her face in disgust and I wait for her to make a snide comment.

'Ever heard of toothpaste?' she says as Jake pulls the comforter over himself.

'I've got your toothpaste right here,' he mutters, and I'm positive he's grabbing his dick under the covers.

Rachel rolls her eyes then turns back to me. She's not going to let this go.

'Give me her number. I want to take her to lunch when we get back.'

'I'm not giving you her number. If she wanted you to have her number she would have told me to give it to you.'

'Whatever, Chris. I'm going to look her up in the directory and you're going to be kissing my feet when she comes crawling back to you.'

I crumple up the note before I toss it into the waste bin. 'She's changed.'

'You've both changed,' she says as she walks toward the bathroom door. 'But I'll bet you Jake's drum set that she's just waiting for you to make your move. Trust me when I say that Claire worshipped you.'

I sigh as I lean forward and rest my elbows on my knees. 'Well, she's really fucking pissed at me right now. Besides, she just wants to move on. I have to let her do that or I won't be able to forgive myself if I mess things up for her again.'

My phone vibrates and my stomach flips inside me. Taking a deep breath, I try to drown the hope that it's her. I pull the phone out of my pocket and smile when I see the text message.

Claire: Are you seriously trying to bribe me to go see your jam session?

'Is that her?' Rachel asks, but I ignore her as I type my response.

Me: I want to apologize properly and I can't do that in a text message.
Claire: I don't want to hear your apologies. Just tell me what Tasha told you.
Me: I can't. It's too important.
Claire: You're an asshole.
Me: I know, but I'm trying really hard to change that.
Claire: I don't want to see Tristan.
Me: He never sticks around after the shows. You know that.

108

The thirty-eight minutes she makes me wait for her response are pure torture.

Claire: When and where is the jam session?

Chapter Thirteen

Chris

'I'm telling you, that's not my mic. That's Jake's. Mine is the 5200. Please get my mic.'

The new crewmember keeps mixing up my mic with Jake's. This is the third time he's done it this week and I'm about to lose my shit. Xander had the brilliant idea of hiring local sound and backline crews we've never worked with for this Home Sweet Home tour, to support the local economy, but I don't need this kind of stress right now. I just want this tour over with.

I'm nervous as hell. Not only am I going to be jamming with the legendary Neil Hardaway, but Claire will be out there watching me. My palms are sweating and I haven't even tuned up.

Keith brings the correct mic this time and I slide it into the mic stand. I sit down on my stool and rest Lucille, my Gibson SG electric guitar, in my lap. I only use the stool for acoustic sets, but I'm feeling a little unsteady on my feet today. Keith hands me the amp cable and I plug in.

I brush my fingers lightly over the strings and the sound echoes through the empty club. Nothing in this world is more soothing to me than holding a guitar in my hands, except being inside Claire or even lying next to her. The worst part of being apart from her this past year was the knowledge that I probably never would have gotten where I am if we'd stayed together. My songwriting improved by a million percent after we broke up. There really is nothing more inspiring to an artist than a shattered heart.

By the time I'm done tuning the guitar, Jake and Tristan are on stage and ready for a warm-up. We're not performing any of my songs today. The studio put too much of a pop spin on most of the songs on the *Relentless* album. Neil Hardaway is a local blues legend. He can't play that shit. He actually called me himself last night to tell me what we would be playing, and I nearly pissed my pants. We rehearsed last night in his home studio and I swear I had an out-of-body experience, as if I were watching someone else living their dream.

'"Firefly"' I say over my shoulder and I immediately hear the clack of Jake's drumsticks behind me and the shuffle of Tristan's feet to my left as they prepare.

'Firefly' is one of the many songs I wrote about Claire where I changed a lot of the details so she wouldn't know it was about her. This song is about a

111

girl I call Firefly who writes me love notes and leaves them in random places for me to find. Of course, in the end, she leaves a note that's not a love note at all. Claire used to send me random texts with random words – anagrams. I had to rearrange the letters to figure out what she was trying to tell me. It was one of our favorite games. She always tried to use the longest words to make it difficult for me to guess. The last text she sent me after we broke up was a one-word text, but it wasn't an anagram: Sorry.

When we finish warming up, Neil Hardaway strolls in looking like a fucking pimp. He's got more soul than any white man I've ever met. And, man, is he white! I don't think Neil Hardaway's face has seen a ray of sunshine in fifteen years. He's wearing a midnight-blue suit with a thin black tie, sunglasses, and black newsboy cap. I hope I'm that cool when I'm fifty-seven years old.

'What's up, brother?' he says in that smooth, soulful twang. 'You ready to turn these girls inside out?'

We shake hands then I nod at Keith for him to take my stool off the stage. Neil laughs, a raspy laugh, as another crewmember races up the steps onto the stage and hands him his guitar: a baby blue ES-345.

'Them girls waiting outside are about ready to tear the doors off this mother,' Neil continues.

I'm a little star struck, though not as bad as I was when I first met him yesterday. 'Not interested,' I mutter as I pull a fresh pick out of my pocket and rub it between my fingertips to warm the plastic.

I'm not interested *tonight*, not when one of those girls waiting outside could possibly be Claire. I told her to come through the rear entrance, but she insisted on not getting special treatment. She probably doesn't want anyone to get the wrong idea about us, afraid it will get back to surfer boy.

'Chris?'

Keith is looking at me weird as if he's been trying to get my attention.

'What's up?'

'There's a girl out back asking for you.'

I can't help but smile as I toss the pick to Keith and he catches it in one hand. 'Take me to her.'

I set Lucille down before we cross the empty space designated for general admission ticket holders then past the bar. He takes me through an adjacent lounge with a few pool tables and then along a corridor with some restrooms. At the end of the corridor, we arrive at an exit door and I push it open slowly in case she's standing on the other side.

The cool night air blasts me in the face and I get a strong whiff of garbage and cotton candy. Claire is leaning against the back wall of the club with her eyes closed. We haven't had any long conversations since we got back in touch last month, but she did mention to me that she started meditating after we broke up. The way she dismissed me when I asked her about it made me think it wasn't something she liked to talk about.

113

'Hey.'

She opens her eyes and turns to me. Her hair is pulled back in a ponytail and the light of the street-lamps paints an angelic glow over her skin.

She flashes me a tight smile. 'Hey. Is it okay that I came back here? The sidewalk was packed out front and I started panicking that Joanie was gonna show up.'

'You can do whatever you want. No one here is going to mess with you. Come on.' I hold the door open for her and try not to be too obvious that I'm breathing in her scent as she passes me. 'And Joanie's not welcome here, so you don't have to worry about her.'

She follows me along the corridor and into the lounge area.

'Have you seen some of the signs those girls are holding out front?'

'Nope. I've been warming up. We're about to run through a few songs then they'll open the doors.'

'You should really go see those signs. They're kind of gross and fascinating all at once.'

'Like Jake's sixth toe or worse?'

She laughs for a split second before she remembers she's still pissed at me. We pass the bar where the bartenders are busy setting up. I grab her hand and she quickly yanks it back, throwing me a shocked look.

'Settle down. I wasn't trying to hold your hand. I was just trying to stop you. Do you want anything to drink?' I ask, nodding toward the bar.

She shakes her head quickly. 'I'm fine.'

I narrow my eyes as I try to figure out why the hell she came here when she knows damn well that she could have worn me down and I'd have given up the information from Tasha. I didn't want to say anything about this when she called me this morning to verify the address. I was afraid questioning her motives would make her change her mind. But I'm getting the feeling that there are more problems in her relationship than just the stupid scuffle we got in last week.

'Christopher Michael Knight,' Jake booms into the microphone in his deep voice. 'Get your sexy ass on this stage.'

'You guys remember Claire,' I shout at them from the bar then turn back to her. 'Come on. You can sit on the side of the stage so you don't get squished.'

'I don't want special treatment,' she insists as she follows me toward the stage.

Jake waves his drumstick at Claire and she waves back, but Tristan doesn't acknowledge her. Tristan and Claire have never gotten along well. She always claimed he was trying to corrupt me. Tristan always claimed that I was whipped and Claire was the reason I went solo. They'll probably never speak again after that fight with her boyfriend.

'This place is going to be packed,' I insist.

'So?'

'You don't have to pretend you don't care.'

I shake my head as I climb the steps onto the stage

and pick up my guitar. I can't see Neil's eyes through the sunglasses, but I glimpse a barely-there smile on his lips. We warm up with 'Gimme Shelter'; I take the first guitar solo and we go back and forth on the second one.

The whole time we're warming up, Claire stands off to the side of the stage with a scowl on her face. After a couple more songs, we head backstage so they can open the doors. Claire follows me with a pissy pout on her face.

Once everyone's out of earshot, I grab her arm and pull her behind an equipment rack. 'You want to tell me why you came here if you're still so fucking pissed?'

116

Chapter Fourteen

Claire

I wrench my arm out of Chris's grip and push him back. He's standing way too close. His dark eyes are burrowing into me and making me nervous. I almost forgot how much of an asshole Chris can be when he thinks I'm hiding something from him.

I am pissed at him over what happened with Adam, but I know Adam is the one who opened the car door to get at Chris. Chris didn't even hit him.

'You're the one who bribed me into coming here. Why don't you just give me the information so I can leave?'

He smiles, that you-don't-have-it-in-you smile, and I'm seriously considering punching him to wipe the grin off his face. But somehow I can't stop staring at his lip ring. I wish I could forget the memory of the metallic taste of it in my mouth.

'Come on, Claire. I'm your best friend; at least, I *was*

your best friend. You can be honest with me. Are you having problems with your boyfriend?'

'You can lose the smug grin, Chris. I came here because you bribed me with your information and because you looked like I'd smashed your guitar in half when I told you I couldn't come.'

He lowers his head a little as if he's ashamed then lets out a soft chuckle. 'Sorry. I guess I'm just a little on edge about seeing you after what happened with Abigail's parents. I thought you'd blame me. Then that shit happened with your boyfriend and I thought for sure I'd lost you forever.'

Suddenly, the muscles in my chest tighten and I feel as if I'm about to have a panic attack. I have been trying not to blame anyone for the mess I'm in with Abigail's parents, especially not Chris since I do believe he's only doing what he thinks I want. But I can't help feeling like Chris's fame is the main thing that tore us all apart. If he hadn't been in Los Angeles recording the final tracks on the *Relentless* album when I found out I was pregnant, I might actually have told him about the pregnancy. If I hadn't been completely certain that having a baby would have ruined his career, none of this would be happening.

I don't want to blame Chris. After all, I was the one who encouraged him to leave. But hearing him say that he thought I would blame him for what happened with the meeting makes me feel as if he's giving me permission to hold him accountable. I take a few long, deep breaths to keep the anger from exploding out of me.

I need some serious therapy.

'I don't blame you for what happened with Abigail's parents, but it is really frustrating.'

'That they backed out on us or the reason they backed out?'

'Both.'

Before he can respond, Xander jogs toward us with a panicked look on his chubby face.

Xander has been managing Chris's career since he was a senior in high school playing local clubs. He was a customer in Jackie's bakery and, true to her chatty nature, they sparked up a deep conversation. She found out he managed a few local bands and she buttered him up with lots of delicious cakes and pastries to get him to listen to Chris's band, Blue Knights. Xander didn't need any convincing to sign on with Chris, but he was always pushing Chris to go solo.

Xander's thick brown hair is plastered with sweat along the hairline and the panic in his eyes makes him look like a sitcom character. When he sees me, he doesn't immediately recognize me. Then it clicks.

'Claire? Is that you, sweetie pie?'

Xander has the most melodic Southern accent I've ever heard on a man. It always makes me smile.

'Hi, Xander,' I say as I reach out to give him a hug.

He hugs me so hard I can feel the sweat seeping through his shirt and mine. I pat his back a few times and he lets go.

'Girl, look at you. You look and smell like cotton candy on a stick.'

'Not looking so bad yourself. Have you lost weight?'

'I have!' He twirls around for me and shakes his butt. 'Ten pounds. It's this new trainer Chris referred me to. I mean, if he can get this boy some muscles, he's gotta be able to work his magic on me.'

I try not to laugh too hard at this. Chris was always a bit self-conscious about his inability to bulk up. He's still pretty lean, but even through his T-shirt I can see his shoulders are a bit broader and his chest is bulkier. I have a strange urge to squeeze his arm the way I used to when he was lifting weights in the garage.

Chris squints at me as if he knows what I'm thinking. 'You think that's funny? My trainer kicks my ass and he has me drinking these awful shakes that make me want to chuck the blender across the kitchen. But I do it all for the fans.'

Xander's panic returns suddenly. 'Speaking of fans, one of your fans just got arrested for stripping in front of the club. They're opening the doors early to try to subdue the frenzy. You're on in twenty.'

'What the fuck? Why do I always miss the action?' Chris complains.

I resist the urge to punch him in the arm the way I would have when we were together. Those days are over. He's allowed to make comments like that in front of me now.

*

After the show, Chris insists I allow him to drive me to my car a couple of blocks away.

'Those girls will rip you to shreds if you walk out there alone,' he says as he opens the passenger door of the Porsche. 'You saw how they were looking at you while you were sitting on the side of the stage, like you were a cockroach.'

Sitting on the side of the stage tonight, the way I used to, was an uncomfortable experience for me. Not because I had to watch Chris flashing his crowd smile at the girls in the first few rows of bodies. It was uncomfortable because of the way I felt when the same girls cast dirty looks in my direction while Chris performed 'Relentless.' He kept glancing at me during this song, and the crowd noticed. I should have felt annoyed with Chris, but instead it felt kind of cool to be so envied. I don't want to feel that way.

'Just take me to my car,' I say as I grab the handle to shut the car door, but he holds on to keep me from closing it. 'What are you doing?'

He stares at me for a moment, looking like he's about to say something, then he shakes his head and shuts the door. Suddenly my entire body is zinging with a dreadful nervous energy. I hope he doesn't try anything. I don't want to have to reject Chris.

He slides into the driver's seat and chuckles as he turns the key in the ignition.

'What's so funny?' I ask as I buckle my seatbelt.

'Nothing,' he replies as the engine purrs around us.

He casts me a sideways look that sends chills through me. I rub my arms to feign cold as he pulls out of the parking lot and takes a few side streets to bypass the crowds leaving the club. When we arrive at my car, there's a group of girls passing by and one of them points at the Porsche when she recognizes Chris.

'Don't get out,' he says as I reach for the door handle. 'We'll chill out somewhere for a while, then I'll bring you back.'

He pulls away quickly before I can protest.

'Hey! I don't care about those girls. I need to get back to the dorm to study.'

'It's eleven forty-five.'

'Yeah, I'll probably be studying until four a.m. Even later if you don't take me back to my car right now.'

He turns right at the intersection and passes in front of the club where the sidewalk is almost empty now.

'Claire, we need to talk.' I stare out the passenger window as he continues. 'I know you asked me not to text you or call you out of respect for your boyfriend, but—'

'His name is Adam and he'd be really fucking pissed if he knew what you were doing right now.'

'I don't give a shit what his name is or what he'd do. The hard truth is that you need to grow up.'

I turn to him and he's serious. Not a trace of a smile on his face.

'Don't look at me like you're so surprised to hear me

say that. I know you made some tough decisions this past year, but you've been running from the consequences of those decisions instead of facing them. And you're *still* running. We should be able to have a fucking adult conversation concerning our daughter without worrying if we're going to piss off your boyfriend. By the way, he needs to grow up, too.'

I want to tell him to fuck off. I want to plug my ears or punch him or jump out of his Porsche as it speeds down the boulevard; anything not to have to hear another word of this.

The only thing stopping me is that he's right.

I take a moment to gather my thoughts before I respond. 'You don't know anything about the decisions I've made or what it's been like living with the consequences of those decisions,' I begin. 'After the baby was born and ripped away from me, I . . .' My throat constricts painfully as I recall the way I felt right after I gave birth to Abigail last April. 'I thought I had nothing left to live for.'

This is the first time I've spoken to anyone about this. Not even Senia knows how close I came to taking my own life the first week after I moved to Wrightsville Beach. Lately, I'm struggling to make it from one day to the next, but back then I was grasping for every second. It wasn't until I met Fallon and she taught me how to meditate that I managed to claw my way out of the dark hole I'd almost buried myself in. Just thinking of all the nights I sat in the bathroom staring at the razor blade and the bottle of pills on the linoleum floor in front of me fills me with shame.

Chris pulls into a supermarket parking lot and triple-parks across a few spaces in the empty lot. He kills the engine and stares at me.

'I should have been there for you.'

'It would have ruined everything you had going on.'

'In April, I was touring in Asia. I didn't have to be there. I should have been here.'

I unbuckle my seatbelt because I'm starting to feel claustrophobic in the tiny cabin of this sports car.

'I need some air.'

I throw the door open and jump out of the car. The asphalt sways beneath me and I swallow the sour vomit stinging the back of my throat. Chris arrives at my side just as the vomit comes back up and explodes out of my mouth. Some of it splashes onto the side of his beautiful car, but he doesn't seem to mind as he holds back my ponytail and one more pocket of spew streams from my mouth.

I spit out the bitter traces still lingering on my tongue then swipe the back of my hand across my lips. 'Sorry.'

'For what?'

'For handling this so poorly.'

His eyes soften as I lean back against the car to steady myself. 'For someone who's been through what you've been through, I think you've handled this well. But I do wish you wouldn't close yourself off to me. Sometimes I need someone to talk to about all this stuff and you're the only one who'll understand. I need you, Claire.' He takes a step toward me and I hold my breath as he brushes a sweaty lock of hair away from my face. 'And I know you need me too.'

His hand is warm against my cheek and it makes me want to lose myself in him. I close my eyes to attempt to block out this longing, but I still see his face. I have so many memories, though most of my memories from my first fifteen years on this Earth are painful. I didn't really start creating happy memories until I met Chris and Jackie.

After Chris and I broke up, I saw him everywhere. When I watched a movie and saw a man kayaking, I thought of how Chris promised to take me whitewater rafting. When I opened the refrigerator at Senia's parents' house and saw her little sister's Capri-Sun pouches, I thought of how Chris was addicted to those. Every time I'd lie in bed at night, I thought of how Chris would sing me to sleep. Every time I looked down at my growing belly, I saw him. Every time I listened to her heartbeat during a checkup, I heard him.

I'd gotten so used to imagining my future with Chris that every reminder of him seemed like a slap in the face. Like someone laughing and pointing at me while showing me all the beautiful things and the all-consuming love I would never have. By the time I had Abigail I was thoroughly beaten down by the memories.

125

Then I met Adam.

I open my eyes and Chris is watching me with that look of concern that I've grown accustomed to. You don't grow up with a heroin addict for a mother without becoming very familiar with that look.

'All of this is insanity,' I whisper as I stare at his chest. 'I should be able to have a conversation with you about . . . Abigail. I don't know if I deserve to meet her. I think it will drive me crazy. Seems I'm more like my mother than I thought I was.'

He places his fingers under my chin and tilts my face up. 'You are nothing like your mother, babe. You put Abigail's needs before your own. You made the selfless choice, not the selfish one. Please tell me you believe that.'

I shake my head. No, I don't believe that.

He pulls me into his arms, a place I practically lived in for four years. My home. I clutch his T-shirt in my fists, afraid I'll collapse at any second.

'I'll make you see it,' he whispers into my ear.

The drive back to my car is filled with an uneasy silence. I can't stop thinking that I shouldn't have come to the club tonight. And I can't stop wishing I were going home with Chris, back to a time and place where things were simpler.

When he pulls up next to my car, the sidewalk is as empty as the space between us.

'Can I call you tomorrow? I'll tell you everything Tasha and I have been discussing.'

126

I nod. 'Yeah. I'll be in my dorm all day.'

I reach for the door handle when it dawns on me that my cell phone is about to get cut since I haven't paid the bill. If I tell Chris, he's going to offer to pay it for me. But if I don't tell him, and it gets cut before he calls, he may think I'm trying to avoid him or that something bad has happened to me.

'I might not be available, though. I've got a paper to write for my sociology class.'

'Really? You can't spare a few minutes to discuss the adoption?'

My leg starts bouncing with nerves as I try to think of a better lie. Finally, I sigh as I resign myself to the truth. 'My phone might get cut. I have a couple of job interviews this week, but even if I get one of those I won't get paid for another two to three weeks, which means I'm going to probably be without a phone for a while. I'll call you from Senia's phone tomorrow whenever I take a break from studying.'

'Are you serious? Your phone is about to be cut off?'

'I don't have a job anymore. The scholarship doesn't pay for my cell phone bill.'

He's pissed.

'Don't worry about your cell phone. I'll take care of it.'

Chris knows all my personal information, from my social security number all the way down to my fucking panty size. All he has to do is have someone call and pretend to be me so he can pay the bill over the phone.

127

Part of me is pissed that I know what he's going to do and part of me is grateful that he's willing to go to such lengths to help me.

'Thanks.'

'I'll do anything for you, Claire. You should know that by now.'

Against everything inside me, I lean over and kiss his cheek before I jump out of the car. My hands are shaking as I hit the unlock button on the key fob. I slide into the driver's seat and slam my door shut before I allow the first tears to fall.

Chapter Fifteen

Adam

This is my fifth trip to Hawaii. The first four trips were packed with exhausting competitions and late nights with plenty of booze and girls. This time is different. My first two days in Hawaii were spent unpacking and grocery shopping for my training diet. My coach, Remmy Dufrense, won't be here for another three days. I need to keep up my routine until then, but I'm already feeling the urge to toke or down a bottle of vodka.

After what happened last week with Chris, I'm getting a strong feeling that this trip will be the biggest mistake of my life. I'm not imagining things. Claire's voice sounds different today than it did yesterday morning.

'What did you do yesterday?' I ask as I grab an apple out of the fruit bowl on the kitchen counter and bite off a huge chunk.

At least the house the company rented for me in Kekaha is less than a block from the beach and a market with an awesome selection of pokē. I don't plan on spending much time anywhere else, besides work, for the next two months.

'I studied and went . . . I went to a concert.'

The word *concert* and the hesitation in her voice confirms my suspicions.

'Who'd you see?' The long pause on the other end of the line just makes the frustration build inside me, spreading through my arms and down to my fingertips. I have to stop myself from throwing the phone. 'Claire?'

'I saw Chris. He asked me to watch a jam session with one of his idols. I went as his friend. You said that was okay.'

She's not asking if it's okay; she's telling me I already said it was okay. I knew this was going to happen, I just didn't expect it to happen so soon.

'So you just went to watch?'

'Yes, of course. Are you mad?'

'I'm not mad, just not sure how to feel about it yet. I don't like the idea of the two of you hanging out.'

'We didn't really hang out very long. I left once the crowds were gone.'

I want to know every fucking detail about what happened. I want to know if he touched her, even if it was just a friendly hug. But I can hear in the tone of her voice that Claire doesn't want to be grilled on this.

'Adam?'

'Yeah.'

'I need to ask you a favor.'

I sit down at the writing desk in the living room and lean back in the wooden desk chair. 'You can ask me anything, babe.'

'I feel really embarrassed asking you this, but can you pay my cell phone bill? Chris found out my service is about to be cut and I don't want him to pay it. I'd rather you do it. I should be able to pay you back in a few weeks.'

'Stop.'

'Stop what?'

'You don't have to explain and you don't have to pay me back. I'll call and pay the bill as soon as we hang up.' *Sneaky little fucker.* 'Thanks for asking. I want you to come to me whenever you need help. Okay?'

'Okay.'

She gives me her account information and I call as soon as we hang up. By the time I hang up with the cell phone company, I'm feeling a little better about the fact that she doesn't want to depend on Chris, but still uneasy about their proximity to each other. But it's nothing a long therapy session with the Pacific Ocean can't cure. I'll get ready while I wait for my company car to be dropped off.

I change into my bodysuit and I'm about to grab the house key off the hook in the kitchen when the doorbell rings. It must be Sam, the project assistant, with my car.

'Coming!' I yell as I slip the key into my backpack and head for the door.

I pull the door open and I'm a bit confused for a second. I had assumed Sam was a guy, but the brunette standing on my doorstep is definitely not a guy unless she's clenching her bulge under that peach bikini.

'Adam?' she says as she dangles a car key in front of the screen door. 'I have the right house, don't I?'

'Yeah, I'm Adam.' I open the screen door and hold out my hand for the key. 'Are you Sam?'

'Uh, yeah. Were you expecting a guy?' She shakes her head. 'You don't have to answer that. I was just on my way to the sand so I thought I'd drop off your car. I actually picked it up yesterday, but then my aunt came over and made all this food and it was this big thing with all my cousins and . . .' She looks at me as if she's just seeing me for the first time. 'Oh. I'm blabbing. Sorry. Anyway, I'm just dropping off your car. I guess I'll see you at work tomorrow.'

She's awkward as hell. Everything from the way she talks to the way she gestures wildly is awkward. She squints at me as I wait for her to leave.

'Are you going surfing?' she asks, as she looks me up and down.

I don't normally wear my bodysuit to surf unless it's really early in the morning, which it is. The fact that she doesn't seem at all embarrassed about showing up at my door at 7:30 a.m. in a bikini just makes this girl even more awkward.

'Yeah, I was just getting ready to leave. Thanks for bringing the car.'

I shut the screen door, but she doesn't leave.

'Can I go with you?' Her brown eyes are wide as she waits for my response. 'I mean, if you don't mind. I was going to walk, but if you're already going.'

'I'm walking. It's less than a block away.'

'That's cool. I can walk with you.'

Fuck. This girl doesn't take a hint well.

'All right. But I'm going to surf, not to hang out.'

'What does that mean? Is that your subtle way of telling me you're going to ignore me?' She laughs, a low, snorting chuckle, and I try not to cringe.

She's definitely good looking, but she's strange, like a tomboy who doesn't quite understand the rules of engagement between guys and girls.

'Look, I have a girlfriend.'

'Cool! So do I. Well, not a girlfriend; I have a boy-friend. Well, we're not really exclusive yet, so it's not a big deal. Plus, he's been getting on my nerves lately. He always wants to spend the night at my place.' I stare at her for a moment and she continues, undaunted. 'Any-way, you'll probably meet Kai soon enough. He stalks me at work.'

'I think I'm going to hang out for a little while,' I say as I reach for the doorknob to close the front door. 'I have to finish reading the specs for the project before tomorrow. Have fun.'

'That's cool. I guess I'll see you at work tomorrow.

133

Don't bring lunch. I'll bring something good from home. My aunt has been cooking like crazy all weekend.'

I nod in agreement as I begin to close the door. 'See you tomorrow.'

I shut the door quickly and stand in the foyer for a moment, confused by how a girl like that, who's more than a bit ditzy, could get a job as a project assistant on the base. I shake my head as I make my way back to the living room to watch some TV for a few hours, at least until it's safe to go to the beach without running into Sam. As soon as I sit on the sofa, the doorbell rings again.

I set down the remote on the sofa cushion and jog to the door. When I peer through the peephole, I'm not surprised to see Sam standing on the porch. I open the door and she's holding out a three-inch stack of mail.

'This was in your mailbox,' she says. 'Looks like you forgot to check it.'

Something about this girl tells me she's desperate for company. 'Thanks,' I say as I take the mail. She stands there for a while like she's expecting me to invite her inside. 'You know . . . Hold on just a sec while I get my board. I can read the specs later.'

She grins as she nods her head and I can't decide if she's prettier when she smiles or when she says something dumb. It doesn't matter. She's annoying as fuck and I have a girlfriend.

After I get my board out of the garage, I eyeball the

green Toyota sedan in the driveway. Good thing I'm by the beach, because there's no rack on that car for my board. I meet Sam on the sidewalk, which is when I notice her silver scooter.

She flips her dark, wavy hair over her shoulder before she grabs the handlebars and hops on. 'I brought it with me in the trunk of the car. My house is about a half-mile from here. It's just faster to get there on this.'

I nod as I take off down Panako Road toward the beach. I don't know if she's trying to get me to offer her a ride home, but it's not going to happen.

'So you came from North Carolina?' she asks as she gently pushes the scooter along the sidewalk so she doesn't pass me by.

'Yeah, Wilmington. You work for Larry?'

Larry Cromwell is the contracting officer on the base whose ass my dad French kissed to get us this job. The guy is more of a prick than my dad, judging by the emails he sent me complaining about politics. I can't even imagine what it must be like to work directly under him like Sam.

'I don't really work with Larry. I work with Ollie. Ollie protects me from Larry.' She snorts again because apparently this must be funny.

We cross Kahakai Road and soon find ourselves on the beach near Waimea State Park, where she folds up her scooter and tucks it under her arm. The waves should be better further north, but I'm really looking forward to just getting this excursion with Sam over with. Then I'll come out again tomorrow morning and find a sweet spot.

'So you're a surfer? Is that why your company sent you?' she asks when we reach the shore.

I stand my board up in the sand and gaze at the glistening ocean. The sun is rising behind us, barely warming my back, and I breathe a sigh of relief at the sight before me. The glimmer of sunlight painted across the surface of the water puts me at ease. This is where I'm meant to be.

'My dad sent me to handle the project startup,' I reply. 'I'll only be here for eight weeks, but, yeah, I have a competition lined up while I'm here.'

'Sweet.' She drops her scooter onto the sand. 'I surf too, but that car doesn't have a rack so I couldn't bring my board. You're lucky you live within walking distance of the beach.'

She takes off, running into the water without another word. I'm just thankful she didn't challenge me to a race or some other corny shit. I'm even more pleased when she allows me to surf in peace. She swims out to a buoy that looks to be about a quarter-mile offshore then back. When she reaches the shore, she collapses and lies on her towel for about an hour before she comes back into the water.

After two hours of my sad attempts to catch some weak waves, I finally give up. But as soon as I start to leave the water, she follows after me. I trudge across the sand, refusing to look at her as she jogs toward the place where she dropped her scooter a few yards away. She snatches it up and quickly catches up with me.

'The waves are way better on the north shore. I can take you sometime. My truck has space for your board.'

'Why didn't they rent me a truck? Who the fuck ordered me a mom car?'

'That was me,' she confesses with a guilty look. 'I assumed you'd be some stick-up-the-ass rich white boy. I didn't think you'd be so . . .'

'So what?'

'So cool.'

I hold my arm out to stop her from crossing the street as a huge truck comes barreling toward us. Once the street is clear, we race across Kahakai Road.

I instantly forget what Sam said about me being cool as my mind wanders to the night I almost ran Claire over with my truck. She was so pissed at me; she almost refused to let me drive her home. I'm here for her and nothing else. Once the startup phase is complete, I can go home to Claire and say goodbye to my dad's bullshit.

We arrive at the wooden fence surrounding the front yard of the rental house and she salutes me like a soldier. 'See you at oh-eight-hundred.'

I shake my head as she scoots off down the street. What an odd girl, yet there's something about her I find strangely interesting. I think it's the way she doesn't seem to have any interest in me. She didn't look at me the way most girls look at me when I first meet them. Maybe it *is* possible for guys and girls to just be friends. Maybe I really have nothing to worry about with Claire and Chris.

Chapter Sixteen

Chris

The phone rings in my ear as I wait for Claire to pick up. I try to remind myself to stay calm, but this feeling that I'm being lied to makes this very fucking difficult.

'Hello,' she says and just the sound of her voice catches me off guard.

Suddenly, I can't remember why I called.

'Chris?'

Then it comes back to me. 'I thought you told me you didn't have the money to pay your bill. My assistant just called to pay it and they said your bill was paid this afternoon.'

She's silent for a moment, probably trying to come up with another lie. 'Adam paid it for me.'

I want to throw the phone at the wall. I'm so sick of hearing his fucking name.

'Good,' I reply, gritting my teeth to bite back an angry retort. 'Can you talk right now? About Abigail?'

'Yeah,' she whispers so low I can barely hear her.

What is it about hearing a name that can provoke such a strong emotional reaction? I hear the name Adam and I want to pummel something. Claire hears the name Abigail and she immediately shuts down. Maybe I shouldn't talk to her about this stuff. She needs a clear head to do well in her classes.

'Are you sure you're okay talking about this?' I ask.

'Yes. I'm fine. I need to talk about it, too.'

I take the stairs down to the first floor and head for the kitchen. I have an apartment in L.A. that's been empty for months while I've been on tour. This Home Sweet Home tour is the last leg for this year. It's over in the end of September. I'm headed back to L.A. in October to record for a few weeks then I'll be back before Christmas.

'I need to get you up to speed on the details of the agreement and I need to give you my schedule for the next few months so you can try to handle some of this stuff alone while I'm in L.A., if necessary.'

'I can't do this alone.'

I open the refrigerator and grab a bottle of water. When I close the refrigerator door, I notice a new picture my mom must have dug up and stuck on the fridge before she left for work this morning. It's a picture of me playing at one of my first paid gigs when I was sixteen. A small piece of the back of Claire's head is visible in the bottom-left corner of the photo. This picture was taken just a few months after I met Claire, when we were still 'just friends.' So much has changed. Claire and I will never be 'just friends' again.

'You won't be alone. You'll be working with Tasha. I'll be gone for less than four weeks and I'll be just a phone call away.'

'Don't you think that's going to look bad? Leaving to L.A. when we're so close to coming to an agreement with her parents? They're already nervous about your . . . lifestyle.'

I laugh as I take a seat on a barstool. 'My lifestyle? What the fuck does that mean?'

'I don't know,' she replies, probably afraid she'll offend me if she elaborates.

'Come on, Claire, you can be honest with me. What the fuck do you think I do when I'm not sitting in my mom's kitchen talking to you?'

'It doesn't matter what I think. It matters what Abigail's parents think.'

'It matters to me what you think.'

There's a long pause followed by a sigh. 'I have to study. Feel free to give Tasha my phone number so she can fill me in on the details. Bye, Chris.'

She hangs up before I can get in another word. When I pull the phone away from my ear I see two text message notifications. The first message is from Amira, a girl I made the mistake of giving my phone number to when we fucked two months ago after a show in Houston. She texts me every now and then to tell me about shows she went to in Houston, like I give a fuck. I think she's waiting for me to tell her the next time I'll be there for a show.

I delete her text then open the next.

Tasha: Got a cryptic message from adoptive mother. She wants to meet me alone tomorrow without her husband. Will keep you posted.

My stomach twists inside me as I imagine what this could mean. Does she want to call off the whole thing or is she going to allow us to visit Abigail without her husband knowing? Maybe she just needs someone to talk to. I hate the idea that this whole agreement might be causing turmoil in their marriage, but I want to see my daughter. Abigail and Claire are the missing pieces of my heart. Even if I only get to hold Abigail once, I think I can live with that.

I slide off the barstool and make my way into the living room where I grab my acoustic guitar, Betty, off the ottoman then sit down on the hardwood floor. Betty was a gift from Claire for my eighteenth birthday. I have at least six better sounding acoustic guitars, but this vintage guitar with the initials she carved into the wood is still my favorite.

I trace my finger over the 'CC' carved into the curve of the body then tune her up. Tristan and Jake aren't coming over to practice for another hour so I have some time to work on a song I began writing in my head while lying in bed last night. I play the opening exactly as I heard it in my head last night, but the transition to the melody of the first verse is all wrong. I start from the beginning again a few more times before I finally get it right and the first verse comes to me.

'This ain't our last goodbye. It's our last hello. I can feel it in my shattered heart; all through my weary bones. You're the missing piece, the final scrap. Someday we'll fit together; someday I'll bring you back.'

I type the lyrics into the notes app on my phone before I continue working on the chorus. 'These pieces of you are promises, whispering endless possibilities. My pieces of you are haunted, just echoes of shattered memories.'

I'll have to work on this later; these are just the bones. The only song I ever wrote that I never changed a word – and it shows – is 'Relentless.' I wrote it in a hotel room in L.A. when we were almost done recording the album. When I played it for the producer he insisted we add it to the album and make it the title track. It took less than an hour to get down the lyrics and the basic melody for 'Relentless' and it's still the one song that gets me the most love from the fans. Maybe people prefer their art a little raw.

As soon as Jake and Rachel arrive, we get to work on an upbeat track that's supposed to be the first single released from the next album, tentatively titled Chris Knight. Jake and Rachel wrote the lyrics for this song – 'Highway 99' – about falling for the wrong girl and how exciting it is to go to their secret hideaway off highway 99. Now that I'm in this fucked-up situation with Claire, I hate this song.

'Is Tristan ever going to show the fuck up?' I ask.

As much as I love Tristan, he's unreliable as hell. His sex life always gets him in some kind of drama that keeps him from showing up to practice sessions. Technically, Tristan is easily replaceable now that I'm considered a solo act, and the shit that happened with Claire's boyfriend hasn't made things better. But so many of our old fans – the ones who followed Blue Knights from the beginning – go to the shows just to see him. And he's still my oldest friend.

'I'll text him,' Jake says, grabbing his phone off the coffee table.

Since my mom refuses to allow Jake to set up a drum set in her house – the way we used to have it before I went solo – Jake is just here to hang out and watch. Without Tristan here, this practice session is a big fucking waste of time.

Tristan never responds to Jake's text and finally, after my eighth time quitting at the bridge, Jake groans.

'What the fuck is going on with you?' he asks. 'The bridge starts on C7.'

I shake my head as I drop the guitar onto the wood floor and one of the pins pops out. 'Fuck this song.'

Rachel glares at me through her icy blue eyes, which are partially obscured by her bangs. 'Did something happen with Claire?'

I storm into the kitchen and grab the key for my bike off the hook. 'I don't want a fucking lecture.'

'You'd better not drink if you're taking the bike. Don't be a fucking asshole!' she yells as I open the door to the attached garage.

I slam the door behind me then hit the button for the door opener. The garage door rolls open and I'm pleased to see the sun has almost set. I hop onto my bike and kick the stand back. I'm already pulling my bike out of the cul-de-sac by the time Jake makes it out to the driveway.

Chapter Seventeen

Claire

The buzzing noise breaks me out of my trance and it takes a moment before I realize it's my phone vibrating on my nightstand. I reach for the phone and see I have four missed calls. I must have been really out of it this time. Until now, I hadn't meditated since yesterday morning.

All the missed calls are from an unknown number with a Raleigh area code. I debate ignoring the calls to continue my meditation, but the number of missed calls gives me an uneasy feeling.

'Who is it?' Senia asks from where she's lying on her bed studying for a biochem exam.

I shrug then call the number. Someone picks up right away.

'Claire?'

It's Jackie and she sounds frantic.

'Jackie? What's wrong?'

'Oh, my Lord. I left my phone at the shop. I've been calling you from Rachel's phone. I didn't think you would *ever* call back.'

'Jackie, what's happened?'

'Claire, honey, I'm at the hospital. Chris had an accident.'

'An accident? What kind of accident?' My heart pounds as that uneasy feeling transforms into panic.

'Who had an accident?' Senia whispers.

'On his bike,' Jackie replies. 'We're at WakeMed.'

Just hearing the word WakeMed makes me want to vomit. I haven't been there since I had Abigail five months ago. Jackie doesn't know anything about Abigail.

'Claire? Are you still there?'

'Yes. I'm here. I'll . . . I'll be there in an hour.'

I'm shaking so hard as I pull on a pair of jeans and a clean shirt.

Senia grabs my hand as I reach for my car keys on the nightstand. 'I'll drive.'

'Drive fast, please.'

The whole forty-minute drive there, I keep imagining all the worst scenarios: he's missing a leg, he's in a coma, he's on life support . . . or worse. Senia attempts to distract me with music, but I can't stop my mind from wandering to the darkest places.

She drops me off in front of the emergency entrance then sets off to find parking. I stand outside the sliding doors under the red emergency sign for a moment, unable to move. This is exactly how it happened when I went into labor.

'Are you in labor?' the nurse with the blue cardigan and the straw-colored hair asks.

'Yes. Please put me in a room. Now, please.'

I'm more afraid of running into someone I know than anything else. I just want to get into a delivery room where no one but the doctors and nurses, and Senia, will see me.

'We'll get you into a room right now, sweetie.'

Another nurse comes up behind me with a wheelchair and I'm hit with another contraction right as I sit down. It's the worst pain I've ever felt and I've been suffering through it for the last three hours in Senia's bedroom while waiting for the contractions to come less than four minutes apart. It's 2:30 a.m. now and I can hardly keep my eyes open. My eyes roll back in my head and I feel as if I might actually die from the pain.

I'd rather be dead than be here right now.

Finally, the nurse wheels me away and it feels like it takes an hour before she arrives at the Women's Pavilion. They set me up in a spacious room and hook me up to a zillion monitors. Every beat of my baby's heart is like a hammer driven into my heart, breaking it into a million pieces. I finally ask the nurse to lower the volume on the heart rate monitor and she does it, but not without a judgmental scowl.

'Have you decided on any names?' another dark-haired nurse asks, putting on some gloves as she gets ready to probe my cervix for the third time since I arrived.

Senia throws her a look of disgust before she pulls the nurse outside. I don't know what Senia says to her, but the dark-haired nurse, Sybil, is overly nice for the rest of my two-night stay. The entire staff *is overly nice after that. Sybil must have shared the news about the adoption with everybody. But their kindness doesn't soothe my anxiety or my guilt. I almost wish they would tell me what an awful person I am. Just to confirm what I know they're all thinking about me.*

She's just a stupid college student who got knocked up by having unprotected sex with some guy who probably wants nothing more to do with her.

If they knew the truth, if they knew that I kept the whole pregnancy a secret from Chris, they wouldn't be this nice to me.

'Claire?'

Senia places her hand on my back and leads me toward the emergency entrance. The doors whisper accusations as they slide open. *Unfit.* They slide shut behind me. *Liar.*

'It's okay,' Senia whispers. 'Nobody knows what happened. That's between you and Chris.'

Chris. Oh, God. Where is he?

I break away from Senia and race to the long counter where a woman in a black cardigan watches wide-eyed as I approach.

'Can I help you?'

'I'm looking for Chris Knight.'

Her eyebrows knit together as if she has bad news

for me, but then she points at a set of double doors. 'Go through there and you'll find the nursing station. They can help you.'

I powerwalk across the lobby to the double doors and shove my way through them. The hospital smell is more intense in here. The woman in the lobby didn't say they would tell me where Chris is. She didn't say he's okay. She just said they would help me at the nursing station. Maybe that's her standard response after dealing with so many people who come in frantic looking for loved ones who've . . . I have to stop thinking like this.

The nursing station is a huge L-shaped counter with Plexiglas panels stretching from the counter to the ceiling. A woman with short red hair is standing behind the counter wearing a midnight-blue nursing uniform and staring at the inside of a manila folder.

'You looking for someone?' she asks as she looks up from the file.

'Yes. I'm looking for Chris – Christopher Knight.'

Everyone knows him as Chris Knight, not Christopher, but there's no way she doesn't know I'm talking about *the* Chris Knight.

'Are you family?'

I hesitate. Am I family? Technically, Chris was my foster brother, but Jackie never adopted me. And I haven't lived with her or Chris for more than two years.

'No. I'm . . .' Senia watches me as she waits to hear exactly what I am to Chris. 'I'm his wife.'

Senia's eyes widen, which doesn't go unnoticed by the nurse. Senia drops her gaze to my hands as I tuck them behind my back. The nurse cocks an eyebrow before she closes her folder and picks up the phone to dial an extension.

'I have Chris Knight's . . . *wife* here.' She looks up at me. 'What's your name, honey?'

'Claire.'

'Claire is here to see her husband. What's his status?' She purses her lips as she listens to Chris's status then hangs up the phone. 'They just moved him out of the trauma unit and into the OR.' She grabs a piece of paper off the desk and hands it to me. It's a floor plan of the hospital. 'You can wait in the Critical Care Waiting Room. They'll keep you updated on his status and when you'll be able to see him.'

Senia and I follow the map through a few more corridors.

'Claire Knight,' Senia remarks with a shake of her head. 'Nope. I don't like the way it sounds.'

'How else are they going to let me see him?'

We reach another quiet lobby where a woman with poufy brown hair is sitting behind yet another counter.

'May I help you?'

'I'm here to see my husband, Christopher Knight,' I reply without hesitation.

'Claire!'

I turn my head at the sound of Rachel's voice. 'Rachel?'

She looks exactly as I remember her, messy brown bangs and clothes that fit too loosely over her tiny frame. Jackie stands from her chair and they both stride toward me. Rachel throws her arms around me first, but I note that her makeup seems untouched as if she hasn't shed a tear. I look over Rachel's shoulder at Jackie and her makeup also seems to be intact.

'What happened?' I ask Jackie and she smiles a bit sheepishly.

'They're resetting his fibula.'

'His *fibula*? You mean, he broke his leg?'

Rachel lets go of me and Jackie holds her arms out for a hug. I give her a quick hug then look up at her questioningly.

'When I called you I didn't know his status yet. If I had known it was just a compound fracture I wouldn't have asked you to come.'

'*Just* a compound fracture?' Rachel says. 'That's some serious shit.' Typical Rachel, always eager to speak her mind. 'Did you just call Chris your husband?'

I'm sensing some hostility from Rachel, but I don't want to make any incorrect assumptions. 'I didn't think they'd let me see him otherwise.'

Her lip curls up in disgust. 'Don't let him know you did that. It will kill him.'

Jackie purses her lips at Rachel. 'Come now, Rachel. Be nice.'

'It's true. He's been miserable the past few weeks. Claire's the reason he was upset when he got on his bike.'

'What?' Jackie looks confused as she glances back and forth between Rachel and me.

'What the fuck are you talking about?'

Jackie's eyes widen at me. '*Claire!* Watch the language.' She turns back to Rachel. 'But, yes, what are you talking about?'

Rachel shakes her head. 'Nothing. He was just upset when he left and I know it's because of everything that's happening between you two.'

'What's going on between you?' Jackie asks me.

There's no way Rachel knows about Abigail. Chris told me he hasn't spoken to anyone about her and I believe him. She's probably referring to Adam. I don't think Chris would tell Rachel about the fight, but I wouldn't put it past Tristan to blab about it to everybody he knows.

'Nothing. We're still trying to work things out. We're just friends.' I whisper the last sentence like it's a dirty secret because it *is*, as far as Jackie is concerned.

'Just friends? Did you friend-zone my baby?'

Rachel cackles at this remark and I probably would too if it didn't make me physically sick.

'No, Jackie. It's just that a lot has happened since we broke up.' Oh, no. This is not how I wanted her to find out. 'I don't know what to say. I'm sorry.'

Jackie looks as if she can't decide whether she should be confused or disgusted. I want to sink into the floor or disappear. I can't bear to see the scrutiny and disappointment in her eyes.

'I'm so sorry,' I repeat this mantra a few more times before she pats my shoulder.

'It's fine. I know you two will work this out. You can't just throw away four years and an engagement without trying to work things out.'

Engagement? Chris told her we were *engaged*?

I don't want to be pissed at him right now. He probably had a good reason to tell her this, though I can't figure out what that could be. Jackie knew Chris and I were having sex the last two years we were together. She told us to be safe and that was the end of our birds and bees discussion. Why would he tell her that? I was nineteen when we broke up. We did promise to love each other forever, and we talked about getting married many years down the road, but there was definitely never an engagement. I would never have put myself through the pregnancy and adoption alone if we were engaged.

Poor Jackie. Chris and I have kept so many secrets from her and told her so many lies, we should both be hanged.

'You're right. We'll try to work it out. I promise.'

She smiles even though I can see in her eyes that she knows I'm humoring her. 'He should be out of the care unit in a couple of hours. I'm sure he'd love to see you when he wakes up.'

I bite my lip as I attempt to stop the tears from spilling over. Of all the lies I've told this year, I think I regret the ones I've told Jackie the most.

Chapter Eighteen

Adam

When I arrive at the guard station at Barking Sands Missile Range, Sam Crowe meets me at the entrance as an escort, since it's my first time there. She signs a waiver assuming responsibility for me then I follow her truck down the narrow roads to the project trailer on the south side of the base. I pull into the dirt lot and park my green sedan in an unmarked space next to Sam's old Chevy pickup truck.

'I'll call the rental company today to see if we can switch out your *mom car* for something a bit more rugged,' she says with a snort as we climb the steel steps up to the door of the project trailer.

The inside of the trailer is cool and quiet and filled with the rich aroma of fresh coffee and the sweet smell of fresh blueprints. Four desks line the opposite wall of the trailer. On my immediate left is a water cooler and a foldout table topped with a coffee machine and various creamers and coffee supplies. The fourth desk at the end of the trailer is occupied by Larry Cromwell, who is currently on the phone. He nods at me and I salute him even though my dad already told me Larry doesn't like to be saluted. Larry doesn't know that I know this about him so I'll just wait for him to tell me himself.

'That desk on the other end is for Ollie,' Sam says, nodding toward the messier desk at the opposite end of the trailer from Larry. 'He had a meeting with the surveyor this morning. He'll be in soon. These two desks in the middle are for us.'

Great. I'll be listening to that snort eight hours a day for the next two months.

After I boot up my laptop, I open my email to find a message from Claire.

Claire: Good morning, babe. I'm on my way to bomb this test on binomial distributions, but I wanted to shoot you a message to tell you how much I miss you. Call me on your lunch break. I should be back in the dorm by then. Love you.

She doesn't normally send me good-morning emails, but then again she doesn't normally wake up five hours before me on a Monday. I make it through a few more emails from the grading and rebar subcontractors before I get to the last email from my cousin Jamie.

Jamie: Just thought I'd give you a heads-up that Lindsay
and Nathan are going to be at that competition on
Koki Beach. Also, I spoke to Pauline (not about
what you told me) and they're doing okay.

That's it. Even though we had a nice heart-to-heart
about Myles, she's still a little pissed that I didn't tell
her the specifics of his death. She thinks I should have
trusted her not to tell anyone. She doesn't understand
that I still feel like I got away with manslaughter.
There's no way I would have stopped Jamie if she went
to the cops because that's pretty much all I've hoped
for these past five years since Myles fell to his death.
I wish someone stronger than I would confess on my
behalf.

So Lindsay and Nathan are going to the competition
and Pauline and the rest of Myles' family are doing
okay. I don't believe that Pauline is okay, but I have
no doubt that Lindsay and Nathan will be at the Koki
competition. Lindsay and Nathan are the reason I
moved to Wrightsville Beach. On one hand, catching
Lindsay cheating on me with Nathan was one of the
best things that ever happened to me because it led me
to Claire. On the other hand, I really don't want to see
her fucking smirk or the scar on his face from the day
I beat the shit out of him. Mostly, I don't want to be
reminded of how out of control I was back then.

After a few hours of phone calls spent trying to
work out permits and temporary utilities, Larry in-

vites me to lunch while Sam stays in the trailer to hold down the fort. We each take our own vehicles because Larry has a meeting on the other side of the base after lunch. I follow him to Wrangler's Steakhouse on Kaumualii Highway just a few blocks away from my rental house. Once we're seated at our table, it only takes a single sentence uttered from beneath Larry's craggily gray mustache to know that I'm going to regret this lunch.

'So how long have you been working for Daddy?'

The waitress arrives and takes our drink order, giving me a moment to think of an appropriate response to this inappropriate question. Larry orders an Arnold Palmer and I order a glass of water.

'I've been working with my dad part-time for more than two years and full-time since June.'

I'm tempted to add that I started working at Parker Construction after graduating from Duke with my bachelor's in architecture, but I doubt it would do anything to convince Larry that I deserve this position. Larry smiles as he sits back in his chair and folds his thick hands over his belly.

'I've known your dad for quite some time and I know he's got plenty of other guys more qualified to do this job. Why'd he send you?'

I grit my teeth together as I try to remind myself that I will only be working with this prick for eight weeks. I dealt with the skeptical looks from employees in the Wilmington office for the first year or so, but everyone there knows I worked my ass off to get my degree and help my dad out for nearly three years and they respect me for it. This asshole doesn't know that and it's not my job to school him. But one good thing my dad did teach me was that we teach people how to treat us. Larry Cromwell will not treat me like a spoiled dumbass for eight weeks.

'I assure you that I am the most qualified project engineer for this project. I handled the startup on the Camp Lejeune training center project in June and, no disrespect, but this project is a walk in the park compared to that. My father sent me here because I'm the only one he trusts to oversee the dredging.'

He doesn't look convinced, but at least this shuts him up. We make it through the meal without any further questions about my qualifications. We talk about the meetings we have scheduled for the week and when the drilling subcontractor is set to start their work. By the time I get into my car I'm annoyed. I don't want to call Claire when I'm like this, but she asked me to call her on my lunch break.

I pull out of the steakhouse parking lot behind Larry's new Cadillac and punch Claire's number. I put her on speakerphone before I set the cellphone into the cup holder.

'Hey, sexy,' she answers.

'Hey, baby. What are you doing?'

'Studying to retake the exam I just failed this morning.'

160

'Why did you fail? I thought you were studying for that last night.'

She's quiet for a moment. 'I was gone for a while last night. I didn't get a whole lot of studying done.'

'Were you partying on a Sunday?'

The silence on the other end of the phone puts me even more on edge. She's hesitating and I can only imagine why.

'Chris was in an accident yesterday so I was at the hospital for a few hours. I didn't get to study.'

Fuck. I hate that I feel even the slightest bit happy that he was in an accident. That's fucked up.

'What happened? Is he all right?'

'He's fine. He just broke his leg and they had to reset his fibula.'

'You went to the hospital to visit him for a few hours when you had a test to study for and all he has is a broken leg?'

'I didn't know until I got there.'

'But you stayed for a few hours.'

'I was already there.'

I take a deep breath as I attempt to focus on the road. The ten-mile drive back to the base and the conversation with Claire were *supposed* to calm me before I got back to work.

'Adam?'

'What?'

'You're mad.'

'How did you even visit him at night if you're not

161

family? I thought his mom never adopted you.'

'Adam, please.'

'Please, what? I just want to know if you've been lying to me.'

'I have not been lying to you. I lied to the hospital staff.'

'What do you mean, you lied to the hospital staff?'

She sucks in a loud breath then lets it out slowly. 'It's not a big deal. I just told them we were family so that I could get in to see him.'

'I don't fucking get it. Why was it so important to see him if it was just a broken leg?'

'Because I ran into Jackie in the waiting room and she wanted me to see him so I lied to the hospital staff and said we were married. *Okayy?* Are you happy now or are you going to keep grilling me?'

Am I happy now?

I blink my eyes to keep the silvery road in front of me from blurring with rage. They taught us in anger management to take a moment to collect our thoughts. Step away until you can work things out calmly. I've had to use the shit I learned in anger management a lot lately.

'I can't talk about this right now. I have to get back to work. I'll call you when I get off work.'

'Adam, please don't shut down. I had to deal with Jackie the best way I could. You have to understand what a tough situation I'm in here. She doesn't know anything about the baby or us.'

162

'Why doesn't she know about us?'

'Because I already broke her heart and I'm just be-coming a part of her life again. And I need her. She's the closest thing I have to a mother. Please don't make me put that in jeopardy.'

'If she's like a mother to you she'll understand that you've moved on. I think you haven't told her because you're not sure you're ready to move on.'

'What? That's ridiculous. I . . . I can't even believe you would say that. Chris and I are over. We're just friends and we have to stay that way if we want to have any chance of seeing Abigail.'

Her voice cracks when she says her daughter's name and I feel awful. Even if I'm still not totally convinced that there's nothing between her and Chris, I can't make her feel even guiltier than she already does. I can't give her a reason to go running to him.

But I also can't fucking stand knowing that she was at the hospital, lying to the staff, and sitting there with him for God knows how long, all over a broken leg.

'I'm sorry. I feel like you're slipping through my fingers and I don't know how to stop it. I don't . . . I don't even know if I should.'

'What does that mean?'

I pull the car over onto the grass along the highway because I'm getting close to the guard station and I'm not supposed to be using a cellphone when I pull up.

'I mean that I don't know if I should be trying to

163

fight this. If you feel yourself being pulled to him, maybe I should just let it happen.'

I grab the phone out of the cup holder and take her off speakerphone. I suck in a deep breath and close my eyes as I lean my head against the headrest.

'I don't want to be with Chris. I want to be with you.'

'I don't want you to be with him. I want you all to myself, and I'm beginning to see how selfish that must seem. But it's the fucking truth. I can't stand that he gets to have you at his side whenever he needs you. I'm just not comfortable with it.'

'Are you saying you want me to stop seeing Chris?'

'Babe, I don't think you see what's happening be-cause you want to think the best of him. He's your first love and the father of your child. I get it. But this is exactly what he wants.'

'He *wanted* to break his leg?'

'No, he wants to tear us apart.'

'He *does* want to tear us apart and you're allowing him to do just that.'

'I'm not allowing him to do shit, but I can't do anything from here. You don't understand the fucking lunch meeting I just had.' My stomach clenches as my mind goes over the last hour spent with Larry Cromwell. 'I'm chained to this fucking island for the next eight weeks. I can't blow this job. I can't swoop in and take you back if Chris gets his way with you, but I want to. I want to show up at your door and take you

164

in my arms. I want to kiss you till you can't breathe. I want to be next to you and on top of you and inside of you. I want to fucking inhale you and every moment we spend together. But I can't do that from here. I'm at a huge disadvantage. And I'm not giving up; I'm just telling you that I don't think I can deal with this shit right now.'

'I don't like where this conversation is going. I—' Her voice cuts off for a moment before it comes back. 'It's Chris calling me on the other line. He's supposed to call me and tell me what happened with the meeting between Tasha and Abigail's mother.'

'Go ahead. I know you have to take this. I'll call you tomorrow.'

'I love you.'

'I love you too.'

I shake my head as I drop the phone into the cup holder. This is way too much stress to put on a two-month relationship. Claire needs to take care of this stuff with her foster mother and Abigail and Chris. And she needs to study. I need to focus on getting this project set up and training for Koki Beach. If we want to have any chance of coming out the other side of the next eight weeks without hating each other, we need a break.

Chapter Nineteen

Chris

Claire's voicemail greeting comes on and I immediately hang up. She's probably meditating or talking to her boyfriend. I told her I would call her with the news about Tasha's meeting. I move to lay my phone on the rolling table next to my hospital bed and just this small movement sends a bolt of pain shooting through my right leg and up my spine.

'Fuck!'

The phone vibrates in my hand as Nurse Fran walks into my room. 'Is everything all right in here?' she asks as I answer the phone.

'Claire, you have to come down here,' I say into the phone, the pain pulsating throughout my entire body giving my voice a hard edge.

'Why? I already saw you yesterday and that was only because your mom insisted. It's a broken leg, Chris. You're not going to die. I have to study.'

'Not for me.'

Nurse Fran gives me a pointed look through her swooped black bangs. She ordered me to get some rest since this is my last night in the hospital, and here I am on the phone again. She already jokingly threatened to toss my phone out the window earlier today.

'It's not for me, Claire,' I continue. 'It's Abigail. She's here. That's what the meeting was about. She's having surgery tonight at eight and Abigail's . . .' I hesitate to refer to this woman as Abigail's mother, though she was nice enough to offer us a chance to see Abigail tonight. 'Abigail's mother is letting us see her tonight before she goes into surgery. You have to get down here.'

Claire is silent and I wish I could be there to give her this information in person instead of lying in this fucking bed. I wish I could have picked her up in my own car and held her hand as I delivered this news, but time is running out. This might be our only chance to see our daughter.

'Claire?' A soft sob comes through the speaker and it feels like a fucking knife in my chest. 'Claire, can you get Senia to bring you?'

'I'll be there.'

I hang up the phone and Fran glances at my chest and I'm pretty sure she's just putting together my conversation with Claire and the tattoo over my heart. 'You need a wheelchair?'

'Yes, please.'

As soon as she leaves the room, the aching in my chest spreads through my throat, choking me, until it reaches my face, stinging my eyes. I clear the thickness in my throat and try to compose myself before Fran returns. Then I hear the click of someone's heels in the corridor and I know who's coming.

Tasha enters my room wearing a cleavage-popping green dress that makes her red hair look even redder. The navy-blue cardigan she wears buttoned at the waist does nothing to hide the soft, round flesh bulging out of her neckline. A blue sweater, green dress, and cherry-red heels . . . somehow she pulls it off. It's the sexy red-framed glasses and red lipstick that pulls it all together.

'Is she coming?' she asks as she walks right up to my bedside and stares at my bare chest.

I swallow the lump in my throat before I answer. 'She's on her way. You didn't have to come here.'

The last thing I need right now is for Claire to feel intimidated by Tasha, if that's even possible. I'm pretty certain Claire knows she has me wrapped around her finger.

'I know I didn't have to come, but I want to be here in case they try to make a verbal agreement,' Tasha replies as she peels her gaze away from my chest and takes a seat in a chair. 'You have virtually no rights here, Chris. I'm just protecting your best interests.'

'Yeah, you've told me that before.'

Fran walks in with the wheelchair and I grit my

teeth as I attempt to sit up. 'Hold on there, bad boy. I'll lift you up.'

'I don't need you to lift me,' I say as she reaches for the button on the side of the bed to lift the head of the mattress, but she's too late. I'm already sitting up and reaching for my leg in the splint.

'You can't move your leg. I'll do it.' I attempt to lift my leg out of the splint and the pain stops me cold. 'Just hold your horses and I'll do it for you. For crying out loud, eight o'clock isn't for another ninety minutes. You've got time. Do you want something for the pain?'

'No. I want to go in there with a clear head.'

She nods and I try not to grimace too much as she slowly helps me into the wheelchair and props my leg up.

'I looked up the information for Abigail and I can take you straight to her as soon as your friend arrives,' Fran adds as she moves toward the door. 'You may want to put a shirt on.'

She leaves and I look down at the jeans that Fran allowed me to put on earlier today. The right pant leg is cut off below the knee.

Tasha and I make small talk for a while as we wait for Claire. I want to ask her if Abigail's mother told her how serious Abigail's condition is, but I almost don't want to know.

'Can you hand me that shirt you're sitting on?' I ask Tasha.

She quickly stands and hands me the black NOFX

shirt that is now nice and warm from her ass. It's already hot as fuck in this hospital room so I wait a minute before I pull it on. Claire and Senia walk in as I'm shaking out the T-shirt and Claire instantly looks away from my chest. She hasn't seen the new tat yet. I know this isn't the right place or time to show her so I quickly pull my shirt over my head to cover it up.

I lean back a little and hit the nurse call button.

'Claire, Senia, this is Tasha Singer,' I say, nodding toward Tasha who's standing on my left.

Senia ogles Tasha's cleavage for a moment, as they shake hands. 'Nice to meet you,' Tasha says before she turns to Claire.

Claire doesn't seem to be in the mood for introductions, but she holds out her hand. 'Nice meeting you.'

Fran arrives and immediately starts pushing me out of the room. No one speaks as we travel through the cold hospital corridors. Fran takes us down to the first floor, past the gift shop, and to the children's hospital. We pass straight through the lobby and to another corridor toward the Heart Center.

I'm afraid of what we'll find when we finally see her. I don't want this to be the first and last time I ever see my daughter. I look to my left and Claire's face is twisted with worry. I wonder if broken hearts are genetic.

Chapter Twenty

Claire

The squeak of the nurse's Crocs on the shiny floor is making me even more nervous. I already feel as if I might collapse at any moment. My thoughts keep rewinding to the day I gave birth and I can't remember if the nurses ever said there was something wrong with my baby.

Not my baby. She's not mine.

A burly man stands with his back to us in the corridor about forty meters ahead. He's speaking to a doctor who stares at us as we approach. There are too many of us. I wonder if we look intimidating to them. The burly man turns around and the worry in his eyes turns to annoyance.

We're not welcome here. We're just the stupid kids who gave Abigail up and now we're crashing motorcycles and trying to ruin their lives.

I stop in the middle of the corridor and Senia stops next to me.

'What's wrong?' she asks.

The burly man with the dark hair and four days' worth of scruff on his jaw watches me. Senia catches me around the waist as my knees begin to buckle under the weight of his glare.

'He hates us,' I whisper, my shoulders weakening as the resolve drains from my body.

The nurse pushing Chris stops and turns back to look at me. She sees Senia holding me and immediately switches into 'nurse-mode.' She comes back to help Senia as they attempt to hold me steady.

'Do you feel like you're going to pass out? Do you feel cold or dizzy?'

Chris looks over his shoulder at me and immediately turns his wheelchair around.

'I'm fine,' I say as I push away the nurse and I finally see her nametag: Francesca. Chris attempts to push himself up from the wheelchair and I throw my hand out to stop him. 'I'm fine. Sit down. Please.'

He grimaces with pain as he sets himself down in the wheelchair. 'Claire, come here.'

'I am here.'

He shakes his head. 'No, come here,' he says, beckoning me with his finger.

Senia and Francesca let me go and Tasha watches me as I step forward. He beckons me closer so he can whisper something in my ear. I lean forward and his fingers hint against my skin as he pulls my ear closer to his mouth.

'I need this. I need you to be strong like you were the day I met you and the day you broke up with me. You're not that broken girl your mom left in the trailer. You made the right choice giving her up, but I need you to be strong right now because I fucking need this. It's just you and me, babe. Okay?'

I nod as I blink furiously to staunch the tears. 'Okay.' Francesca comes to turn the wheelchair around and I stop her. 'I'll do it. You guys can stay here.'

I turn the wheelchair around and Tasha falls in step with me.

Chris turns to her and shakes his head. 'We're going in there on our own.'

'This is a bad idea,' she warns him, and I try not to glare at her burgeoning cleavage.

'Tasha, this isn't about the adoption,' Chris says; then I push him toward the doctor and the burly man.

My feet seem to sink into the hard floor as I walk, holding me still, yet somehow I keep getting closer. *Help*, I want to cry out. *Please help me get through this.*

The doctor holds out his hand to Chris. 'I'm Dr Buchik. I'll be handling the surgery today.' Buchik holds his hand out to me and I shake it. His hand is dry and warm and, as stupid as it is, this gives me comfort.

The burly man looks conflicted, like he's not sure he wants to meet us. Maybe he can deny our existence just a moment longer.

Chris pushes himself up from the wheelchair and I hold the chair steady as he offers the man his hand while standing on one leg. 'I'm Chris.'

The man looks a bit annoyed by this gesture, but he takes Chris's hand. 'Brian.'

It seems both of them want to introduce themselves as Abigail's father and I want to run away and never show my face again for what I've done to them.

I take a deep breath as I try to compose myself. I have to control the guilt. I have to get through this, for Chris.

I hold out my hand to Brian and he takes my hand. 'I'm Claire . . . Nixon.'

Somehow, I feel as if saying my last name will establish a modicum of trust between us. I know Chris didn't introduce himself as Chris Knight because he didn't want to remind Brian of the reason they backed out of the meeting two weeks ago. I blame myself one hundred percent for getting pregnant and having to give Abigail up. But, though I'd never tell Chris this, I do blame Chris Knight for that failed meeting.

'Lynette is in the room with Abigail,' Brian mutters as he nods toward the open door on his left.

Dr Buchik smiles at me. 'I'll take you in.'

Buchik has thin lips and short gray hair, but I can't decide if his gray eyes are filled with pity or skepticism. He knows this will not end well.

The room is small and a woman with light-blonde hair, lighter than mine, is hunched over the bed. Her pink cardigan hangs loosely on her shoulders and arms as if she's lost weight recently.

I didn't want to meet the adoptive parents when I decided on a couple to adopt Abigail. I didn't want to know their names or even see a picture of them. I wanted to know nothing other than their stats. I didn't want to be tempted to look them up.

'Mrs Jensen?' Buchik whispers.

Lynette Jensen. Brian Jensen.

Abigail Jensen.

The woman turns around and she appears frightened at the sight of Chris. 'Oh, my God!'

She claps her hand over her mouth and glances over her shoulder at the bed, probably to make sure she didn't wake Abigail with this outburst. She turns back toward us and I can't help but notice the striking similarities between Lynette Jensen and me: the blonde hair and blue eyes, the small frame, the pouty upper lip, the exhaustion. She's at least ten years older than me, but she's actually quite beautiful – much classier than Tasha Singer.

She turns back to us and I can see now that she's star struck. 'Chris Knight?' she whispers as she moves toward us. 'Oh, my God. I can't believe this.'

It's as if I don't exist.

She takes his hand in both her hands to shake it and I'm almost waiting for her to kiss his pinky, but she eventually lets go. Chris bows his head a little as he gives her a humble smile.

'It's a pleasure to finally meet you, Lynette,' he says and I breathe a sigh of relief that I have Chris, and his fame and charm, to make this introduction smoother. 'This is Claire,' he says, looking up at me.

He flashes me a quick smile, but I know in that one smile he's saying, *You can do this. I'm here for you.*

I hold out my hand to her, to Abigail's mother, and I feel the emotions building inside me, threatening to thwart me. I bite my lip to hold back the tears as I imagine all the times she probably rocked my baby to sleep, kissed her forehead, made her smile. I hold out my hand to her and she can see how difficult this is for me. She reaches her hand out slowly and I do something so stupid, but I can't stop myself.

I pull her into a hug. 'Thank you,' I whisper through the tears. She hugs me weakly and I know she wants me to let go. 'I'm sorry. I'm just really grateful for . . . for this.'

I want to thank her for taking care of Abigail, but I'm afraid this might come across as patronizing since it's their job to take care of her – because I wasn't able to.

'You don't have to apologize,' she says as she takes a step back so I can't hug her again. 'I was really scared about doing this, and Brian was pretty dead set against it, but I've been up many nights these past few weeks just . . . agonizing over what I'd want someone to do if I were in your position.'

Brian comes in and kisses Lynette's forehead as he

wraps his thick arm around her shoulders. Buchik steps forward so he's standing off to the side between us.

'Would you like me to explain the procedure for the birth parents?' Buchik asks and I nod, even though he's obviously not asking me.

Lynette looks uncomfortable with this, but she nods.

'You can explain it to us out in the corridor,' Chris says, nodding toward the door.

I don't want to go out there. I want to stay in here with Abigail. I haven't even seen her yet. But I follow reluctantly as everybody shuffles out into the corridor where Buchik explains the procedure for correcting an AV canal defect.

'Does your family have a history of congenital heart defects?' Buchik asks us and Chris immediately shakes his head. Buchik turns to me, awaiting my answer. Everybody is waiting for my answer, but I don't have one.

'I don't know.'

Is that what this was about? Did they ask us here under the guise of allowing us to see Abigail so they could find out our family history?

'I don't have a family history. My mother died . . . She's dead. I never knew my father.' *Stop it, Claire.* 'He raped my mother and she died of a drug overdose when I was seven. I don't know anything about my family history. I'm sorry.' Chris grabs my hand and squeezes. 'I'm sorry.'

I take off, running down toward the exit door at the far end of the corridor.

177

'*CLAIRE!*' Chris calls after me, but I keep running.

My legs fly across the floor as silent as my past. Not a single secret given up. No history to speak of. I'm a ghost. A phantom. A flicker of an actual soul.

The exit doors slide open and I rush out onto the pavement then into the parking lot. I don't stop until Senia grabs my arm and I'm wrenched backward.

'Claire!'

I cover my face in shame. 'Get me out of here.'

'I thought you wanted—'

'Just get me out of here!'

I don't want to face the judgment. The look in their eyes when they realize I gave up Abigail because I'm no better than my mother. Lynette and Brian didn't really care about letting us see her. They just wanted to know our family history. Well, now they know. And now they can go home and breathe a sigh of relief as they realize how much better off Abigail is without us.

Senia throws her arms around me and I lose it. 'You're a good person. You deserve to know her.'

'Please just take me home.'

I ignore Chris's phone calls and texts on the ride home. I keep telling myself it's over now. They will never want us around Abigail. Now I just have to focus on school. I have to study for a test. I have to write a term paper on the importance of the father in the family unit. I have to call Adam.

I need him so much right now.

Chapter Twenty-One

Adam

I'm woken by the pinging sound of a voicemail message. I glance at my phone on the bedside table and see the screen is lit up. I slide it off the table and squint at the screen as my eyes attempt to adjust to the brightness. Claire just left me a voicemail at one in the morning.

I touch the screen and it automatically plays the message in my ear: *I'm sorry to call you at this time. I just need to hear your voice. Call me later.*

I can hear the anguish and uncertainty in her words. She has to be upset if she's calling me at six in the morning, her time. I should never have come here.

I call her back right away and she picks up on the first ring. 'Adam?'

The way she says my name with such relief is both comforting and worrying. 'What happened?'

I've been going over our next conversation in my

head all day, thinking of how I'm going to break it to her that I think we need a break from each other, to get things straightened out in our lives. She has so much going on and I want to be there for her, but I can't. She needs someone there. If it can't be me – *fucking hell* – it should be him.

'I just wish you were here,' she whispers.

'You don't want to talk about it?'

'I think I just needed to hear your voice.'

Fuck. How am I going to do this?

'I love hearing your voice,' I say as my stomach clenches with anticipation. 'I wish I was there, too.'

'You sound tense.'

I take a deep breath and sit up in my bed. This room is a lot bigger than my bedroom in Wrightsville Beach. Most people think that they want spacious homes, but they don't realize how the emptiness of a large room just amplifies the emptiness in a broken heart. And we're all broken, in one way or another.

'I am tense.' She's silent as she waits for me to elaborate. 'Are you sure you're okay?'

'When am I ever truly okay? I'm a mess, as usual.'

I want to say, *'You're my mess, and that makes you a beautiful mess,'* but I don't want to get distracted. I need to get this over with before I lose my nerve.

'Claire, you know I love you, don't you? You know I'd do anything for you?'

She pauses for a moment, probably trying to figure out where I'm going with this. 'What are you doing?'

'I'm trying to talk to you. I'm trying to talk about what's best for you.'

'What best for *me*? Are you trying to talk to me or are you trying to *tell* me what's best for me?'

She's not going to make this easy, not that I expected she would. I can hear each of her breaths, soft and quick on the other end of the phone, and it's killing me. She can already anticipate what's coming.

'I don't want to be another distraction. You need to focus on school. You can't keep failing tests and losing sleep. You need to be healthy, physically and emotionally, if you're going to get through this semester and all this stuff with Abigail. I just want you to have everything you need.'

'And you think that I don't need you? How could you ever think that this would be the solution?'

'Because I can't do anything for you from here and it's killing me. I don't want to worry that you're not getting everything you need. I want to know that you're okay. I want to know that you're being taken care of.'

'And dumping me is supposed to ensure that I'm taken care of? Are you handing me off to Chris? Is that what this is? You're tired of dealing with my shit so you're just pawning me off?'

I grit my teeth as I climb out of bed and make my way to the window. I have a view of the ocean from here that's much nicer than the partial ocean view in my Wrightsville apartment. But no ocean view is beautiful enough to paint this ugly moment pretty.

'I'm not tired of your shit. How could you even say that? And I'm not pawning you off. I'm just trying to be mature about this. This was really bad timing for me to come here. You need to focus on school and I need to focus on this project and the competition.'

My muscles are wound up so tight I could probably punch straight through this wall.

'I don't fit into your world. Is that what you're telling me?'

Her voice is small and dark with despair.

'Claire, you *are* my world, but that world is crumbling and I'm just trying to do what needs to be done to stop it.' I take a deep breath as I watch the waves roll in and out. 'I'm trying to throw you another lifeline.'

The sniffle on the other end of the line makes my stomach ache. I've gone over this conversation a thousand times in my mind since we talked yesterday. In my mind, she got pissed and hung up on me.

'So what are we supposed to do now? Just go on with our lives as if we never knew each other? Am I still going to know you? If we break up now, we'll never see each other again, even when you get back. Wrightsville is a hundred miles away.'

'When I get back, I'm moving to Raleigh as soon as I can find Cora a new tenant. I would love for you to wait for me, but I don't expect you to.'

She's full on sobbing now and my arms ache with the thought of holding her. I want to soothe her pain and make her feel loved. I want her to know that this is not permanent because I fully intend to fight for her and for our future when I get back. But we will have no future if we don't get through this separation.

We will definitely not get through this if I have to keep hearing about all the things she's doing with Chris and how he doesn't give a shit about her failing a test. I don't actually know if he doesn't give a shit, but I get the impression that he's less concerned with her doing well in school than he should be, probably because he never had to go to college.

'I don't want to wait for you. I want you here now. I *need* you here now,' she whispers.

'Hey, let me tell you a story.'

'I don't want to hear a story.'

'Please?'

'A story about what?'

'When I was eight years old, there was this little girl, Victoria, who used to ride her bike up and down our street every day. She would do this for hours sometimes and one day I asked my mom why Victoria always rode her bike alone.' I pause as I try to remember the exact words my mom replied with. 'My mom told me that sometimes being alone is more desirable than being in a roomful of people who aren't there. I thought I understood what she meant by that, but it turns out I didn't really understand it until now.'

I get back in bed and lie down as I await her response.

'Are you going back to sleep?' she asks.

'Not a chance. Did you sleep okay?'

'I haven't slept at all and I have a class in two hours.'

I don't say it aloud, but this is exactly why we need to break up. She already has enough to worry about without having to worry about what I'm doing or if I'm going to be pissed about what she's doing.

'I would tell you to take a day off and get some rest, but I know you won't.'

'I don't want to go to class.'

She sounds like a child when she says this, fragile and frightened of what awaits her. I know we have to end this conversation before I change my mind, but I can't bear the thought of hanging up the phone. She has to be the one to say goodbye first.

'Can I tell you a secret?' I say, trying to keep my voice from wavering. 'I chose to move in to Cora's building because of you.' She lets out a soft whimpering sound and I continue. 'I drove down Lumina a few times searching for rental signs and I spotted you walking home from work. You were pretty lost in thought, like you were carrying the world on your shoulders. You reminded me of Victoria, like you just needed someone to be there, completely, but everybody was gone. Now I realize why you looked like that.'

'Why?'

'Because you're the one who was gone.' I listen for a few minutes as she cries softly. When she's finally quiet, I speak up. 'I love you. Do you believe me?'

'Yes.'

'Do you believe me when I say that I would never do anything to hurt you?'

'Adam, you're not hurting me, you are *killing* me right now.'

'Please don't say that.'

'It doesn't matter. This was inevitable. And I totally get why you're doing this, so you don't have to keep trying to make me feel better about it. I know you wouldn't do this unless you truly believed it was for the best. I just happen to disagree with you on what's best for me.'

I pull the pillow out from under my head and throw it onto the floor as I lie back on the mattress and stare at the ceiling through the darkness. 'I'm willing to do whatever it takes to make sure you get the future you deserve, babe. Even this.'

She lets out a loud sigh. 'I guess I should let you go so you can get some rest or train for your competition or whatever it is you're going to do now that you're free.'

'I'm just going to lie here and regret this for a while before I go to the beach.'

'I'm going to get ready for class and try not to think of dozens of ways of murdering you.'

I chuckle, but it's a weak laugh, weighed down by this impending sense of sorrow. 'Before you start plotting my death, can I tell you a blonde joke?' She sniffs loudly and I know she's crying again. 'Why did the blonde get excited after she finished a jigsaw puzzle in six months?' I wait a moment, but she doesn't ask why. 'Because the box said two to four years.'

She lets out a congested chuckle. 'Oh, God. I can't believe this is happening.'

'I'll be back in less than two months.'

'I have to go.'

Before I can respond, she hangs up. The silence left in the wake of this conversation is louder than the crash of a thirty-foot wave. It presses in on me and I hold my breath as I wait for a sound, any sound, to break the silence. But I'm all alone here.

I get out of bed and head for the garage where I wax my surfboard for far too long, lost in the rasping noise as I rub the wax back and forth over the surface. It doesn't take long to realize this is just the first hour in a series of hours that I will have to fill with things that don't involve Claire. Knowing that she was waiting for me to come back was all that has kept me going these past few days.

At least Remmy will get here soon and I can throw myself into training. Remmy will kick my ass and pretty soon I'll be too exhausted to think. And if that doesn't work to shut off my mind, then I'll have to consider the possibility that I made a huge mistake. Then I'll consider going back.

Chapter Twenty-Two

Claire

I squeeze my fist tightly around the heart-shaped locket dangling from my neck. I put this locket on before I went to see Abigail, but now I have a strong urge to rip it off. Instead, I lie down on my side and curl my knees up. It doesn't take long before the bed squeaks behind me and Senia wraps her arm around my waist.

She doesn't say anything. She just lets me cry.

I sometimes wonder why Senia has stuck with me through the chaos of the last year.

After a while, she finally speaks. 'You have to go to class. My class doesn't start till ten. I can sit in with you for a while if you want. Even if it's just so I can raise my hand to make sure Mr Collins never calls on you.'

'I wish I could laugh.'

'Come on, it will be fun to watch me get all the

answers wrong. You can even record me and put it on YouTube.

'I can't go.'

'Okay. We'll both stay here today.'

'No, you have to go. I know you have a test today in Bromley's class.'

'Nope. I'm staying here and we're going to wallow in self-pity over our ex-boyfriends until our tears, and the tequila, run dry. I'm off to the market to stock up. Do you want anything besides hard liquor?'

'Red Vines,' I say before I can change my mind.

I know it's a stupid choice because it reminds me of Adam and all the times he brought me Red Vines after work when we were neighbors in Wrightsville. If there's one thing I'm great at it's torturing myself.

As soon as Senia leaves, I curl up on my bed and press the blanket into my eyelids to absorb the tears that seem to never stop. I try not to think that this breakup has anything to do with the fact that I'm not good enough for Adam. He has a degree and a successful job that keeps him busy and traveling. I'm a year behind in college and I've got enough baggage to weigh down a 747.

Not to mention the fact that I have no family.

As if on cue, my phone makes a tinkling noise; my text message tone. I turn over and snatch the phone off the nightstand. I close my eyes so I can't see the screen. I make a stupid wish that it's Adam telling me he changed his mind or even that he was just kidding.

I could forgive a joke like this. It might take a few days, but a few days is better than eight weeks – or forever.

I open my eyes and it's Chris. The notification has a picture icon, which means there's no text, just a photo attached to the message. I hit the notification and it takes me to my messages app where Chris's text message opens up. It's a picture of Abigail.

Senia arrives as I'm just beginning to doze off. I don't turn around in my bed, but I can hear the door slam shut and the sound of glass bottles clanking together as she drops some bags onto her bed.

'Get up, get up! It's time to get shitfaced and plot our revenge. I say we get even by moving on with some really hot guys – ahem, Chris – then we can plaster kissing photos all over our Facebook walls.'

'That is so immature and totally pathetic,' I say, as I turn over in my bed, still clutching tightly to my blanket because it still smells a little like Adam. Not at all pathetic.

I sit up in bed as she pulls a bottle of silver tequila out of a paper bag along with some limes, a bag of ice, margarita mix, and some plastic cups. She tosses a pack of Red Vines at me and it lands on the foot of my bed.

'I forgot the salt,' she says apologetically. 'But I thought of a great game on the way over here. We take turns saying one thing we hate about Adam or Eddie and every time we stumble or stutter we have to take a shot.'

'I can't do that. I don't hate anything about Adam.'

Senia stands between our beds: five-feet-ten inches of Amazonian woman glaring down at me.

'What? It's true. I love everything about him and miss him like crazy so that game just sounds stupid to me.'

Senia heaves a deep sigh and I can tell she's not happy with this response. 'Okay. I think I heard what went on with Adam during that conversation, but why don't you break it down for me. Did he really dump you because he thinks that's what's best for you?'

I draw in a long, stuttered breath as she reaches into a small paper bag and pulls out something that looks like a burrito wrapped in foil. She hands it to me then sits down on her bed. The bottles in the bags clang against each other as she makes herself comfortable. I unwrap my burrito and the smell makes me sick. I immediately wrap it up and set it down on the nightstand.

'Yes, he dumped me because he thinks he's just another distraction that I don't need and I kind of got the feeling that he was trying to tell me I'm a distraction for him. He thinks we're going to end up hating each other if we try to stay together while he's in Hawaii.'

'You have to eat something if we're going to drink.'

'I'm not drinking. You know that.'

'He's right,' Senia says, and by the look on her face she's totally serious. 'It's too painful to hear about everything that's going on with you and Chris and Abigail while he's five thousand miles away. If you

190

two try to stay together through this, you'll probably end up breaking up before he gets back. At least this way, there's a chance you may still want to be with him when he comes back.'

'Stop applying your logic to my relationship.'

She smiles, but it's a weary smile. She's right. I'm just torturing him with all this stuff. He has a job to do and I have schoolwork and legal business to attend to.

'Being mature sucks,' I say, pouting. 'I want to go to sleep and wake up in eight weeks.'

I really am deliriously tired from not having slept. The idea of food or alcohol in my stomach is only making it worse. I lie back in bed and pull the covers up to my nose.

'I'm going to shower and get ready in there so you can sleep. Do you need me to drop off any assignments to Collins?'

'I already emailed him the chapter review. Thanks.'

I clench my teeth as I attempt to hold it together for just a few more seconds until she leaves. She looks at me with that motherly concern that reminds me of Jackie.

'It's okay to cry, Claire.'

As soon as the door closes behind her, I reach for my phone again and stare at Abigail's picture. She's asleep and there are a million tubes coming out of her body, but she looks so peaceful, so blissfully unaware of the turmoil caused by my decisions. Will she grow up to resent me for giving her up? If we do come to an agreement on the open adoption, will she resent her adoptive parents because they're not rich and famous like Chris?

I pull the phone against my chest and the covers over my head before I close my eyes, trying not to think of all the studying I'll have to do whenever I wake up. Instead, I imagine Adam beside me, holding me, and whispering jokes in my ear.

Chapter Twenty-Three

Chris

Three weeks later

The ride to Xander's office is uncomfortable. I refuse to take the pain pills they prescribed me. I've seen too many people strung out on that shit to touch them. The last thing Abigail or Claire need is a junkie for a father or a . . . I don't know what the fuck I am to Claire anymore. But I hope what I'm about to do will help Claire make up her mind.

She won't return my calls these days unless I have specific news about Abigail, and I haven't had any since Claire's meltdown in the hospital. Lynette and Brian don't want to agree to an open adoption at this point. They think that my fame and Claire's past make us 'unstable.' That has to be the worst fucking insult I've ever had lobbed at me, and Claire doesn't deserve it either. I'd like to see Lynette and Brian suffer through just a fraction of what she's had to endure.

I make it out of my mom's SUV and onto my crutches easily enough. The doctor wanted to put my leg in a full cast, but there's no way I was going to be wheeled around everywhere. If it takes one to two weeks longer to heal this way, so be it. I'll do the extra time in order to hang on to a shred of dignity.

I laugh to myself as we make our way to the elevator in the lobby and I punch the button. I wrote a song last week about being *injured*, so I guess this broken leg stuff isn't a total loss. If Claire knew this, she would say it's my insistence on turning every negative into a positive. I think I have a pretty good track record with that, considering how broken she was when she came to us five years ago. But you can't mend a broken heart like you can a broken leg.

'I'm going to the café next door to use their WiFi. Will you be okay?' my mom asks as we wait for the elevator to descend eleven stories.

My mom is a crazy mobile gamer. She downloads every new game that has enough sparkly jewels or flashy colors to get her attention. She insists that some of her games require WIFI, even though my assistant got her the largest data plan available. She's always sneaking off to ask people for the nearest hotspot whenever I'm out with her, which has been quite often lately.

'I'll be fine. Go ahead.'

She sets off out of the building and turns right

toward the café next door. The elevator doors open and I hobble into the cabin then punch the button for the eighth floor. I make it to the Greenway Management office and Cheryl holds the door open for me to get into the back office area. I knock on Xander's door even though it's wide open. He's on the phone and it's hard to lose the manners my mom drilled into me. She always insisted I had to be a good example for all the foster children she took in.

Xander waves me in and I sit carefully in an armchair across the desk from him then lean my crutches against the desk. I shake my head as I think of me being an example for dozens of foster kids and unfit for my own daughter. I run the tip of my tongue over the thin ring in my lip and wonder if Lynette and Brian found my piercings and tattoos offensive. Probably.

He ends the call and lays the phone on the desk as he studies me for a moment. 'What the heck are you here for? You should be lying in your bed with a bell while your momma brings you cold beers.'

'I'm not going to L.A. on Monday.'

Xander's eyes widen. 'I have a bad feeling this has nothing to do with your leg.'

'I have to be here to see this adoption thing through.'

'And Claire?'

'She's starting to shut me out again. If I leave her she's going to think that nothing's changed and that I'll always choose music over her. I can't do that to her again.'

195

Xander closes his eyes as he leans back in his leather desk chair. 'You may lose the deal if you do this.'

'I'll take full responsibility. I'll give you your portion right now if you want. I just need some time to work things out with Claire and Abby.'

This is the first time I've called her Abby aloud and it catches me by surprise. I kept hearing Brian and Lynette call her Abby and I kept wishing I had that kind of familiarity with her. That level of comfort. Something happened when I touched her soft fingers and she latched onto me. I will never be the same and I haven't been able to think of anything else for three weeks.

Tasha relayed the information that Abby is healing well and should make a full recovery from the gaping hole in her heart. I wish I could say the same for Claire and me.

Xander opens his eyes and looks at me. 'I don't understand throwing away ten years of hard work for a long shot. You've worked hard for this, Christopher, and you're crazy if you don't think you deserve it just because you left Claire last year. Isn't she the one who broke up with *you*?'

'She broke up with me so I could do the shit I've been doing for the past year. She made me who I am. I can't thank her for that by abandoning her when she needs me most. Right now, she needs me more than I need a second hit album.'

Xander shakes his head with disappointment. 'You

know I love Claire, but I don't like this one bit. You're going to lose a lot of momentum if you hold off on this album for personal reasons. The release date has been circulating for weeks. Everybody's expecting it early summer. If you skip the trip to L.A., there is no way you'll get it done by then.' He stares me in the eye for a moment before he continues. 'Are you absolutely sure that this is what you want?'

'As sure as I am that you're going to cry like a bitch when I leave this office.'

He shrugs. 'I guess you're pretty sure.'

His brow furrows and I don't think he can hold the tears in much longer. 'I promise I'll work on the rest of the songs as much as I can while I'm getting fondled by my physical therapist.'

I grab the crutches and chuckle as I leave Xander's office, the sound of his sobs growing softer with each hop of my crutches. Cheryl scrambles to open both exit doors for me and I soon find myself back at the elevator, waiting. On the way down, I try to think of how I'm going to break the news to Claire. I can call her, but I'll probably have to leave it as a voicemail message. I can text her, but that's too impersonal. I have to see her, but that means asking someone to drive me to her dorm.

Why couldn't I have broken my fucking left leg? I could drive with a broken left leg.

The elevator doors open onto the first-floor lobby and I immediately spot my mom sitting on a cushy chair, her fingers moving furiously while her eyes are

197

glued to her phone. I make my way to her and she looks up.

'Did Xander have a heart attack?' she asks.

'No, but he may need some extra happy pills or some chocolate cake tonight.'

She stands and I'm struck by how much I admire my mom for taking everything that's happened with Claire and me in her stride these past two months. It's time to tell her everything.

As soon as I get myself settled into the passenger seat, I reach out to stop her from turning the key in the ignition. 'Mom, I have something to tell you; something you may not like to hear, but I want you to keep in mind how much I love Claire – how much *we* love Claire. Okay?'

She looks at the dashboard in front of me instead of straight at me because she can sense I'm about to tell her something really bad.

'Christopher, if you tell me something that makes me upset with Claire, I'm going to take it out on you. I just got her back. Please don't do this to me.'

I draw in a deep breath and let it out slowly as I contemplate this, but she needs to know. 'Mom, Claire had a baby in April. She gave her up for adoption and she's been suffering with this secret for over a year.'

'*A* baby or *your* baby?'

'*My* baby. Her name is Abigail. I saw her for the first time three weeks ago and she's the most beautiful thing I've ever seen. I got to hold her hand and I think

'. . . I don't think I've ever loved anything more than I love this little girl who I don't even know. Not even Claire or music.'

Both her hands fly up to cover her face as she begins to cry. I reach over and squeeze her knee and she shakes her head. *Fuck.* I hate seeing my mom cry.

'Mom, please don't cry. We're working it out. I just wanted to tell you because I can't keep it inside any longer.'

She curls her fingers a little so they're not covering her eyes, then she looks at me. 'I have a granddaughter? And you're just telling me this now?' She pushes my hand off her knee and scowls at me. 'I am so disappointed in you right now. I never thought you would keep something like this from me.'

'I wanted to tell you, but I wanted to wait until I knew what was going to happen with the open adoption. But I see now that we're no closer to knowing what's going to happen than we were two months ago.'

'Two *months* you've kept this from me! I knew something was going on when Rachel told me that Claire has a new boyfriend.'

'Rachel told you that?'

'I weaseled it out of her. Is that why this open adoption thing isn't settled yet, because she has a new boyfriend?'

'No, it's nothing like that.'

'Don't you lie to me to protect her. I can't believe she would keep this from me.'

'Don't you dare get mad at Claire. She only did what was best for Abigail *and* me. I wouldn't be where I am if she hadn't made the difficult choice she made.'

She grunts with frustration. 'I want to call her.'

'No, you're upset right now. Call her tomorrow or whenever you've cooled off.'

'You're right. I don't want to call her. I want to hug her. My God, Chris. Why didn't she tell me? I would have been there for her.'

'Come on, Mom. She obviously didn't tell you because you would have told me.'

She wipes the tears from her face and shakes her head as she attempts to collect herself. 'I need to see her.'

This is exactly what I was hoping for. Claire needs to know that her secret is not a death sentence marking the demise of all her previous relationships. We will always love her because even if Claire and I never get back together, we will always be her family.

'I'm going to ask Farrah to take me to go see Claire tonight. I'll tell her that I confessed to you then I'll ask her to come visit us at the house this weekend. I need to tell her in person.'

Farrah, my personal assistant, has been sitting on her heels without much work to do since I broke my leg. She was all set to go to L.A. with me next week, but that's not going to happen anymore. She may as well get used to being my new chauffeur because I'm not giving up on Claire and I still have three weeks in this fucking cast.

'Give her a big hug from me,' my mom says as she turns the key in the ignition. 'And if you ever keep something like that from me again, I will skin you.'

'If you skin me, who's going to pay for your gaming addiction?'

She shakes her head, but I see a reluctant smile barely tugging at the corners of her lips. It's hard keeping the women in my life happy. They're high-maintenance. But I don't think I would want it any other way.

Chapter Twenty-Four

Adam

I sit in the Hurley sponsor tent and try to mentally prepare myself to go out and compete. This morning was a mess. I woke with a start at 3 a.m. from a nightmare where Claire and I ran into each other years from now and she didn't recognize me. For the past three weeks, I've been living in the worst kind of hell. I can't talk to anyone about what happened with Claire, except Yuri, but I don't want to burden him with this crap before the competition. I've been totally and utterly alone. At least when I moved to Wrightsville, I ran into Claire on my first day there. This is a kind of loneliness I've never had to deal with.

Remmy walks into the tent, laughing as he glances over his shoulder at someone. Remmy was my trainer before I quit competing. After we parted ways, he moved to Florida to work at a surfing academy near his ex-wife's house to try to work things out with her.

I didn't understand this since they didn't have any kids together, but I guess love makes us do crazy things. When I called him two months ago to see if we could start training again, he moved to Wilmington the following week. I get the feeling he was looking for a way out of whatever situation he was in with his ex in Florida. It seems that being near the one you love doesn't solve everything.

Remmy is half-French and half-Brazilian, born in Brazil and raised in North Carolina. He's entirely mixed up, but he's also the best of the four trainers I've had in my lifetime.

'Hank is sitting at the judge's table,' he mutters to me so the group of people handing out Hurley T-shirts on my right can't hear.

Hank Langley loves me. When you're in a business where you have to do a lot of traveling, you find yourself latching onto people you feel drawn to. It helps make the constant change, the long plane flights, and the loneliness bearable. Hank is one of those who I was naturally drawn to when I was competing. He used to tell me about all his problems with his daughters and their boyfriends. The guy is hilarious. He once told me that I should never tell a girl that she's beautiful unless I'm willing to commit to her because girls don't know how to take a compliment from a handsome guy without falling in love. With Hank sitting at the judges' table, my chances at placing just increased significantly.

Somehow, this makes me more nervous and more determined to prove myself.

I haven't bumped into Lindsay or Nathan yet, but the prospect of seeing them is weighing heavily on my mind. I just keep telling myself that they're nothing to me. I've moved on. Claire is all I care about and getting back to her is my number-one priority.

By the time the heat begins and my group comes up, I'm ready to kill it. I jog across the sand toward the water and close my eyes for a moment to drink in the moment. If I place here, I can enter the ASP World Tour. Of course, that would mean more time away from Claire.

The sand has a slightly pink tinge due to the run-off from the red rocks that surround this small stretch of sand at Koki Beach. I block out the cheering as I trot across the sand, my eyes completely focused on the waves ahead. I make it past the bleachers, just a few dozen yards to the water, when I see her.

Lindsay is standing at the edge of the water further down the beach, her blonde hair flowing out behind her as the ocean breeze washes over her. She's wearing a one-piece bathing suit, probably because she's pregnant as fuck.

Chapter Twenty-Five

Claire

Professor Linda Coldwater insists we call her Linda because Professor Coldwater makes her question her decision to quit the theater. When the class lets out, I approach her to ask something I've never asked a teacher in my life.

'Um, Linda?'

She looks up from the small table next to the podium where she's putting away her notes and laptop. Her blue eyes fix me with a puzzled look. I've never really participated in this class in the eight weeks since classes began, but something – *someone* changed me and I finally understand that I don't just want to make it through this semester. I want to make this semester count.

'Yes?' she asks, her light-brown hair bouncing around her face as she continues to slide stuff into her laptop bag.

I swallow the knot in my throat and take a deep breath. 'I was wondering if you'd be willing to meet with me sometime this week? This is a required course for my major, so I was hoping I could pick your brain about your days as a caseworker.'

She immediately stops what she's doing and stands up straight so she doesn't have to look at me through a curtain of hair. 'Claire Nixon.'

'Yes.'

'Is this for the final?'

I know if I tell her it's for the final that she will probably reject me, but the truth is that the final is only a tiny factor in this request.

'No, I just have some questions about what path you took and how you liked it. I'd love to get some insight from someone who lived it and walked away.'

The truth is that I've been having doubts about whether I'll make a good caseworker. I'm so screwed up and I cry at the drop of a hat these days. I know this is partially due to the botched adoption agreement and the breakup, but I sincerely doubt whether I will ever have the strength to tell a child that they're going to live with strangers because their mother died of a drug overdose. I need some reassurance that I haven't picked the absolute wrong field.

She looks at me as if she's seeing me for the first time yet she obviously knows my name. 'Come to my office on Friday at two thirty. Does that work for you?'

'That's perfect. My last class lets out at one on Friday. Thank you so much.'

I set off toward the door when she clears her throat behind me. I'm not sure if this is meant for me so I wait until I reach the door before I turn around.

Her expression has softened. 'I just wanted to tell you that the paper you turned in last week on parent–child relationships was the best paper I've ever received for this unit.'

I don't know if she knows how little I actually know about parent–child relationships. She certainly doesn't know how I assumed my paper would come across as the biggest load of crap she'd ever read.

'Thanks,' I whisper, then quickly push through the door and into the corridor.

I make it halfway across the yard in a daze before my phone vibrates in my pocket. I slip it out and glance at the screen.

Chris: What time are you going to be in the dorm tonight?

I consider ignoring his text the way I have been for the past few weeks, but he's lucky Linda just put me in a really good mood.

Me: In about twenty minutes. Why?

He doesn't respond right away so I tuck the phone back into my pocket and continue toward Spencer Hall. When I open the door to room 330B, he's sitting on my bed with his leg propped up on some pillows and a baseball cap and sunglasses lying on the bed next to him. Senia is sitting on her bed and staring at me with a skeptical look on her face.

'What's going on?' I ask as I drop my backpack onto my desk.

Senia stands suddenly. 'I have to go call my mom about this weekend. I'll be back in a few minutes.'

She leaves and I'm left even more confused than when I walked in. 'Why are you here?' I ask Chris.

He flashes me a tight smile as he adjusts his position on the bed so he's sitting up a little straighter. 'Claire, I have something to tell you. Well, two things. Depending on how you take it, this could be considered good news and bad news. Which do you want first?'

I hate when people say they have good news and bad news. The bad news always cancels out the good.

I sit across from him on Senia's bed and curl my legs up so I'm cross-legged. 'Give me the bad news first.'

'I was afraid you'd say that.' He leans forward a bit, but he keeps his eyes locked on me. 'I told my mom about Abigail.'

The relative lightness I was feeling after leaving class is gone, replaced by a panic I haven't experienced in a very long time.

'Why? How could you? I just— Oh, my God. She hates me now, doesn't she?'

'She doesn't hate you. She could never hate you.'

'This is so embarrassing.'

My heart is pounding so hard my chest hurts. Suddenly, the necklace around my neck feels constrictive. I slide my fingers between the silver chain and my neck as I take deep breaths. I need to meditate.

'Are you okay?'

I shake my head. 'No, I am *not* okay. I can't believe you would do that. I wanted to be the one to tell her.' I cough in an attempt to clear the trapped sensation building in my chest, but it doesn't help. 'Oh, God. I can't breathe.'

He rises from the bed so suddenly it startles the last bit of oxygen from lungs. My hands and feet turn ice cold right before I pass out.

I open my eyes and I'm no longer on Senia's bed. I'm lying in my own bed with my blanket tucked tightly around me. Chris is watching me from where I was sitting before I passed out, as if we magically traded places. His jaw is set and I can't tell if he looks more pissed or worried, or if he's in pain.

'Did you put me in this bed?'

'Are you okay?' he asks, and I can definitely tell that he's in pain.

'Are you crazy?'

'Yes.'

I sit up and resist the urge to throw my pillow at him. 'You're so stupid. You're going to mess up that leg forever.'

'I'm fine. Are *you* okay?'

I nod. 'Thanks for catching me.'

'I should have let you fall.' The half-smile on his face makes my stomach flutter. 'But I love you too much.'

I close my eyes and take a deep breath. 'I need to meditate.'

'Go ahead.'

'I'm not going to meditate with you here.'

'Why not? I promise I'll be quiet.'

My chest aches as I remember the first time I meditated on Adam's living-room floor while he watched. It took me a while to get used to tuning out noise while meditating. The obvious way to deal with this is to focus instead on the steady rhythm of your heartbeat or breathing. Fallon taught me to create noise in my head to drown out the outside world. Then I gradually lower the volume on the noise until I'm fully relaxed. The deepest moment of peace always comes right after the blast.

I fold my legs so I'm sitting cross-legged and close my eyes. I take a few deep breaths and attempt to think of something peaceful. The ocean is usually my favorite thing to meditate on. You're technically not supposed to think of anything when you meditate, but I haven't reached that level of nirvana yet. So I imagine the waves crashing, but the first thing I see is Adam riding a wave. I shake my head and imagine a glass of water in a sink. The faucet drips into the glass, filling it up one drop at a time. Suddenly, Adam is there washing dishes in Cora's apartment.

I open my eyes. 'This is useless. I can't meditate with you here.'

He leans forward and rests his elbows on his legs. 'Do you want to hear the good news now?'

'Shoot.'

'I'm not going to L.A. I'm staying here until everything is sorted out with Abby.'

Hearing him call her Abby, with such familiarity, is painful. I'm so jealous that he got to touch her.

'What about the album?'

'If they can't wait then I'll have to scrap it, for now.'

His eyes are locked on mine, gauging my reaction. A warm sensation spreads from my belly and outward into my chest as I finally realize he's still in love with me. He's not just doing this to be competitive or out of a sense of obligation.

'I don't know what to say.'

'You don't have to say anything, but I'd love it if you could come over this weekend to talk to my mom.' I narrow my eyes at him and he chuckles. 'What?'

'Why did you tell Jackie that we were engaged?'

His eyes widen for a moment then he tilts his head. 'I never told you this, but after we started having sex she made me promise that I would ask you to marry me.'

'This is a joke, right?'

'No, it's no joke. She didn't want to tell you because she really thought I was going to ask you and she wanted it to be a surprise.'

I think back to the months after I turned eighteen, after Chris and I started having sex. Two months after my eighteenth birthday, he took me to Moore Park and gave me a promise ring, but he insisted it wasn't an engagement ring. It was just a symbol of our promise to love each other for the rest of our lives, even if we broke up. I wish I could say that this was a stupid promise to make when we were so young, but somehow I've found it to be a very hard promise to break.

'Don't let that scare you,' Chris says as if he can read my worried thoughts. 'My mom knows you've moved on, and she's dealing with it – like me.'

My fingers reach for the heart-shaped locket as I wonder how Adam would feel about me going to see Jackie. He broke up with me so I wouldn't have to worry about what he would think. Still, I can't help but feel like I need his blessing. But I need Jackie now just as much as I need Adam. I need to know that I haven't broken her trust in me.

'Okay. I'll go.'

He puts on his hat and sunglasses then grabs his crutches from where they're leaning against the foot of the bed.

'Hey, you never told me why she thinks we were engaged.'

He stands up on his crutches and his expression is serious. 'I'll tell you some other time.'

We stare at each other for a moment before I decide to let it go. 'Whatever.'

He sets off for the door and I scurry over to open it for him. He stands on the threshold for a moment, staring at the floor, before he turns to me.

'Remember when we went to Tristan's sister's birthday party two years ago?'

'Molly.'

'Yeah, Molly. When we were leaving, I had to go back inside to get your phone and Molly asked me if you could spend the night. I told her no because you were spending the night with me before you went away to college. She told me that I was lucky and Tristan nearly kicked me when I told her she had no idea just how lucky I was.' He pauses for a moment as his gaze wanders over my face. 'You may not be mine anymore, but I'm still lucky to have you in my life.'

I didn't think it was possible to feel guiltier about my decision to give up Abigail. But as I watch him shuffle away on his crutches, I realize that he is much stronger than I gave him credit for.

Chapter Twenty-Six

Adam

By the time I reach the water, I can't feel my hands. I'm not sure if I'm more stunned or angry. I trudge through the water, forcing myself not to look back in Lindsay's direction, then I do the math in my head. Lindsay and I broke up in the end of March. It's now the end of September. Six months. There's no way she's less than six months' pregnant. *Fuck!* How long was she cheating on me?

I duck dive under a ten-footer then resurface next to Carlos Ferreira. I nod at him and keep paddling until I'm past the breaks. The sun warms my skin between each breeze and I breathe in the salty fragrance of the Pacific Ocean. As much as I love the Atlantic, the Pacific Ocean just seems to have an electric quality, a *life* that the Atlantic doesn't have. If I could live on the Pacific I would. I'd pack up all my things, sail out to sea, drop anchor, and never look back.

My gaze keeps darting across the shoreline to where Lindsay dips her toes in the water. She used to bitch at me all the time after I quit competing. She actually called me a quitter once. I should have dumped her then, but we'd been together for a year and a half and I had the stupid idea that we should try to work things out since we'd already invested so much time in the relationship. It was just a few weeks later that I caught her cheating on me with Nathan Jennings – number 86 in the world ASP rankings.

I'm not even ranked anymore. It was depressing watching my rank drop from 47 down to nothing. I should never have let my dad deposit my winnings into my trust fund. I never thought he'd put the stipulation on the account that I'm not allowed to touch a single penny of it until my thirtieth birthday. I'm pretty certain he also put a stipulation in there saying I'll gain access to the funds if I have a child. I guess he assumed that I'd be less inclined to confess my sins to Myles' family when I'm thirty or when I have a child of my own to consider. At least, come Thursday, I'll only have seven more years to wait. Unless Lindsay has a secret she's been keeping from me. Then, by the looks of it, I may gain access to my trust fund in about seven days.

A jet ski whizzes past me with someone in tow. Whoever it is lets go and I'm hit with a small wave from the jet ski's wake. I wipe the water from my face to see who had to get towed out here – the water's not that rough – then I see Nathan's shoulder-length brown hair and the cross tattoo on his right bicep.

I'm tempted to look away so I don't see the scar on his face, but I don't. It takes him a moment before he notices me.

I throw him a cool nod. 'Good swell today.' *And I hope you get bombed out there.*

He smiles and I see that fucking gold tooth he got to replace the one I knocked out. 'Perfect conditions for schoolin' some seniors.'

Nathan's only a year younger than I am. I don't know who he's calling a senior, but I'm not playing into that bullshit. I feel the frustration building in my arms. I've suppressed that sensation for six months, only slipping up that one time a few weeks ago. I've controlled my temper since March by moving away from everyone I know, smoking a fuck-ton of weed, and keeping myself busy with work and Claire. Weed and Claire were my addictions for the past six months and now I've given them both up. I'm fucked.

'Don't let that grille weigh you down,' I shout over my shoulder as I paddle away to get a better view of the swell.

I count the seconds between the first few breaks then close my eyes to listen. The crashing of the waves forms a rhythm that corresponds with the motion of the water under my board. The sun warms my shoulders as the ocean sways beneath me until I'm totally relaxed. The siren blasts to signal the beginning of the heat and my nerves fire up again.

I open my eyes and Carlos Ferreira is riding inside the barrel, racing to stay ahead of the spit coming off the wave. The barrel closes in on him, or so it appears. He emerges two seconds later wobbling as he fights to stay on his board. Even all the way out here you can hear the cheering from the crowd.

I paddle out to the line-up and wait to see if Jordan Muzo is going to take this next wave. He hesitates and, since I'm on the inside of the wave and have the right of way, I take it. I push the nose of the board down into the water and stand up as the wave curls up behind me. I flip a hard left then right to get some momentum as the tube forms. I kick faster so I can stay ahead of the curl because I need more than just a clean ride if I want to place today.

I get ahead of the wave and ride it up to the crest then flip my board into a 180. The sensation from that half-second I'm in the air is pure exhilaration and terror. Then everything fades and suddenly all I see is the terror in Myles' eyes as he teeters on the edge of the cliff. The moment when he realized he was falling too fast.

My board comes down on the crest of the wave facing backwards and I try to right myself before the wave closes in on me. Then I bail.

The rest of the heat doesn't go much better as I attempt to drown my thoughts of Myles and Lindsay. I try to think of Claire as motivation, how I'd love to bring back a trophy to her, but I keep getting confused

217

by my desire to be with her. If I do well, I'll be seeing a lot less of her when I go on tour.

I place ninth overall; enough to move on to the ASP qualifier in Australia. While everyone hangs out around the judges' tent during the award ceremony, I set off to find Lindsay. Nathan placed thirteenth, so they probably took off before the ceremony began. I head toward the park area and spot them behind a sponsor tent where Nathan is changing in the shade of the tent. I set off toward them, but a photographer cuts me off.

'Parker. We need you at the Hurley table for photos.'

I make it back to the hotel at 8:30, having refused four different offers to hang out and celebrate. It doesn't even occur to me that the contest coordinator may have booked a block of rooms for us on the same floor until I get to the tenth floor and find Nathan at the ice machine with a bucket under the dispenser. This is my chance to make things right or make things worse.

'Hey.'

Nathan whips his head around, his eyes wide as the ice tumbles out of his bucket, half of it spilling onto the floor. 'What the fuck?'

Nathan was always a nervous little shit. He used to smoke speed a few years ago. He thought it gave him superpowers in the water. He ended up finally making it to the ASP tour a few months after he quit meth, though he placed near the bottom. I try not to rub in my former ASP ranking because it's just that, a *former* ranking. It's the surfer I *used* to be. It's not the surfer I am now, though I'm sure I have it in me to get back up there. I'm just not sure I have the desire to get there.

In some ways, Claire makes me a better man. In other ways, she makes me want to give up everything just to be with her. I'm not sure if these two aspects of our relationship cancel each other out. All I know is that my love for Claire is quickly gaining on my love for surfing.

'You have something you want to tell me?' I say as he places the bucket back under the dispenser to get more ice.

'I don't know what the fuck you're talking about.'

'Save the posing for the cameras. I'm talking about Lindsay.'

He stands upright once his bucket is overflowing with ice and looks me in the eye. 'She didn't do anything wrong. She's just waiting for the baby to be born. Then she's going to get the test and if it's yours she was going to call you. She ain't trying to keep it from you.' I open my mouth to respond, but he cuts me off. 'She said you guys used condoms all the time so it can't be yours.'

I want to clock him in his gold mouth. 'Fuck yes, I used condoms with her. I always knew she would do some shit like this.'

He looks at me with what might be a trace of sympathy in his eyes. 'She knows where to find you and you know where to find her. We don't need to make a big fucking deal out of this. She's due in two weeks and then this will all be settled.'

I can't help but think of Claire and how she kept the pregnancy from Chris then gave the baby up. 'And if it's mine? She'll call me?'

'Dude, what the fuck kind of question is that? Of course she'll call you.'

He looks at me warily as if he's not sure if I'm going to hit him or walk away. I run my fingers through my hair and grit my teeth against all the volatile impulses I'm suppressing.

'Two weeks?' I mutter, mostly to myself. I look him in the eye and he looks about ready to cover his face to block the blows. 'I guess I won't see you in Gold Coast since you placed thirteenth. Good luck in Fiji.'

He looks confused by this calm response, but I don't bother sticking around to explain. I've got the most beautiful girl in the world waiting for me at home. I don't need to get into any more shit with Nathan and Lindsay. If the baby turns out to be mine, I'll deal with it because I'm not a quitter – contrary to what Lindsay and Nathan might think.

I make it to my room without further run-ins. After a long, hot shower, I lie down on the bed and stare at my phone. I haven't spoken or texted Claire in three weeks, but I need to hear her voice right now. I want to call her and tell her how much I miss her, but I don't want to call just to find out she's already moved on with Chris. Maybe I'll wait until I fly back to Kauai tomorrow. If I still feel the need to hear her voice then, I'll call her.

Who the fuck am I kidding? Of course I'll still want to hear her voice tomorrow.

I heave a deep sigh as Myles comes to mind. If he were here he would probably tell me to stop being such a pussy and call her already. The only time you'll discover you've waited too long is when it's already too late.

I open up a new text message to Claire and begin typing.

Me: I came in 9th today. It reminded me of your birthday. I left something for you in my apartment.

I lay the phone on my bare stomach and close my eyes as I await her response. A few minutes later, the vibration startles me awake.

Claire: You broke my heart.

Chapter Twenty-Seven

Chris

My mom comes home from the bakery early on Saturday with a lemon cake – Claire's favorite. She makes room for it in the fridge then insists on bringing me breakfast in bed. She sets a tray next to me on my bed with some scrambled eggs and protein pancakes my trainer gave her the recipe for.

'Hurry up and eat so you can get ready for Claire. You don't want her to smell you like that.'

'Seriously, Mom. Don't start with this. I already told you, Claire has a boyfriend.'

'So you say. I've never seen her with him. I'm practically her mother. If she's so serious about him, she should bring him here to meet me.'

'You'd better not tell her to bring him here unless you want me to end up in jail.'

She purses her lips as she fluffs a pillow to put under my leg. 'You will not do a thing if she brings him here.

Claire is allowed to move on, though I really don't see how she can just throw you and your child away like that.'

'She didn't throw our child away.' I snatch the pillow from her hands before she can attempt to place it under my leg, and she throws me a surprised look. 'If you say anything like that to her today, I swear to God I'm getting a hotel room tonight.'

'You're not getting a hotel room.'

I shake my head at her and she rolls her eyes as she leaves the room. I can already feel I'm going to regret asking Claire to come today.

I eat my breakfast then shower and get ready. As I look in the mirror at the tattoo on my chest, I imagine taking Claire aside to show it to her. She traces the letters and I shiver at the sensation of her fingertip on my skin; something I've been craving so badly for the past year has turned into an obsession since I saw her again two months ago. I press my lips to her fingertips then lay a soft trail of kisses all the way up her arm until I reach her shoulder. Her perfect shoulders. Then I taste the skin on her neck and she moans softly. That's when I take her face in mine and kiss her the way only *I* can kiss her.

Fuck. I want her so fucking bad. Rachel's right. I have to man-up and tell her.

The doorbell rings and I pull on my T-shirt. I grab my crutches and hobble out of the bathroom. When I reach the top of the staircase, my mom is leaning out the front door, hugging someone.

'Let her in,' I say from the top of the stairs.

My mom lets go and opens the front door wider, but it's not Claire.

'Come on in, honey,' my mom says, beckoning the girl inside.

Her loose, light-brown curls are pulled back into a neat ponytail that tumbles down her back. She looks a bit timid as she steps inside and flashes me a shy smile. Something about her looks very familiar.

'This is my new assistant manager at the shop,' my mom continues. 'Do you recognize her?'

I do my little hop routine down the stairs until I reach the foyer to get a better look at this girl. She looks very uncomfortable as I look her over, taking in her round brown eyes and full lips. I can't tell if she's wearing makeup and she's dressed pretty plainly in jeans and a black T-shirt bearing the bakery logo.

'Melina?'

Her eyes light up when she smiles. 'I can't believe you remember my name.'

I can't believe I remember it either. She stayed with us for less than three months when I was fourteen. She was twelve and I tried my hardest to stay away from her because I was going through all sorts of changes. Girls were just beginning to change from pests to conquests and I didn't want to go there with her. She was incredibly awkward – braces, frizzy hair, hand-me-down clothes.

She's still a little awkward, but only in the way she carries herself, not in her appearance.

My mom closes the door behind Melina. 'Come on in, hun. I have that cake stand in the kitchen.'

I'm tempted to watch her as they walk into the kitchen, but I restrain myself, which is a good thing because right then the doorbell rings again.

'I'll get it!' I shout toward the kitchen.

I open the door and Claire is standing on the doorstep looking more beautiful than ever. Her soft blonde hair hangs loose over her shoulders and she's wearing a regular pair of skinny jeans, but it's the shirt that makes me want to take her upstairs and rip her clothes off.

I stare at the shirt for a moment, incapable of tearing my eyes away. 'You cannot do this to me.'

'Do what? Senia gave this to me a couple of days ago and I thought we'd get a good laugh out of it.'

She steps inside and I sigh as I get a closer look at the Chris Knight T-shirt she's wearing.

'Where's your mom?' she asks as she sets her purse and car keys down on the small table in the foyer.

I want to pull her into the coat closet and slip my hands under her shirt, but then a dark thought hits me. Maybe she only wore the shirt so my mom doesn't go ballistic on her over Abigail.

'She's in the kitchen with one of her employees. Come upstairs with me. I want to show you something.'

225

She eyes me and my crutches warily. 'Maybe I should go alone. Is it in your bedroom or mine?'

'I'm not a cripple. I go up and down these stairs all day long.' I hand her my crutches. 'You can carry those.'

She rolls her eyes then follows after me as I make my way up the steps, gripping the handrail so I have to put very little pressure on my right leg.

'That leg is never going to heal if you do this all day.'

'It's healing up just fine. Cast should be off in eighteen days.'

'Claire!' My mom's voice is a bit shrill with surprise. 'Was that you who rung the doorbell?'

I look over my shoulder at Claire and she looks a bit frightened. 'Yes, ma'am.'

My mom shakes her head. 'Oh, stop with the ma'am stuff and you should not be ringing the doorbell. This is your house. Come here and meet Melina.'

Melina comes out of the kitchen carrying a large white cake stand. I recognize it as the one my mom used for my birthday cake in May. It was the first cake stand she got before she opened her bakery. There must be some big event going on at the shop for her to allow Melina to use it.

Claire looks at Melina for a moment before she glances back at me. It's just a split-second look, but I swear there was a trace of jealousy in her eyes.

She leans my crutches against the handrail and descends the stairs. She gives my mom a hug before she turns to Melina and holds out her hand. 'I'm Claire.'

Melina takes her hand and my mom beams as if she's introducing long lost sisters.

'Claire, this is Melina. She was with us for a few months just two years before you showed up.'

Melina and Claire share a quick handshake before Melina casually moves toward the door. 'I should get going back to the shop now. Nice to meet you, Claire.'

She glances up at me and I raise my eyebrows, but I don't say anything. I don't want to give Claire the idea that I know this girl even though she did stay with us a billion years ago.

'Nice to meet you, too,' Claire says as my mom opens the door for Melina.

My mom closes the door and looks up at me with utter contempt. 'Jesus, Christopher. She came to me a few weeks ago because she had aged out and needed a job. She's going through a really hard time. You could have been just a little more courteous.'

I roll my eyes because I am not going to be courteous to a strange girl who obviously makes Claire uncomfortable.

Claire squints at me for a second before she rushes out the front door. My mom looks confused then quickly follows after her.

Damn this leg! I hop down the steps and grab my crutches from where Claire left them. By the time I make it onto the front doorstep, Claire and my mom are returning up the front walk. They both look serious, then I spot a hint of a smile on Claire.

'What was that?' I ask as she enters the house ahead of me and holds the door open for me.

'I just wanted to give her my number in case she needs someone to talk to.'

My mom enters behind me and I stand inside the foyer watching them. I know my mom. She wants to be angry with Claire because of Abigail, but Claire is not going to allow that.

God, I fucking love her.

'That was very kind of you,' my mom says to Claire. 'But we still have some things we need to talk about. You go ahead upstairs and let Chris show you his little surprise then we can talk.'

I make my way upstairs as quickly as I can, before my mom can interrupt again. Claire follows me into my bedroom, though I sense a bit of reluctance as she enters.

'I'm not going to try anything. I know you have a boyfriend.'

She winces at the word boyfriend then shakes her head. 'I don't have a boyfriend. Adam and I broke up.'

I want to tell her how happy this makes me, but her face screws up, as if she's in physical pain, and I'm suddenly mad as hell. Did this motherfucker break her heart?

'I didn't know that. I'm sorry.'

'No, you're not. This is what you wanted.'

'Claire, I want you, but I don't want to see you in pain.'

She closes her eyes as she heaves a deep sigh. She's trying to hold it together. 'What's the big surprise?'

I think of the box of photos my mom found in her room the other day while searching for Claire's diary. I was so pissed when I found out what she had been doing, but I quickly got lost in the pictures. It was the box of photos I hid in her room after I left for L.A. because I knew my mom would leave Claire's room as is. I didn't trust her to do the same with my room. I looked through that box of pictures the other day and found moments I'd long since forgotten. I hoped that giving her the pictures might spark some forgotten feelings inside her, but now I can't bring myself to put her through that. She doesn't need me pushing myself on her right now. What she needs right now is a friend.

'It can wait,' I say as I nod toward the bed. 'Sit down so we can talk.'

'I don't need to talk.'

'Don't pull that on me, Claire.' I rest my crutches against the dresser and sit down on the edge of the bed as I pat the mattress. 'Talk to me.'

She sits next to me, but she stares straight ahead at the mirror above the dresser. 'I can't talk to you about this.'

I don't want to hear about her problems with Adam. I think I'd rather break my leg again than talk about this with her, but I'm nothing if not a complete fool when it comes to Claire.

'You can talk to me about anything, babe.'

She glances at me and I nod to encourage her. 'He left for Hawaii four weeks ago and everything just fell apart. He said we should take a break so we don't hate each other by the time he gets back.'

'So you two are getting back together when he gets back?'

'I don't know.'

She looks miserable. This is not how you treat someone you supposedly love. This guy is a fucking idiot.

'Do you *want* to get back together with him when he gets back?'

She sighs again as she stares at the carpet. 'I don't know. I . . .' She looks at me then shakes her head. 'I can't talk about this with you. This is too awkward.'

'Awkward?'

She smiles. 'Yes. It's very awkward.'

'You know what's awkward? You sitting there talking to me about your breakup while wearing that shirt. I think you should take it off and this would get a whole lot less awkward.'

She presses her lips together to suppress her smile. 'Really, Chris? You're talking to me like that at a time like this?'

I can sit here and argue with her and make little cute comments back and forth or I can do something.

I reach across and trace my finger lightly over the side of her cheek. She only flinches a little, but I can see her body tense.

'I'm sorry, but I've been dying to touch you since we

230

broke up.' She leans forward and hides her face in her hands. 'I'm sorry, I didn't mean to upset you.'

She shakes her head as she takes a moment to compose herself. Finally, she pulls her hands away from her face and wipes a few tears away.

'Claire, I love you and I just want you to be happy.'

She looks at me, her eyes are rimmed red, and it's as if she's seeing me for the first time. 'How can you still love me after everything I've done to you?'

'How can I not? You're the fucking love of my life. You don't stop loving someone just because they've hurt you. Yes, what you did hurt me, but I gain nothing if I stay angry with you. But I might gain everything by forgiving you. You're my everything. I just want you back.'

She gazes into my eyes and before I can change my mind I take her face in my hands and kiss her.

Chapter Twenty-Eight

Claire

He tastes minty and I recognize the flavor of his brand of toothpaste – the toothpaste I had to stop using last year because it reminded me too much of him. I want to push him away. I don't want to kiss Chris. But my curiosity gets the best of me.

Not counting the kiss that didn't really happen two months ago, this is our first kiss in over a year. How can we still be so in sync? I can anticipate the movement and pressure of his lips, every graze of his tongue, and I respond exactly the way he wants me to. No one can kiss me the way Chris does.

This thought makes me sick and I instantly push him away. 'Stop.'

'Why?'

'Because I want you to.'

He looks as though he can't decide whether he

should be pissed or understanding. 'You felt that. Don't tell me you didn't feel that.'

'Please don't do this,' I say as I stand. 'I came to talk to your mom.'

'Go ahead and walk away. You're still mine, Claire, whether or not you admit it to yourself.'

I want to tell him to fuck off, but I can't ignore the nagging voice inside my head telling me he's right. Why else would that kiss have felt so good?

I leave his room, still attempting to make sense of this. I'm just feeling lonely. I miss Adam. Of course, I wanted to be kissed. And who better to do it than Chris? Someone who's kissed me a million times. Someone who knows exactly what I want. But that's all it was, just a kiss. We are not in love anymore. I love Adam.

Even if he did break his promise never to hurt me.

This is not exactly what I wanted to happen when I showed up here. I should never have worn this stupid shirt Senia bought me. I glance down at my chest at the gray T-shirt with a black silhouette of Chris playing the guitar and the letters CK behind the silhouette. I thought it would be kind of funny, but apparently I gave Chris the wrong idea. I should never have told him that Adam and I broke up.

I should have taken Linda Coldwater's advice.

I think back to the conversation I had with my professor yesterday and I can't believe I allowed myself to get so emotional in front of someone who holds such a large piece of my academic career in her hands. I'm a complete emotional wreck lately. Linda insisted that she didn't quit her job as a caseworker because she didn't enjoy it. She insisted that she loved the job, and the children she worked with, too much.

'It's no secret that it's a tough job. You can see that from watching any damn movie about orphans,' she said as she leaned back in her desk chair. 'What you don't see in movies and what most people who've worked in this job won't tell you is that there is very little you can do for these children other than placing them in decent homes and performing thorough inspections. What happens the moment you leave a foster home or when they leave your office is not up to you.'

That's about where I lost it. Then Linda handed me her business card with the name and number of a campus therapist scrawled on the back.

If I had had someone there to watch over me during the eight years I was shuffled through the system, I might have found a forever home sooner. I think back to all the homes I came through to get here, to Jackie and Chris.

When I was eight years old, I was placed with an artist, his wife, and their two young sons who were toddlers. They had a nice home in a quaint suburb where he painted mock-ups for large-scale murals. I was fascinated by these paintings, until he picked me up to set me on a stool, to watch him paint, and he accidentally touched my butt. I punched him and kicked down the stool and threw a hellish tantrum until they called my caseworker.

Eight years of these episodes. It's no wonder my caseworkers hated me, and any wonder how Chris and Jackie got through to me.

Jackie sits at the table in the breakfast nook going over some paperwork, probably bills or something for the bakery. She looks up at me over her reading glasses and I feel like a child about to be chastised, full of shame and guilt over my indiscretions.

'Sit,' she says, pulling out the white wooden chair next to her.

I sit down and resist the urge to launch into a long apology. Jackie hates excuses and she doesn't want to hear that.

'Jackie, I know you don't hate me, but I can't bear the idea of you being disappointed in me.'

She pulls her eyeglasses off and looks me in the eye. 'I'm not disappointed in you. I'm hurt that you didn't feel you could come to me.' Her eyes begin to water and my chest tightens. 'Even if you and Chris aren't together, you will always be like a daughter to me. You're the little girl I always wanted but couldn't have.' I make no effort to stop the tears once hers begin to fall. 'After Chris was born, I had three miscarriages and it tore my marriage to his father apart. When Michael left, I gave up on finding unconditional love in a man, so I decided I would give unconditional love to those who needed it most.' She grabs my hand and my body shakes as I attempt to keep from sobbing. 'I'm not angry with you. I love you, unconditionally.'

She stands from her chair and beckons me into her arms. I rise and we hug for a while as she strokes my hair and rubs my back.

'So are you ever going to bring this boyfriend of yours here to meet us?' she asks and I freeze.

'Boyfriend?'

She lets go of me and looks me in the eye. 'You don't have to pretend, honey. Rachel and Chris already told me you have a boyfriend. I want to meet him.'

Shit.

'I don't have a boyfriend. Chris just assumed we were still together, but we're not. He's in Hawaii right now for business, anyway, so he wouldn't have been able to come.'

'For *business*? How old is he?'

'Twenty-two.' It dawns on me that Adam's birthday is coming in just a few days. October tenth. He's going to be twenty-three.

She narrows her eyes at me. 'So you *don't* have a boyfriend?'

If I were being honest I would tell her that I don't have a boyfriend, but that I desperately still want Adam to be my boyfriend. I miss everything about him. My heart and body ache for his voice, his jokes, his touch.

'He's not my boyfriend anymore, but I miss him. His name is Adam.' I want to say that he brought me back

236

to life, but I don't want to drop too many bombshells on Jackie today. 'I think you'd really like him.'

The look of sympathy in her eyes makes my heart squeeze in my chest. 'Well, I hope for your sake that you two can work out your differences.'

I nod as Chris shuffles in on his crutches. I don't tell her that Adam and I don't have differences, we have distance – too much distance.

'I see tears have been shed. Does that mean I missed the good part?' Chris says as he passes me on his way to the fridge.

Jackie looks at me and I see a glimmer of something in her brown eyes. I think she's silently asking me not to tell Chris that we were talking about Adam.

'I should get going,' I say and Chris immediately closes the refrigerator door.

'I'll walk you out.'

'Walk?' Jackie says with a chuckle, and I can't help but laugh.

'Real funny. Make fun of the cripple.'

He waits for me to give Jackie a hug and say goodbye before he follows me to the door. I grab my purse and keys from the table in the foyer and pretend not to notice how uncomfortable Chris looks when I open and close the front door for him.

I follow him out to where my car is parked next to the curb and he looks over my car. It needs to be washed, but I haven't gotten my first full paycheck yet from my new job at the used textbook store.

We stand in silence for a moment while we both try to think of something to say. Finally, he looks me in the eye and I recognize that look. It's the same look he gave me the day we broke up – the look that broke my heart – and it has the same effect on me now.

'I'm sorry that I never called you after I left last year. I know I fucked everything up.'

'I think we both did a pretty good job of that.'

'No, this is my fault. If I had fought harder for us, we wouldn't be in this situation with Abigail and everything would be different. We'd still be together. You know that, don't you?'

I sigh then nod, because it's true. It's Saturday. If we hadn't made all these stupid mistakes, we'd probably be lying in bed in my dorm or hanging out at Tristan's house entertaining whatever girl he'd brought home that weekend. We'd be wrapped up in each other, two ribbons of the same color twisted and tied together, inextricable and indistinguishable.

He leans his crutches against the side of my car and holds out his hand. I stare at it for a moment, my heart pounding as I try not to think that this is one of those moments where everything changes – a turning point. I reach out and he takes my hand in his then pulls me toward him. I wrap my arms around his waist and bury my face in his shoulder.

'Can I call you tonight?' he asks in that soft, sexy voice he uses when he's on stage.

I try not to laugh. 'Yeah, I guess that's okay. You still haven't heard anything from Tasha?'

'Not yet,' he says as he pulls his head back to look at me. 'But I swear I'm working on it. I'm not giving up.'

'I should go.'

He kisses my forehead and I sigh as his fingers trail down the side of my face and land on my neck. 'Drive safely, babe.'

He grabs his crutches and steps back as he watches me get into the car. I turn the key in the ignition then jump when he knocks on my window. I roll it down and he smiles.

'Please wash your car.'

'Way to kill the moment, douche.'

'I put some money in your bank account yesterday, which you probably didn't notice because judging by the negative balance you probably never check your account.'

I don't know if I should punch him or kiss him or cry from embarrassment. 'That's not funny.'

'I know. That's why I took care of it. Please don't let it get to that point again.' He smacks the top of my car. 'And wash this thing.' He leans his head through the window and kisses my cheek then whispers in my ear, 'I'll always take care of you.'

Chapter Twenty-Nine

Adam

After that text message from Claire, I was about ready to completely give up on her, if it weren't for the talk I had with Yuri last night. Sometimes I feel like Yuri's the craziest person I know and other times I feel like he's the only person I know who has any sense. His nuggets of wisdom come mostly from his upbringing. Both his parents were humanists and his mother was a surfer when she was younger.

'Dude, the quickest path to self-destruction is to push away the people you love,' he said as he lay on the bed in the hotel room in Maui and I sat in the desk chair, both of us sipping beers and admiring the view out the hotel window.

'You sound like your mom.'

'Because my mom is the shit.'

I finish off my beer and pull another one out of the bucket of ice on the desk. 'I think I fucked up majorly, but I don't know how to fix it other than jumping on a plane and going back to her.'

'You can use my ticket and I'll stay here and pretend to be you.'

'Do you think Lena would mind me pretending to be you when I get there?'

'She doesn't like small dicks.'

'Then how the fuck are you two still together?'

'She doesn't know about my inflatable implant.'

I can always count on Yuri to say what I need to hear, but now I'm faced with the biggest decision of my life. I can quit this project and go back to Claire. That means I'll have to keep working for my dad and I'll be tied to Wilmington and the secret that binds me to my father until I'm thirty. Or I can stick it out here for four more weeks and risk coming back to find that Claire can't forgive me – or worse, that I've been replaced.

After driving Yuri to the airport at 5 a.m., I just want to get back to the hotel room and go to sleep before I make any important decisions. I have to take this rental car back tomorrow and catch a flight back to Kauai at 8 p.m. But a text message from an unknown number changes everything.

Unknown: We decided not to catch the flight back because Lindsay was having some pain. We're at Maui Memorial.

It's Nathan. I don't want to respond and I definitely don't want to go. The odds of the baby being mine are so fucking slim, it's not worth putting myself, or them, through it. I always used condoms with Lindsay. I did love her, but I'm not stupid. It's not a trust issue. I just know I'm not ready to be a father.

Of course, this just makes me think of Claire. What if she *does* work out an open adoption agreement with Abigail's parents? If I want to be with her, I'll have to support that. I have no idea how open adoptions work, but I assume the parents wouldn't want Claire's boyfriend around their daughter mixing her up even further than she'll already be by having two sets of parents. What if I'm not what's best for Claire at all?

Fuck that. That's the kind of thinking that got me into this mess.

I pull over to look up the directions to Maui Memorial Medical Center then turn my truck around. I pull into the parking lot a half-hour later and find a parking space as far from the entrance as possible before I text back.

Me: What room are you guys in?
Nathan: I don't know. Just ask for her name at the nurse's desk in the waiting room.

I sit in my car for a minute and think about what I'm getting myself into. In the years since Myles'

242

death my life has been a series of train wrecks. I quit competing. I got together with Lindsay. I nearly killed Nathan. I started smoking weed to calm down after I realized I was on a collision course. My life only started getting better when I met Claire. I feel like being here at this hospital is just a way for me to get sucked back into that old life. It's another train wreck waiting to happen.

As much as I want to pull out of this parking lot and go home, more than anything I want to do what I think Claire would want me to do.

I find the nurses' desk outside the maternity waiting room and the nurse wants to know if I'm family.

I look her in the eye and try not to sound too annoyed when I say, 'I could possibly be the father.'

She raises her eyebrows as she leans forward and points down the hall. 'Third room on the right.'

I make it within a few feet of the door when the realization hits me. If this baby isn't mine, I'm going back to Wilmington and calling my dad's bluff. I'll quit my job at Parker Construction and take the job in Raleigh. I don't think my dad will tell the cops the real version of what happened to Myles, but I wouldn't put it past him to completely dissolve my trust account. I can live without the millions so long as I have Claire.

I knock on the door and Nathan comes out looking frazzled as fuck. 'Lindsay doesn't want you in there, but I already booked the paternity test for tonight 'cause the baby's coming soon. You can wait around until then or you can go home and we'll call you on Thursday with the results.'

'Thursday? That's five days from now.' And it also happens to be my birthday. I'd rather be in Raleigh on Thursday.

'It takes the lab three business days from the day they receive the blood to get the results. That's three days from Monday.'

'Fuck,' I whisper. 'When are you all going back?'

He runs his hand through his hair as a guilty look washes over his face. 'I have a competition on Wednesday so I'm leaving Tuesday. Lindsay's sticking around here until Friday. They won't give the results to anyone but the three of us.'

I sigh as I realize where this conversation is going. 'You want me to pick up the results on Thursday.'

The guilty look on his face is replaced by relief. 'Dude, I know you'd rather do pretty much anything other than help me, but I don't want her to have to stay here alone.'

'And you can't miss one fucking competition?'

'It's my last chance to qualify. You already made it. You don't have to worry about this shit anymore until March. I've only got one more shot. I'm paying the entire eleven hundred dollars for the test.'

As much as I want to tell him to go to hell, I know that he and Lindsay probably didn't think they'd have to deal with this because she wasn't supposed to be due for another two weeks. And they sure as hell didn't expect to run into me here. If this is what it takes to get some peace of mind, I'll do it.

I don't even know if this kid is mine and I'm already stressed out. I can't imagine what Claire has gone through this past year. I should be there with her right now, but I have to handle this first.

'All right. Text me the address for the lab and I'll pick up the results on Thursday.'

'Thanks so much, bro. You don't know how much you've helped us.' He reaches out to shake my hand and I can't bring myself to do it.

'I'm not your bro.'

I make it back to the hotel in Hana around two and immediately lie down to watch some TV. I should probably be booking a flight back to Raleigh for next Saturday – after I've gone back to Kauai to get my things – but I need to chill out first and think about what I'm going to do if this baby is mine. I have to prepare myself for the possibility that Claire will want nothing to do with me.

I scroll through the pictures on my phone and find the last picture we took together in the Busy Bee Café. Lena took the picture for us. Claire is hugging my arm as she leans her head on my shoulder. I've looked at this picture a million times over the past four weeks, but tonight she looks more beautiful than I remember.

Maybe it's the prospect of seeing her next Saturday that is giving me a false sense of hope, giving everything a rosy tint.

Even if this baby is mine, I'm going to try to get Claire back. I can't live without her.

Chapter Thirty

Chris

I don't like talking on the phone, but I'll do it if that's what it takes to hear Claire's voice and to make sure I stay on her mind. She picks up on the first ring: a good sign considering this is the first time she's answered any of my calls since the day we met Abigail's parents.

'You deposited ten thousand dollars into my account?'

Not the greeting I was hoping for, but not totally unexpected. 'It's not a big deal. I'll make it back by tomorrow night.'

'That's too much. I can't accept that. I *won't* accept that.'

'Why do you always have to make everything so difficult? Just take the money and you can pay me back later.'

'I will never be able to pay you back ten grand. That's not pocket change to me. In my world, that's a lot of money.'

'I didn't say you had to pay me back in money.'

'I'm hanging up now.'

'That was a joke,' I say, though I'm trying my hardest not to laugh. 'Claire, you will never have to pay me back.' She's silent for a long time; so long that I begin to think she hung up. 'Are you still there?'

'Yes,' she whispers. 'Chris, I didn't tell you about what happened the day I ran into you at the concert on my birthday.'

'What happened?'

She pauses again and I'm starting to worry. 'Before the concert, I went to Northstar Bank in Raleigh because I got a letter from them saying I have a trust fund in my name worth more than two hundred grand.'

'What? How is that possible?'

I don't say it aloud, but we both know that Claire grew up with nothing, even when her mother was alive. I don't like bringing up her mother. I never have. It upsets her just the way she's obviously upset right now.

'My father has been depositing money into the account for years. I guess he did it so my mom would keep quiet about the fact that he raped her when she was seventeen.'

Fuck. The last thing I wanted to do when I deposited that money into her account was bring up these kinds of memories.

'I'm sorry, Claire. I feel like a total dick now.'

'That's not the worst part.' She heaves a long sigh

248

before she continues and I wish I were there to comfort her. 'My mother's overdose wasn't a mistake.'

'I'm coming over.'

'You can't drive. Don't be stupid.'

'That's what taxis are for. I don't like hearing you like this.'

'I'm fine.'

'You are obviously not fine. How could you be? Claire, you don't have to pretend with me.'

'It's almost nine o'clock. I'm not finished studying and Senia's coming back soon.'

I sit up in bed and reach for my crutches. 'I promise I'll let you study. And you know I have no problem with Senia being there. I haven't hung out with her in a while.'

Senia loves me. I don't know how she feels about surfer boy, but I remember her being pissed as hell the day Claire broke up with me. She was always on my side when Claire and I fought. It drove Claire crazy.

'You'd better not try anything like what happened earlier today. That is not going to happen again so just get that out of your mind.'

'I just want to be there for you.'

'I should be done studying by eleven.'

'Good, because that's about how long it's going to take me to hobble there on my crutches. See ya, babe.'

The sound of her laughter as I hang up makes me happy. She needs someone there. She probably doesn't want to burden Senia with this stuff since they're both carrying big workloads with their classes. But she needs someone to talk to and I'd rather it be me than him.

The taxi drops me off near the entrance at Spencer Hall at 10:44 p.m. It's a Saturday, so people are still coming and going and I wait less than ten minutes for someone to open the door to let me in. Unfortunately, it's a group of girls who look about ready to go partying and they instantly recognize me.

'Oh. My. God!' a blonde girl in a purple blouse cries. 'You're Chris Knight!'

The other girls snap their heads in my direction and fix me with hungry stares. 'I'm just here to see a friend.'

'You have a friend in this dorm? OMG!' the blonde girl cries.

'That is so cool!' says another girl with auburn hair and red lipstick. 'Can you tell us who it is?'

'So we can stalk him?' the blonde girl says, and all four of them roar with laughter.

'Sorry. I'm trying to keep a low profile. You ladies understand, right?' I flash them my crowd smile and it seems to work as they all let out a collective sigh. The blonde girl holds the door open for me to hop inside on my crutches and I nod at her. 'Thanks, girls. Be good tonight.'

The blonde girl sighs as she lets the door fall closed behind me. I pull my hood up over my head so I don't have any more run-ins and quickly make my way to Claire's dorm. Claire opens the door wearing plaid green pajama pants and a pink tank top.

'I dressed up for you,' she says when she catches me checking her out.

'You know how much plaid turns me on.'

'If you weren't crippled, I'd kick you.'

Senia gets up from her bed and she's as tall as me now that I'm hunched over these crutches. 'Christopher, Christopher, Christopher. Two visits in one week. Tell me, why have you stayed away so long?'

She holds out her arms for a hug and I grab both my crutches in one hand so I can give her a one-armed hug.

'Because I've been a huge ass, but I'm working on not being one anymore.'

She lets go of me and smiles. 'Right answer. It's almost as if you always know the perfect thing to say.' She winks as she turns to go back to her bed.

'Aw, come on. I was counting on you being nice to me.'

She grins as she grabs her phone off her bed, stuffs her headphones in her ears, and slides in under her covers. 'I'm going to read now so I'd appreciate it if you all could keep the sex noises down.'

I turn to Claire and she shakes her head. 'Don't get any ideas.'

She grabs a textbook and her laptop off her bed so I can sit. She sets the book and the laptop on a desk then leans against the desk as she stares at the floor.

'You can sit down. I'm not going to try anything. I promise.'

She narrows her eyes at me for a moment before she relents and sits near the pillow while I sit at the foot of the bed. There's at least two feet of safe distance between us, but it may as well be two miles.

'I don't want you to have to use the money in that trust account, but I think it should go to good use.' I begin the speech I've been rehearsing in my head since I got into the taxi thirty minutes ago. 'I want to match that two hundred grand and we can donate everything to a charity for victims of sexual assault.'

She pulls her legs up onto the bed to sit cross-legged. Her gaze slides over my face as if she's remembering something then she smiles, the smile that I love so much.

'You look different.'

'I do not.'

'Yes, you do,' she insists. 'You look older. Wiser.'

I don't want to tell her that it's probably the dismal year I spent without her that aged me. Then again, maybe she needs to know how completely miserable I was, to know how serious I am about never letting her get away from me again.

'I'm only a few months older than you and I didn't get to spend my birthday with you this year for the first time in five years. Worst birthday of my life.'

Her smile disappears and she looks down at where her hands are folded in her lap.

'I didn't mean that the way it sounded. I just mean that I wanted you with me. And now that I know what

252

you were going through in May, I wish I could have been there for you.' I scoot closer to her and she looks up at me warily. 'I wanted to call you every day that we weren't together, but I didn't work up the nerve to actually do it until a couple of months after we broke up and by then you'd already changed your number. I should have tried to hunt you down, but I figured you changed your number because you moved on. Then my mom told me you weren't calling her anymore and I began to have crazy thoughts, that you were planning the breakup for a long time.'

'That's stupid.'

'I know, but I wasn't in my right mind.' I pause as I think of all the times I fucked a girl in the dark hoping to convince myself for just a minute that she was Claire. 'The worst part is that I've never been more inspired than when I was deep in that darkness. You did do what was best for me when you let me go. And as much as I hated being without you, I'll always be grateful for that.'

I look her in the eye and wait for the right moment, that moment where her breathing slows and the connection is made.

'I'm so confused,' she whispers as she closes her eyes. 'Sometimes I want everything to be the way it was before we broke up. Other times, I want everything to be the way it was before . . .'

'Before what?'

'Before Adam left.'

253

She opens her eyes and I have to look away because I don't want her to see the mixture of pain and rage that's boiling inside me right now. I grind my teeth together to keep from saying something I'll regret. Part of me wants to kill him for taking her away and another part of me wants to thank him for being there for her. Mostly, I just want to kill him. The thought of the two of them together makes me sick.

I take a deep breath to drown this burning jealousy then look her in the eye again. 'I want to know everything you went through while we were apart. Everything since the day we broke up.'

She's quiet for a moment then she begins. 'I was sitting in my SOC 101 class of all places when I started feeling sick to my stomach. I didn't think anything of it until I got back to the dorm and Senia offered me some of her leftover Chinese food. The smell in our room made me so sick, I threw up in the wastebasket.

'I thought it was some kind of virus, so I stayed in the dorm the next day and slept pretty much all day. The whole day I lay in bed thinking about how I hadn't gotten my period since you and I . . . since the day we broke up.'

I think back to that day and I wish we had never had sex. Not just because of what happened with Abigail, but because I'm sure both of us were haunted by the memory of that day for months afterward. I couldn't stop thinking of the taste of her skin and the pure bliss of being inside her. The memories were torture and

I can only imagine what they were to her knowing she was carrying our child – the result of that overwhelming passion we shared.

'How did you find out?' I ask.

'I went to the clinic and the doctor walked into the examination room and told me I was pregnant. She looked at me with such pity when I started crying instead of jumping for joy. I wanted to slap her.' I reach forward and grab her hand and I'm surprised she doesn't flinch. Instead, she looks up at me with the most painful look in her eyes and says, 'Everyone judged me. At least, that's how I felt.'

'You didn't do anything wrong. I'm the one who should have been there for you. None of this is your fault.'

Her face is blank as the tears roll down her cheeks. 'I hated myself for so long. I thought I deserved that judgment.'

I pull her into my arms and she buries her face in my neck as she sobs. I try to hold it together, but I can't. Even though she's the one who broke up with me, I feel like I destroyed her. After everything she went through with her mother, she didn't deserve that.

'You didn't do anything wrong,' I whisper into her ear and she whimpers. 'The biggest mistake you made was loving me enough to let me go. I'm so fucking sorry I wasn't there for you.'

We talk for a few more hours and, though the subject of what went on while we were apart is difficult to discuss, I can't help but feel like this is the happiest I've been in a very long time. It's after 3 a.m. when we realize we're both too tired to carry on. She folds down her blanket and I know she's inviting me into her bed for the first time in nearly fifteen months.

I slide in next to her and we lay in silence for a moment, just staring at the ceiling, before she speaks. 'Thank you for coming. I so needed this.'

'So did I.'

I turn my head through the darkness and glimpse a smile. I kiss her temple and she turns her back to me.

Turning onto my side, I lean forward and whisper in her ear. 'Goodnight, Claire-bear.'

I lay a soft kiss on her earlobe and she pulls my arm around her waist before we fall asleep.

Chapter Thirty-One

Claire

I wake with my head on Chris's chest and my arm draped over his belly. His shirt is off. He must have taken it off in the middle of the night because it was super hot in here. I peel my cheek away from his chest and find him awake.

'Good morning,' he whispers.

I glance down at his legs to make sure he's still wearing pants and I'm relieved to see his jeans. As my gaze follows the thin line of hair under his belly button up his torso and over his chest, a new tattoo catches my eye.

'When did you get that?' I ask, unable to tear my eyes away from it.

The letters CC are interlocked, one facing forward and one facing backward. Both the Cs are twisted through the letter A. All the letters are covered in thorny vines that drip with blood.

He places his fingers under my chin and tilts my face up. 'I got it when I was in London a few weeks ago. I got it for you.'

I glance at Senia's bed and it's empty. 'Where did she go?'

'She left a few minutes ago to meet her mom for brunch.'

Chris and I are alone. On a Sunday. And all my studying is done. Nothing good can come of this.

'I need you to leave,' I say as I sit up on my knees.

'Why?'

'Because.' I close my eyes so I don't have to see that disappointed look on his face. 'I'm afraid of what will happen if you stay.'

I feel him sit up so I open my eyes. He's leaning against the wall behind my bed. I have no headboard and I try not to think of how convenient this was when Adam and I spent the weekends in this bed.

'Why are you afraid? It's not like I'm some guy you picked up at a club. I'm not a one-night stand. I'm your first love and the father of your child. And I'm in love with you.'

I swallow hard and try to catch my breath. 'I can't do this.'

'Come here,' he says, beckoning me into his arms.

I shake my head and he purses his lips. 'Claire. Don't make me tickle you. I still know your spot.'

I roll my eyes and he takes the opportunity to catch me off my guard and pull me toward him. I laugh as

I attempt to get away, but he quickly and lightly digs his fingers into the soft flesh just below my ribs and I bellow with laughter.

'Stop!' I shriek.

He laughs as he grabs both sides of my waist and pulls me on top of him so I'm straddling his hips. We stare at each other for a moment. I don't know what he's thinking about, but I'm thinking of that kiss we shared yesterday. I just want to feel that way again. Like nothing has changed.

He grabs my face and pulls my lips to his. 'I love you,' he says into my mouth between kisses. 'I love you so fucking much.'

I'm so lost. This is wrong. I would lose my mind if Adam knew what I was doing right now. But I don't want to stop. I want to kiss Chris. I want to feel like things can be this good again. I want to feel this good forever.

He pulls back and looks me in the eye. 'I want you so bad right now. I want to make love to you, Claire.'

His hand traces the curve of my jaw and I sigh as my heart races. I've missed his touch, electric on my skin. This is what I dreamed of almost every night for a year before I met Adam. Even now, after learning Adam's ways, becoming accustomed to his kiss and his intensity, I still crave the familiarity of Chris.

I shake my head as I pull away. 'I can't. I'm sorry. I just don't know what I want right now and I don't want to hurt you,' *or Adam*, 'again.'

He nods solemnly, but I can feel the disappointment rolling off of him. 'We don't have to make love. I just want to be here with you.'

I glare at him warily. I remember how often Chris liked to have sex. I don't know how he's been keeping himself satisfied for the past two months, but I know he's bullshitting when he says he just wants to *be here* with me.

'What?' he says as I continue to glare at him. 'I can go without sex. I don't want to go without you, but I'll do it. As fucking painful as it will be, I will wait for you, the same way I waited until you were eighteen.' I move to get off his lap and he grabs my waist to stop me. 'Are you hungry? Let's go to Angie's.'

'Angie's is far.'

'But you have all day.'

Chris and I used to go to Angie's for Sunday brunch at least once a month until I went to UNC. It was our monthly meeting with the band: Chris, me, Jake, Rachel, Tristan, and whatever girl Tristan felt like bringing. It's strange because most people think that Chris's band fell apart when he decided to go solo last year, but the truth is that they began growing apart as soon as I went off to college and Chris had to spend more time with me in Chapel Hill. I was their Yoko Ono.

'Fine,' I say, then something overcomes me.

I don't know if it's guilt from not having sex with him or from being so instrumental in the breakup of

260

the band, but I take his face in my hands and kiss him, slowly, as a deep sigh and longing builds inside me. Finally, I pull away and press my lips together as I attempt to catch my breath.

He kisses the corner of my lips then smiles with that signature gleam in his eyes. 'Sorry, babe, I'm not in the mood.'

We arrive at Angie's Restaurant just before ten and, to my surprise and horror, the waitress who seats us in our booth recognizes us.

'Chris,' she says, poking Chris's arm before she turns to me. 'And Claire.'

I don't recognize her and judging by the puzzled look on Chris's face he doesn't recognize her either. Her cheeks are hollow and her brown hair hangs all the way down to her butt in a long ponytail. Nothing about her is familiar to me, but Chris quickly recovers his wits – or his memory – and gives her his crowd smile. *Ugh*. I have a love/hate relationship with his crowd smile.

'Priscilla,' he says, and her gray eyes light up. 'Can you believe how long it's been?'

She hands me a menu without taking her eyes off Chris. 'Where the heck have you been? Oh, wait. I know where you've been. You're a friggin' rock star now! But you look exactly the same! Except that leg. What the heck happened there?'

Chris goes into a brief explanation of the motorcycle

accident, carefully leaving out the fact that he was out riding his bike that day to try to forget how upset he was over Abigail and me. She asks if she can sign his cast before she finally takes our order.

He orders the usual Denver omelet then turns to me. 'Do you want the usual?'

I don't know if he really remembers what I used to get, so I decide to test him. 'Sure.'

He turns to Priscilla and she waits with a curious expression as he thinks for a moment. 'Belgian waffle with bacon and eggs over-medium.'

Priscilla shakes her head as she jots it down. 'Too cute.'

Once Priscilla is gone, I glare at him across the table. 'Do you always have to show off?'

'I'm a performer. What do you expect?'

'A little humility.'

'Hey, I'm humble. I don't go around bare-chested, wearing fucking leather pants with my shirt hanging out my back pocket.'

'Because you know I'd make fun of you if you did that.'

'No. I only do it on Wednesdays.'

Hump day.

I ignore the jealous roar inside me as I imagine how many girls have been on this end of his charming little act.

'Are you okay?' he asks as Priscilla shows up with our coffee. He flashes her a tight smile and she quickly sets off.

'I'm fine.' *Just getting a glimpse of what life with you would be like now that you're God.*

'You don't look fine. I know what you need.'

I need to not be here. I should be in my dorm moping like I have been the last few Sundays since Adam broke up with me. Instead, I'm sitting across the table from the one person, other than myself, who I can actually hold responsible for breaking us up. What is *wrong* with me?

'Chris, no offense, but I'm beginning to think that even *I* don't know what I need.'

His smile fades and he stares at my hands for a while before he reaches across the table and grabs my left hand. He rubs his thumb over my knuckles for a moment before he brings my hand to his lips and lays a soft kiss on my ring finger.

'I know what you need.' He keeps rubbing my ring finger between his thumb and forefinger and it's making me nervous. 'It's the same thing you've always needed since the day we met. You need your home.'

I swallow hard as I try not to let him see how relieved I am that he didn't do something crazy like proposing to me in Angie's Restaurant. A year ago, I would have loved for Chris to propose to me over a casual breakfast. I was deep in the throes of self-pity over the breakup and I wanted nothing more than for him to walk through my door and tell me he couldn't live another day without me. Now, the thought of Chris proposing actually fills me with panic.

'I have a home. I live with Senia.'

'Yeah, but how about the holidays and the summer. You're coming home, aren't you?'

I pull my hand out of his and he narrows his eyes at me. 'I promised your mom I would be there for Christmas. I'm not going to break my promise.' He shakes his head then stares out the window. 'Why are you shaking your head? You can't expect me to commit to spending every holiday at home. You're really putting me on the spot here.'

He sighs before he turns back to me and looks me in the eye. 'You want everything, Claire. And to me you *are* everything. Do you have any fucking idea what that feels like?'

'Are you trying to make me feel guilty for being confused?'

'Did you not hear what I just said? This is it for me. I've probably blown my record deal and even my career to be here with you. I know you didn't ask me to do it and I'm not asking you to drop everything for me, but can you at least pretend to care?'

'I *do* care. I—'

Priscilla arrives with our plates of food, one of her eyebrows raised, as she is keenly aware she has interrupted a heated discussion. She sets our plates down and leaves without asking if we need anything else.

We eat in silence, though both of us seem to have lost our appetites. When we make it back to my car, he grabs my hand before I can turn the key in the ignition. I close my eyes as I wait for him to speak.

'Can you look at me?' I open my eyes and turn to him as he releases my hand. 'I need to tell you something I probably should have told you a few weeks ago.'

'What?'

He looks down at the console between us for a moment and I recognize that expression of guilt. 'After I saw Abigail, I wasn't in my right mind. I didn't sleep that whole night.'

I think back to that day and remember how I lay awake the entire night cursing myself for running out of the hospital instead of holding it together for just a few more minutes.

'I didn't sleep either.'

'Yeah, but I did something.'

'What did you do?' I ask carefully.

'I checked out of the hospital early and called Tristan to pick me up.'

He doesn't have to say anything else. I already know where this conversation is leading.

'You fucked someone?'

He winces at these words. 'Not *technically*. Tristan took me home and some girls came over. I was fucked up on pain pills and one of them gave me a blowjob.'

I was with Adam when this happened so I *technically* shouldn't care, but I'm furious.

'Is that how you deal with stuff now? By getting fucked up?'

'No, it's not, but you were with . . . *him* and you

265

weren't answering my calls. I knew that it could possibly be the last time I ever see my daughter again and you didn't even get to share that moment with me. I was fucked up even without the pain pills.'

'Why can't you say his name?'

'I don't want to say his name.'

I turn the key in the ignition and try not to think the obvious. Chris is the love of my life, but he's still not ready to grow up.

'Are you mad?' he asks as I pull out of the parking lot.

'Of course I'm mad. And don't act like I have no right to be angry either because that will only make me more angry.' I shake my head as I change lanes so I can head for the highway entrance. 'No one knows how to love me like you and no one knows how to hurt me like you.'

He's quiet the whole drive home. I park next to the curb instead of in the driveway because I don't know if I can go in right now. We sit in silence for a while before he turns to me.

'I'm sorry if I hurt you, but I'm not sorry for being honest with you. You deserve nothing less.' He kisses my cheek then reaches into the back seat to grab his crutches. 'You don't have to come in if you don't want to, but I know my mom would love it if you did. I'd love it, too.'

His lips slowly curl into a smile and I press my lips together to keep from returning the favor.

'Come on. You know you want to come in,' he coaxes me.

'I hate you,' I mutter as I pull the keys out of the ignition.

'I hate you, too,' he says with a soft smile that makes the breath catch in my throat. 'I hate you from the bottom of my heart.'

Chapter Thirty-Two

Chris

I don't want Claire to do anything she'll regret later, which is why I'm going to make sure this is too good to regret.

When we step inside the house, I'm hit with a cool gust of air-conditioned air, but the house is completely quiet. Claire enters after me and I hand her my keys.

'Take the house key off the chain and make a copy for yourself.'

'I don't need a house key,' she says, pushing the keys back into my hand. 'I'm too busy to come visit when no one's here.'

'You're not visiting. This is your house.'

She looks away from me as she closes the front door. 'Where's your mom?'

'I thought she was here. She probably left to run errands.'

I set off toward the kitchen on my crutches, but

I don't hear her footsteps behind me. When I turn around, she's still standing just inside the front door.

'Oh, come on. It's not like we've never been alone in this house.'

She rolls her eyes before she follows me into the kitchen and takes a seat on the barstool at the breakfast bar. She doesn't look much different than she did the first time we had sex three years ago. I lean on the other side of the bar just staring at her for a moment as I remember that day.

'Why are you looking at me like that? You're creeping me out.'

I chuckle as I push off the bar and limp to the other side. 'I was thinking of the first time we had sex. You were sitting right there before I took you upstairs.'

She glares at me, unblinking, before she replies. 'We are *not* having sex.'

'I know, but you asked why I was looking at you.'

'You know, Chris, if you wanted to be nice you'd keep stuff like that to yourself, even if I ask you.' She scoots her barstool farther away from me. 'Can you call Tasha to see what's going on with Abigail?'

'I called her last night before I went to your dorm. I wanted to see if she had some good news I could give you in person.' She looks at me with that heartbroken expression because she knows what's coming. 'Nothing.'

'You should be lying down,' she says as she slides off the barstool and rounds the breakfast bar to retrieve my crutches from where they're resting against the counter. 'Do you need me to help you upstairs or are you good?'

'You're leaving?'

She nods curtly and I can tell she's trying to hold in her disappointment long enough to make it out to her car where she'll probably cry.

'You don't have to try to be strong. I feel like this whole situation with Abby is the worst thing I've ever had to go through and it's not even close to how you must be feeling. You can talk to me.'

'I'm not going to cry. I've been crying *way* too much lately. I need to just be strong for a little while. Can you please just let me do that?'

I shake my head. 'You're such a nerd.' I get onto my crutches and nod toward the stairs. 'Come watch a movie with me. I bought a TV for your bedroom so you have something to watch when you're home.'

I don't tell her what else I bought for her room because I'm sort of regretting buying it now.

'When do I ever have time to watch TV?' she says as she follows me up the stairs.

She must be curious about the TV.

'You used to watch that *Vampire Diaries* shit all the time. Don't pretend like you're some anti-TV hipster.'

I open the door to her bedroom and the sight of it makes my heart pound with anxiety.

She looks confused when she sees it. 'You got me a bigger bed?'

'You're going to think this is totally pathetic, but I

270

got it a couple of weeks ago after you stopped taking my calls when I was still planning to go to L.A. tomorrow.'

'Why would you do that?'

I stare at her for a moment, hoping she'll figure it out so I don't have to say it. It takes her a moment before her mouth drops open.

'You . . . you got it for—'

'Please don't say his name.' I let out a long sigh. 'I didn't want you to stop coming over to visit my mom just because I was gone and you had a new boyfriend. And I sure as hell didn't want you two sleeping in my bed. And now that I think about it, I can't even believe I did this. Now I want to burn this fucking bed.'

She looks puzzled for a moment before she starts laughing.

'There is nothing funny about this.'

She moves toward the bed and I reach for her hand. She looks over her shoulder at me.

'I'm sorry. I don't mean to laugh. This is actually really sweet of you.'

'Can we go to my room?'

She tilts her head as she looks at me. She reaches up and brushes her thumb over my eyebrow.

'Thank you for thinking of me,' she whispers.

I turn my face and kiss the delicate skin on the inside of her wrist. She looks at me and I see her breathing quicken.

'I was serious when I said I would do whatever it took.'

I drop the crutches to the floor and clutch her face as I pull her lips against mine. Her lips are so soft and taste like coffee with a hint of maple syrup. I slide my hand behind her neck as I slip my tongue farther into her mouth. She moans softly as her hands find the bottom of my T-shirt.

'I love you so much, Claire,' I say as I kiss her jaw. 'I will always love you. I want you to be mine.'

I bite her neck softly and she gasps. 'You shouldn't be standing like that,' she says as she pulls me toward the bed.

I walk on my cast across the room until we reach the bed. I don't know if I'm in pain because all I can feel is my need for her. She lies on the bed and pulls me down on top of her.

'I officially claim this bed for you and me,' I whisper in her ear as I settle myself between her legs. I kiss her hard and she grinds her hips into me. 'And now I'm going to claim you.'

'Oh, God, Chris,' she whimpers as she pushes my shoulders back and looks me in the eye. 'Please don't hurt me.'

'What? Why would I hurt you?'

'No, not today. I mean, later. Please don't leave me again.'

I kiss her forehead then look at her for a moment.

'You are so beautiful.' I brush her hair away from her face and kiss her cheekbone. 'The first time we had sex I had that song ready to sing to you, but I was so nervous that I was going to mess up.' I kiss her chin and she sucks in a sharp breath. 'When I finished singing and you kissed me, I thought I was dreaming. I didn't think there was any possible way that you could still love me after I fucked up that song so badly.' She smiles and I lay a soft kiss on the corner of her mouth. 'That's how I feel right now. I can't believe you still love me after I fucked up so hugely. I will never do anything to jeopardize that again. That is my promise to you. If you're mine, you're mine forever.'

She shakes her head as she closes her eyes and I brace myself for the rejection. The silence kills me as she leans her head back. A tear rolls down her temple and I quickly wipe it away.

She opens her eyes and my pulse pounds in my ears as I await her response. 'I missed you so much.'

I kiss her slowly, savoring the sweetness and movement of her lips, letting my mind take me back to all the moments we lay in this room kissing. This feels, if it's even possible, better than all those other times. We've hurt each other and stumbled over our emotions and our words, but we've both grown. We're still here, together, the way we always imagined it would be.

'I thought I had lost you forever,' I whisper as I move down to kiss her throat. I slip my hand under her shirt and her skin is so soft, I can't wait to taste her. 'Can I take this off?'

She nods and sits up a little so I can pull her shirt off. She lies back and, with her blonde hair fanned out against the pillow and her breasts burgeoning from her white bra, she looks like an angel. I take her breast in my hand and slide my finger between her breast and her bra to expose her nipple. I take her nipple into my mouth while keeping my eyes on her face to watch her reaction. She closes her eyes and lets out a small gasp.

I suck gently as I slide my hand under her back to undo the clasp on her bra. When the clasp is unhooked, I slowly slide her bra straps off her shoulders then toss her bra to the floor.

'Tell me you love me,' I say as I trace my finger lightly over the skin between her breasts and all the way down to the button of her shorts.

Chapter Thirty-Three

Claire

Chris hooks his finger under the waistband of my shorts then unbuttons them with one hand as he stares at me, waiting for me to say what he wants to hear. I love Chris. There is no doubt about that. But something feels different.

He slides my zipper down and I place my hand over his to stop him. 'Wait.'

He immediately moves his hand up to my waist. 'What's wrong?'

I suddenly feel exposed, lying here with my breasts uncovered in my old bedroom. I grab the front of his shirt and pull him down on top of me, to cover me up, then I wrap my arms around his neck.

'Claire, what's wrong?'

I squeeze my eyes shut and hold him tight. 'I want you. I do, but I don't know if I can do this.'

He plants a soft kiss on my shoulder then whispers

in my ear, 'We don't have to do anything. We can just lay here.' He kisses my jaw then pulls his head back to look me in the eye.

His gaze wanders over my entire face and I allow myself to do the same. He's definitely the pretty boy in the band, even with all his tattoos and the lip ring. He's just too beautiful to be scary. He bites his bottom lip, the way he does when he's turned on, and now I have to have him.

'I love you,' I whisper as I cradle his face in my hands.

It hurts so bad to admit this because I still love Adam, but I can't deny myself the happiness I know I'll have with Chris for something that may never happen with Adam. He gave up on me when I needed him. I know Adam thought he was doing it for the right reasons, but I'm not sure I believe those reasons.

Chris kisses my temple then lays a soft trail of kisses along the side of my face until his lips are next to my ear. 'You make me so happy,' he whispers before he nips my earlobe. 'Let me make you happy.' His fingers skim over my ribs and I shudder. 'I want you so bad. Do you want me?'

I nod vigorously. 'Yes.'

His hand slides down my waist until he reaches the waistband of my shorts again. 'I'm going to go slow,' he says as he kisses my neck and gently tugs my shorts down. 'Can I take these off?'

I nod again and he smiles as I lift my hips for him to remove my shorts. He leaves my panties on and takes his shirt off, which only gets me hotter with anticipation. I can't take my eyes off the tattoo on his chest. He takes my hand and kisses my palm before he lays my hand over his heart.

'Hold on tight, babe.'

He positions himself between my legs and slides his hand behind my knee to pull my leg up. He kisses the inside of my knee and I'm breathing so hard I think I might pass out. His fingers brush the inside of my thigh as they travel up and find my panties. He leans down to kiss me as his fingers stroke me through the soft cotton so gently I feel as if I might burst with frustration.

I grab his hand and pull it out from between my legs. 'What are you doing? I'm ready.'

He smiles and shakes his head. 'I'm going to take my time and you're going to like it.' He kisses me again, but this time he slides his hand inside my panties and eases two fingers into me. 'You're so wet.'

'You're killing me.'

He chuckles into my mouth and I can't help but laugh, until his fingers find my clit. 'Can I take your panties off?'

'You don't have to keep asking. Just do it.'

He slips my panties off and tosses them over his shoulder. 'You might want to grab that pillow so you have something to bite down on because I'm about to make you come so hard.'

'*Chris?*'

'What?'

He's never spoken to me like this before and it's both shocking and extremely sexy. Unfortunately, I can't help but wonder how many other girls have heard this exact line from him. But it's too late now. I have to do this or it will drive me crazy.

'Don't stop.'

He smiles as he leans down to kiss me and I wrap my legs around him. His jeans rub against me as he rocks his hips back and forth on top of me. I moan as his kiss becomes hungrier, his mouth seeking that seed of longing deep inside me. His hand roams over my breast and down my waist until he finds my butt. He pulls me into him, his erection like a rock under his jeans, as he kisses my neck. I lean my head back and draw in a deep breath.

His lips move down my shoulder and over my chest until he reaches the valley between my breasts. He looks up at me as he licks my skin. I hold my breath as he kisses his way down my belly. Finally, his head is between my legs and his mouth is on me, hot and firm, as he takes my clit into his mouth and gently sucks.

'Oh, God,' I cry as my fingers grasp the comforter.

He pulls back and gives me a soft lick before he inserts two fingers inside me. His fingers beckon me, coaxing me further down the path of ecstasy. Then his tongue is on me again. His tongue swirls as his fingers massage me from the inside. He alternates between

278

slow and fast, light and firm, as he lovingly pushes me over the edge.

I snatch the pillow out from underneath my head and cover my face because I know I'm about to scream as if I'm being murdered. Suddenly, he stops and pulls his fingers out of me.

I lift the pillow from my face as he kisses my belly. 'What? What's wrong?'

He reaches into his back pocket and pulls out a condom. 'I changed my mind. I want you to come with me inside you.'

He carefully shrugs out of his jeans and boxers and I watch in amazement as he slides the condom on. His body is amazing. Even after four weeks in a cast, the ripple of his muscles, the way they flex as he moves, is mesmerizing.

He eases himself into position between my legs and takes my left hand in his right hand. He laces his fingers through mine, as if we're about to start dancing, and looks into my eyes.

'I've been writing a song for you, but it's not finished yet.'

I smile the kind of smile that penetrates down to my heart and through my bones. He smiles as he kisses the back of my hand.

'But I want to sing to you. Do you mind?'

'Of course not.'

I can tell right away when he starts to sing that it's not one of his songs. He sings low at first, almost a whisper, then a little louder until I can hear some of the lyrics and I recognize the song: 'Bloom' by The Paper Kites. His eyes and voice are full of such tenderness. I can feel each word, each syllable, wrapped in love as he delivers them to me, fills me with them.

When he's finished, he kisses my forehead. 'I love you.'

He keeps a firm grip on my hand and I hold my breath as he guides himself into me.

'Is that okay?' he asks as he watches my reaction.

'Yes, yes, yes,' I whisper as he grinds into me. 'It's very okay.'

He presses his lips to the inside of my wrist before he drapes my hand over the back of his neck and kisses me slowly. His mouth moves in time with his hips. His breath is hot in my mouth as he speeds up, the friction between us lighting me up.

'Oh, babe,' he breathes. 'I missed being inside you.'

He slows down again, stretching me gently as he plunges deeper. I'm already sensitive from the attention he paid to me a few minutes ago. I'm getting so close to a bone-shaking climax, but I can tell he's only just begun.

I pry his lips away from mine and look him in the eye. 'I'm gonna come.'

He stops moving and smiles. 'Let me help you out with that.'

He pulls out of me and slides his hand between my legs. He barely touches me and I dig my nails into his shoulders as I explode. But he doesn't give me any time to recover as he plunges right back into me. He kisses me hard as he moves in and out of me, until we both orgasm together.

He lies on top of me, tasting my neck and shoulder, as we both attempt to catch our breath.

'God damn,' he says as he pushes up onto his elbows and looks me in the eye. 'I miss the way I fit inside you. You're my missing piece, babe.'

Chapter Thirty-Four

Adam

The lobby in the lab is a lot darker than I expected. The wallpaper is a dark forest green with pink rosettes and the industrial carpet is a dark blue that matches the color of the chairs. The squat woman at the front desk is on a phone call when I approach, but she raises her dark eyebrows when she sees me as if I should make my intentions known.

'Picking up some test results,' I whisper.

She nods and mouths, *Last name*.

'Parker.'

I don't know if Lindsay and Nathan had the sense to put the test under my last name, and I almost wish they hadn't. If this baby isn't mine, I don't want anything left tying me to Lindsay, not even a paper trail to a negative DNA test.

She pulls a folder out of a rack on her desk. 'Adam?' she whispers.

I nod and she opens the folder. There's an envelope clipped to the inside of the folder.

'I.D.?' she whispers.

I show her my North Carolina driver's license and she looks over the details, probably checking that the name and birthdate match. She hands me the envelope and I'm surprised to see that it's still sealed. I guess they take this privacy thing seriously.

'Thanks,' I whisper as I tap the desk and set off to open the envelope inside my rental car.

The car has that new-car smell that I can't stand, like plastic and carpet. I miss my truck, which always smells a little like ocean and coconut sunblock – and Claire when she used to ride with me.

I slide my finger under the flap of the envelope and quickly pull out the paper folded neatly within. I don't waste any time unfolding it and searching for the words I want to see. The words materialize in front of me as if they were spelled out in the heavens with stars. I am not the father of Lindsay's baby.

I kiss the paper and I'm tempted to run back inside the lab and hug the receptionist for giving me the best birthday present ever.

I have never cried from sheer joy, but I'm *almost* happy enough to cry right now. I can't even imagine what Claire must have gone through being pregnant all alone. I don't think I ever realized just how fucking strong she is until now.

My first instinct is to call her and tell her I'm coming

home, but I don't know if she'll even answer her phone. For all I know she's changed my name in her phone to 'Not Worth It' or 'Asshole' the way Lindsay's friend Michelle did when she broke up with her boyfriend. Just the possibility of Claire ignoring my calls or giving me a shitty nickname makes me anxious. I can't call her. Besides, I want my arrival to be a surprise.

I take a picture of the lab results and text them to Lindsay and Nathan then I delete the text messages and their numbers from my phone. Next, I call the airline and book a flight to Kauai so I can get my stuff and hop on a plane back to the mainland tonight. Then I'll arrange for Tina and Cora to help me plan the surprise for tomorrow, Friday, when Claire has the day off.

Just thinking of finally seeing Claire again after four weeks apart makes me ache inside. I hope I haven't fucked things up too badly.

I pull out of the parking lot and head straight for the airport. My suitcase is already packed and tucked away in the trunk. As I head down the highway with the green mountains on my right and the Pacific Ocean on my left, all I can think of is the gift I left for Claire in my apartment.

I actually left it in my apartment the night before I left to Kauai, but I had to ask Tina to go into my apartment to attach a note to the gift a couple of weeks later. I hoped that I could get Claire to go to my apartment and search for the gift while I was gone. I thought that if there were anything that would make her wait for me, the gift and the note would be it. I never expected to be coming home to so much uncertainty. I guess I'll have to save that surprise for another time.

Chapter Thirty-Five

Claire

I lay my finished quiz on top of the stack on Mr Collins' desk and scurry out of the lecture hall. I am so glad it's Friday. All week long, I've had butterflies in my stomach anticipating tonight. I can't believe that after so many years together, Chris and I feel new again. I guess absence really does make the heart grow fonder.

I head back to the dorm to get some clothes and the rest of my textbooks so I can spend the night at home, but when I enter the dorm Senia is sitting on her bed looking totally bummed out. I drop my backpack onto the floor and take a seat next to her.

'What's wrong?'

She looks up at me with an expression that says she's about to tell me something I don't want to hear. 'Tina just called.'

My heart stops as I think of the worst news that Tina, Cora's caregiver, could deliver.

Senia notices the horror in my face and shakes her head adamantly. 'No, Cora's fine, but Tina asked if I could go check on Cora this weekend because she's going to be out of town and . . .'

She doesn't have to finish this sentence. If Adam weren't in Hawaii, he would be the one checking up on Cora. The way he cared for Cora was one of the things that made me fall in love with him.

'I know you're going home this weekend so I offered to go,' Senia continues as she stares at her hands in her lap. 'I guess I'll miss the party.'

Senia's family is having yet another party, but this one is for her parents' twenty-fifth wedding anniversary so it will be huge. I would have gone with her, but I had already made plans with Chris when she asked me to go a few days ago. There's no way she can miss this party.

'I'll go.'

She looks up at me with so much hope, I try not to let her see the utter disappointment I'm feeling.

'Really? I know you had this weekend all planned out. I don't want to mess that up for you.'

I roll my eyes. 'Please. I can see Chris and Jackie any time. If Cora needs me, I need to be there.'

'Thank you.' She hugs me hard and I give her a few pats on the back. 'I'll help you pack.'

She helps me empty out my backpack and toss in some clothes and toiletries. When we're done she looks me up and down, raising one of her perfect eyebrows as she takes in the jean jacket I'm wearing over a dress and some leggings.

'What?'

'Lose the leggings. You're going to the beach.'

'I'm not going to the beach. I'm going to Cora's.'

'Even more reason to lose them. Do you really want Bigfoot rubbing himself all over those leggings?'

I immediately pull off the leggings and put my ankle boots back on, silently thanking myself for shaving my legs this morning.

'Beautiful,' Senia says, pulling me in for one last hug. 'You can pass this hug on to Cora for me.'

She slaps my ass then pushes me toward the door where she hands me my backpack.

'Trying to get rid of me, huh?'

'Cora needs you.'

I'm not looking forward to sleeping on Cora's thirty-year-old sofa tonight, but I've missed the hell out of her. It will be fun to have a nice drama-free weekend with Cora and Bigfoot. Of course, Jackie will be disappointed. Now that Chris and I are back together, she's been dying for me to spend the weekend there. I hate disappointing Jackie.

The two-hour drive to Wrightsville Beach gives me time to call Chris and break the bad news.

'Finally,' he says when he answers my call.

'Finally, what?'

'Finally, I can stop checking my phone. Where are you?'

'Oh, shut up. You were *not* checking your phone.'

He laughs and I'm reminded of the first few months Chris and I were together when we were sixteen. He bought me a cell phone and I threatened to drop it in the toilet because I was becoming obsessed with checking for missed calls and texts from him. He made fun of me, but after that he never made me wait longer than five minutes for a response to a text or voicemail. When I told Senia about this she nearly threw up.

'Okay, I wasn't checking my phone, but I was dying to hear your voice. I can't wait to kiss you and sing to you. I finished your song today.'

And the butterflies are back. I really don't want to have to give him the bad news, but Chris will still be there next weekend. In fact, I'm pretty sure I can count on Chris to be there for me forever.

'Chris, I can't make it out there today.'

He's silent for a moment before he responds. 'Why? What are you doing?'

There's a note of suspicion in his voice that makes me wonder if he'll even believe me when I tell him where I'm going.

'I have to check on Cora.'

'Who's Cora?'

'I told you about Cora. She's my old landlady and my friend. Her caregiver is going to be out of town and she doesn't have anyone else to keep an eye on her.'

He pauses again. 'So you're going back to your old apartment?'

289

'Chris, I'm going to Cora's apartment. I'm only going because *he's* not there. If he were there, he would be the one checking on her.'

It really bugs me that I don't feel I can speak Adam's name around Chris, but I understand feeling like you despise someone so much you don't even want to hear their name. I feel that way about Joanie Tipton and, though I don't know his name, I feel that way about my father. I hope I never know his name.

'I trust you, babe. I guess I'll just have to go see you during the week. I'll help you *study*.'

Study is Chris's code word for oral sex. He used it all the time when we were together. The thought of his mouth on me is enough to make me squirm in my seat.

'I'll call you when I get there.'

'No, call me when you go to bed so I can sing you to sleep. I love you.'

'Love you, too.'

I pull the phone away from my ear to plug it into the stereo and I already have a text message from Chris.

Chris: The song is called 'Pieces of You'. I wrote it for you and Abby.

The closer I get to Wrightsville Beach, the tighter the knots in my stomach become. By the time I pull into the parking lot at my old apartment complex, I feel as if I might vomit. I turn off my car and pull my feet up onto the seat so I can hug my knees. My entire body is shaking with nervous energy as memories of Adam come back to me: all the conversations we had while sitting in his truck in this parking space; all the eye-roll-inducing jokes he told me while hanging out in his apartment; all the times he touched me or kissed me and made me feel like the most beautiful person in the world. Adam and I were only together for eight weeks and we've been broken up for four weeks, but I can't deny how much I miss him and how happy he made me.

I meditate for twenty minutes before I get out of the car. The breeze rolling in from the ocean smells like my old life, but it brings with it a slight chill. I button up my jacket and heave my backpack over my shoulder before I set off for Cora's.

It's almost 7 p.m. If Tina already checked in on Cora today, she'll be gone by now, which means that I may have to wait upwards of ten minutes for Cora to answer her door. I knock on the door three times and stuff my hands into my pockets to keep them warm. My hand hits my phone and I think of Chris's text message. I pull my phone out of my pocket while I wait – to gaze at the name of the song he wrote for me. When Cora's door opens, I drop my phone on the concrete. It's Adam.

291

Chapter Thirty-Six

Claire

I can't breathe. My skin breaks out in a cold sweat as my fingers go numb.

'Oh, shit!' he says, and this is the last thing I hear before I pass out.

I open my eyes and I can hardly see anything through the darkness, but I can feel the scratchy fabric of Cora's sofa under my cheek. I blink a few times and her living room slowly comes into focus.

'How are you feeling?'

His voice is both startling and comforting. I turn my head toward the sound and he's kneeling on the carpet not far from my feet. I'm torn between throwing my arms around his neck and kicking him for breaking my heart.

Cora clears her throat and I turn my head in the other direction. 'You almost took a nasty spill there, honey. Good thing Adam was here to catch you.'

I sit up slowly and he shifts a little so I don't hit him with my legs. Just that small movement and I can smell him. He took a shower recently. I recognize the scent of his shampoo and it actually makes me want to cry. I want to pull my knees up to my face again, but I'm wearing a dress and Adam is kneeling almost directly in front of me. I stand quickly and he stands up right after me.

'Claire, we need to talk.'

'Did you trick me into coming here?'

His skin is more tanned than when he left and I'm suddenly angry as I picture him surfing and frolicking on the beach while I suffered through four weeks of self-doubt.

'I just want to talk to you.' He takes a step toward me and I take a step back, almost falling back onto the sofa, but I manage to regain my balance. 'Are you feeling okay?'

'I'm fine.' I turn to Cora, who's sitting in her recliner with Bigfoot in her lap as usual. 'I came here for you, Cora.'

I stride toward her and give her a big hug. She pats my arm weakly and I try not to cry as I look into her eyes and see the fatigue.

'Senia wanted me to give you a big hug from her,' I say as I kneel next to the recliner and scratch Bigfoot's head. He purrs softly and this makes Cora smile.

'You tell Senia I saw a beautiful dress that would

293

look perfect on her. This girl looked just like Senia and she wore the most beautiful dress to her wedding. Of course, they ended up throwing her in a koi pond at the reception and ruining it, but it was so perfect for her.'

Cora's more than a little obsessed with the TV show *Bridezillas*. She thinks it's the most hilarious thing, women having nervous breakdowns over the color of a dress or the flavor of a cake. She loves to tell the story of how she and her husband, Frank, got married more than sixty years ago in a tiny chapel in Minnesota. She wore a dress that she made herself and he wore the suit his father got married in almost thirty years earlier.

'We had holes in our clothes and our shoes, but our hearts were finally whole,' Cora likes to say whenever she tells the story.

I glance at Adam for just a second and his eyes are locked on mine. My brain knows that he did what he thought I needed, but my heart feels utterly betrayed by him.

I continue stroking Bigfoot's head as I avoid looking in Adam's direction. 'Well, I'm here now, so you can go.'

'I'm not leaving until you talk to me.'

'Adam, that's no way to speak to a lady,' Cora chides him.

'I'm sorry. You're right, Cora.' He looks me in the

eye again, but his expression softens. 'Please come up-stairs so we can talk.'

'That's much better,' Cora says with a smile. 'You two go on ahead. My show's coming on soon.'

My hand shakes as I grab the remote off of Cora's wooden TV tray table and point it at the television to make sure it's on the right channel. I set the remote down and I can't believe how anxious I feel. This is Adam. This is the guy who picked me up off the floor when I was broken and carried me until I was ready to walk again.

I make my way to the door and Adam kisses the top of Cora's head before he follows me.

'Goodnight, Cora. I'll be by in the morning. Make sure you have my birthday steak and eggs ready.'

'Don't you worry. Bigfoot knows just how you like your steak. Goodnight, sonny.'

I can't help but smile before the sadness of how much I've missed Cora and Adam comes rushing back to me. I wait near the front door to my old apartment as he locks Cora's door. He turns around and my heart pounds at the sight of his beauty. The sun is almost down, but the faint warm glow of the sunset makes his golden skin glow.

He gives me a soft smile and I close my eyes so I can't see his face while I think of how he broke my heart and how it would destroy him to know what I did with Chris five days ago.

'Claire, please look at me.'

I take a deep breath as I open my eyes and he's closer, just a couple of feet away, and staring down at me with that intense look in his eyes. I want to wish him a belated happy birthday, but I can't bring myself to do it.

'You hurt me.'

'I'm sorry. I know I fucked up, but I came back for you. I quit my job.'

'You quit your job?'

'I quit. I took the job in Raleigh and I'm moving in two weeks.'

His green eyes search mine for a sign of forgiveness, but I don't know what to say. I can't tell him I wish he had come back a week ago.

'Am I too late?' he asks as the muscle in his jaw twitches.

I want to tell him the truth, but I can't bear to place the image of Chris and me together in his head.

'I don't know.'

He looks confused. 'What do you mean, you don't know?'

I shake my head. 'I just . . . I was so hurt and I thought you had given up on me. I mean, I'm a mess. I've got more baggage than any person should be allowed to carry.'

'And I'm strong enough to carry it. I just got a little scared, but it wasn't because of your baggage. I'm fucked up, too. It had nothing to do with that. It

296

had everything to do with what I heard in your voice that night you called me at one in the morning. You needed me there and I felt so fucking helpless because I couldn't give you what you needed. I didn't want to keep disappointing you like that.'

'How could you ever think that? You never disappointed me until you left me.'

He steps forward and takes my face in his hands. His hands are warm and I close my eyes to breathe in his scent. His lips are soft as he presses them against my forehead. The lump in my throat makes it impossible to speak as the first tears begin to fall. He kisses each of my eyelids and I grab his forearms to steady myself. His arms are so smooth and solid, exactly the way I remember them. I open my eyes as he plants a soft kiss on the corner of my mouth.

'I'm so fucking sorry. I promise I will never hurt you again.' He kisses the tip of my nose then the other corner of my mouth. 'I promise I'll make it up to you. I love you,' he whispers against my lips, but he doesn't kiss me.

His breath against my lips gives me chills and I have to taste his mouth. I lean forward slowly and give him a soft kiss. He slowly slides his hand behind my neck and I kiss him again as I grow more eager. This time he kisses me back, but he doesn't open his mouth and it's driving me crazy. I take his top lip into my mouth and he pulls away before I can taste him.

'I love you, Claire. I want to be with you forever.'

Like a switch going off in my brain, I think of Chris and I want to crawl into a hole. I close my eyes so I don't have to see Adam's face. What the hell is wrong with me? I'm a disgusting person.

I have two choices: I can be honest with Adam about what happened with Chris and hope that he can still stomach me or I can leave now and go home to Chris.

Chapter Thirty-Seven

Adam

I see her mind working like crazy and I know she's going to talk herself out of this if I don't act quickly. Claire is notorious for overthinking every situation. She worked herself into a frenzy trying to figure out why I never visited her during the week when we were first dating. And, of course, she spent nearly a year in hiding from everyone she knew because she was afraid of being judged for keeping Abigail a secret. I need to do something before she convinces herself to walk away, but I also don't want to rush this.

I look into her eyes and her eyebrows furrow. She's worried about something.

Ah, fuck it.

I pull her face to mine and crush my lips against hers. Her lips taste exactly as I remember. I slide my tongue into her mouth and she moans, but then she pulls away.

'Wait.'

'I'm tired of waiting,' I say as I scoop her up in my arms.

She lets out a high-pitched yelp then laughs. 'Hey!'

'Hay is for horses,' I say as I carry her up the stairs toward my apartment. 'And I have a great horse joke.'

'Oh, no.'

I dig my finger into her side, where she's ticklish, and she squirms in my arms. I nearly drop her, but I'm full of too much adrenaline from the anticipation.

'Open the door. It's not locked.'

'No.'

'Claire.'

I give her the most serious look I can muster, but she just laughs.

'You don't scare me.'

She musses up my hair and I turn my face to kiss the inside of her forearm. Her smile fades and she waits a moment before she reaches for the doorknob and pushes the door open.

I step over the threshold and kick the door closed behind me. 'What did one horse say to the other horse when he fell down?'

'What?'

'Help. I've fallen and I can't giddy-up.'

'That is terrible.'

'I thought you'd like that.' I sit her down on a barstool so our eyes are level. 'I just want to make you happy.'

Her smile disappears again and she looks down

at my chest. 'You did make me happy. You made me happier than I thought I could ever be. Then you left.'

I brush her hair off her forehead and she looks up. 'Claire, we both left. You left to school and I left to Hawaii. I'm surprised we both made it back here at all.' I plant a soft kiss on her lips. 'If we break up forever, we'll both probably move on. That's just reality. But I'll never be the same. You changed me and I know I've changed you. You're not the same scared girl hiding in a meditation cave all day long. You're mine, and a piece of you will always belong to me the same way a piece of me will always belong to you.'

I kiss her cheek to catch the tears as they fall. She clutches the front of my shirt, her chest heaving as she tries to decide what to do.

'Come and lay with me,' I say, and she looks at me suspiciously. I shake my head. 'Not to have sex. That was a long drive. You need to rest. Then you can leave if that's what you decide.'

I wrap my arms around her waist and she wraps her legs around my hips as I lift her off the barstool. She rests her head on my shoulder as I carry her to the bed and set her down gently.

I kiss her forehead and step back. 'I'm gonna get you a bottle of water. Do you need anything else?'

She shakes her head as she lies down and curls her legs up. She's so beautiful; it's difficult to tear my eyes away from her. I grab a bottle of water out of the refrigerator and glance at the cupboard above the refrigerator where I hid Claire's surprise gift. I wish she had come looking for it when I told her about it.

I make it back to the bedroom and hand her the bottle of water as I lie next to her. She props herself up on her elbow to drink half the bottle then she screws the cap back on and places it on the nightstand. She turns back to me and I beckon her to lay her head on my shoulder. She does and I kiss the top of her head as I wrap my arm around her.

'Do you remember the first time I walked you to work?'

She lays her hand on my chest and I resist the urge to bring it to my mouth to kiss it.

'Of course.'

'You never asked me how I got Jo to switch shifts with you so we could go on a date.'

'I figured you fed her a dirty lie and I didn't want to know anything about it.'

'That doesn't make sense. You should have asked me so we both had our stories straight.'

She traces her finger in light circles over my heart and I can't resist anymore. I grab her hand and lay a quick kiss on her knuckles before I place her hand back on my chest. She giggles softly and I continue.

'Anyway, I told Jo that I was pretty sure I had just met the love of my life and that I had to take you on a nice, long date to make sure my instincts were correct.'

'You did not tell her that.'

'I did. And she knew I was serious.'

302

We're both quiet for a minute before she speaks. 'I really miss being here. I miss seeing you and Cora and I miss how easy everything was before I went back to school. I miss waking up next to you or in the apartment below you. I miss being close to you.'

'I can get an apartment in Chapel Hill and commute to Raleigh. It's only a forty-minute drive.'

'Why would you do that?'

'To be closer to you.'

She pulls her head away from my shoulder to look up at me. 'You would do that?'

'Of course. I'm very serious when I say I want to be with you forever. I've already tried living without you and it nearly destroyed me.'

She climbs on top of me and lays her head in the center of my chest as she wraps her arms around my waist.

'What's wrong?'

She shakes her head. 'Nothing. I just can't believe I'm here with you. I can't believe you're real.'

I want to ask her if she'd like to take off her jacket and boots to get more comfortable, but I don't want her to think I'm just trying to get her into bed so I can have my way with her. I really want to have my way with her, but I can wait until the time is right.

I run my fingers through her hair and I can feel her body relax on top of me. After a few minutes, her breathing has slowed so much I'm certain she's fallen asleep.

'Claire?' I whisper as low as I can.

'What?'

'I thought you fell asleep. Were you meditating?'

'No, just thinking.'

'Have you eaten?'

'Not since this morning. But I don't want any mac and cheese.'

'Look who's a comedian now,' I say as I try not to think of the surprise I hid for her in the cupboard. 'You want to go out to eat or do you want me to order a pizza?'

'Order a pizza and we can eat in bed.'

The pizza arrives forty minutes later; forty minutes we spend catching up on what's happened in our lives over the past four weeks. I tell her about the conversation I had with my dad when I quit. Then I tell her about the competition, but I leave out the fact that I qualified for the competition in Australia. She tells me about a meeting she had with her professor. Then she gets really quiet when she tells me what happened when she and Chris were invited to go see Abigail in the hospital.

We finish our pizza in silence, both of us scarfing down three slices.

'I've never seen you eat like that,' I remark.

She tosses her crust into the pizza box on the bed, but when she looks up at me she's serious again.

I have an awful feeling there's something she's not telling me, and my gut tells me it probably has to do with Chris. But I don't want to jump to conclusions or accuse her of anything she hasn't done.

'What's bothering you? I can tell something's bothering you.'

She looks up at me with the guiltiest look in her eyes. I don't have to hear a word to know what she's going to say.

Chapter Thirty-Eight

Claire

I can tell by the way Adam's nostrils are flaring that he already knows what I'm going to confess.

'Oh, God,' I whisper as I attempt to gather the courage to say the words he both deserves and doesn't deserve to hear.

He shakes his head slightly. 'No fucking way.'

'I'm so sorry.'

'No, don't say that.' I reach for him and he instantly backs away then rises from the bed. 'Please don't fucking say that.'

'I am. I'm so fucking sorry. I was just so hurt. I thought it was over.'

He clutches chunks of his hair as he takes deep breaths in a vain attempt to calm himself. He's about to explode and I know my heart is going to absorb the full impact of the blast.

'Please just sit down so we can talk.'

He keeps shaking his head. 'I can't fucking believe this. This is what happened in my worst fucking nightmare, but I never expected it to come true.'

I scramble off the bed and he steps away from me. 'Adam, please just listen to me. You were gone. I . . . I thought I wasn't good enough for you. I thought I didn't fit into your life and you were just tired of dealing with me.'

I grab the front of his shirt and he closes his eyes so he doesn't have to look at me.

'Please look at me.'

He shakes his head and I can see the anguish in his face, even with his eyes closed. 'I can't.'

I take his face in my hands and he finally opens his eyes, but he looks at the ceiling. 'Adam. I am begging you to look at me.'

He takes a deep breath through his nose before he finally looks me in the eye. 'I asked you to wait for me.'

'That's not what you said. You said you didn't expect me to wait for you.'

He shakes his head again with sheer disappointment. 'It was four weeks. Four fucking weeks.'

My hands drop to my sides as the tears fall down my face. This is it. I can feel it. I squat down on the floor as I try to catch my breath.

'I'm sorry,' I whisper.

I have to get out of here. I know he doesn't want me here anymore, but I feel like I might pass out again if I stand up.

'I thought I'd understand if this happened,' he says, and his voice is so thick with emotion it makes my entire body ache. 'Maybe I just need to be alone for a while.'

'No,' I whisper as I place my hand on the edge of the mattress to try to pull myself up.

I'm overcome with a hot dizziness and I lean on the bed to steady myself as I try to draw in deep breaths.

'What's wrong?' he asks as he reaches for my arm to help me.

'I'm fine,' I say, pushing his hand away. 'I'll let you be alone.'

I push myself off the bed and take another deep breath. He doesn't look at me as I move around him to leave the bedroom.

Right when I reach the bedroom door, he speaks. 'You didn't come here while I was gone.'

I stop in the doorway as I try to figure out what he means by this. 'What are you talking about?'

I turn around and I want to die when I see the look on his face. He finally looks more hurt than angry.

'I told you I left something for you in my apartment, but you never came.'

'I was hurt.' I can barely speak the words as the knot in my throat swells.

He nods and I take this as my signal to leave, but I don't want to go. We stand in silence for a moment before he comes to me. He stops right in front of me and I draw in a long, stuttered breath. He reaches up and I close my eyes as he wipes the tears from my cheeks with the back of his fingers.

'I'm sorry that I hurt you.' I open my eyes and his eyes roam over every feature of my face. 'You can stay here. I'm going for a drive.'

'Please don't go.'

'I have to.'

He squeezes past me and I resist the urge to grab onto him in desperation. I don't watch as he leaves, but I can hear the front door as it closes.

Chapter Thirty-Nine

Chris

Tristan kicks my foot to get my attention and I look up from my guitar. 'What?'

Tristan is the classic brooding musician, which is why girls can't resist him. He's the one who always sits in the corner at parties with a beer in his hand and a scowl on his face. He's only ever shared one song he wrote with me. He's secretive as hell; even more than Claire. But this is one of Tristan's best qualities. He's extremely loyal. He'll never blab my secrets to anyone, which is why I still can't figure out why I haven't told him about what's going on between Claire and me. It probably has to do with the fact that I've always felt like Tristan had a thing for Claire before we broke up.

'What the fuck is wrong with you? Are you strung out on Claire again?'

I shake my head as I try to also shake the feeling

that Claire is being pulled further away from me by the second. It doesn't feel like there's just physical distance between us right now.

I thought I knew Claire until two months ago when I realized she was in love with a guy she barely knew. It took me nearly a year to break down her walls. Before we broke up, I wouldn't think anything of it if she told me she was going to spend the night next door to her ex-boyfriend's apartment. But Claire is not the same person she was before we broke up.

'Don't talk about Claire like she's any other fucking girl.'

Tristan raises an eyebrow at me. He's not used to Claire and me being back together so I'll let this slide, though I'm feeling unreasonably angry right now.

He sighs before he leans back on the sofa. 'I don't know what the deal is, but the answer is always *call her*. Girls love that shit. Whenever something is fucked up or uncertain, all it takes is a fucking phone call to fix it.'

I don't want to hear him compare Claire to the chicks he fucks so I grab one of my crutches and head for the garage with my guitar. He doesn't ask where I'm going because he probably assumes I'm taking his advice, and he's right.

I flip the light switch inside the garage and feel a pang of longing when I see the empty space where my bike used to be parked. It seems like everything in my life has gone to shit the past couple of months.

Only the past week have things finally begun to turn around – and now this.

I sit on the concrete steps that lead down from the house into the garage, lay my guitar in my lap, and call Claire. She said she would call me when she went to bed. It's not even eight yet, but I don't want to wait anymore.

'Hello.'

Her voice is thick and raspy, like she's been crying.

'Claire, babe, where are you?'

She lets out a soft whimper and I know I'm too late.

'Chris.'

'Babe, just come home and we can talk about it.'

'I can't.'

'Yes, you can. I promise whatever happened we can work it out.' Her sobs come suddenly and like fucking shotgun blasts to my heart. 'Claire, we've been through worse. I don't want to fucking lose you again. Just come home.'

I had planned to tell her about the fact that Abby's parents have decided they don't want to proceed with the open adoption when I saw her this weekend. I couldn't bear to break this news to her over the phone. I was actually a little relieved when she said she wasn't coming over because I was dreading breaking her heart. I should be angry enough to try to hurt her with this news right now, but I can't. Claire and I have been through enough heartache this past year to ever deliberately hurt each other.

'I know you're feeling confused right now, but that's okay,' I begin. I take a deep breath before I continue with the one thing I hope can bring her back. 'I want you to know that no matter what, I will always love you and this will always be your home. No matter what happens between us, please don't forget my mom.'

She's sobbing harder now and I let out a deep sigh as I prepare myself for what will probably be the most painful three minutes of my life.

'This is the song I wrote for you and Abby.' I place the call on speakerphone, lay the phone on the concrete step next to me, and try to ignore the soft sounds of sobs in the background as I play the first notes.

Chapter Forty

Claire

My chest and head ache from the uncontrollable sobbing. I should go to Cora's to get my stuff so I can drive back to the dorm, but I want to wait for Adam. I also can't bear the thought of being alone in the dorm right now. I feel as if it's not just my heart that is breaking in half. My life is being split down the middle and everything that happened yesterday was the before. Tomorrow will be the after. Today, I'm stuck in the hell of knowing there is no turning back.

I sit on a barstool and try to calm myself. The instant I hear the sound of the guitar, I can breathe again.

'*This ain't our last goodbye,*
it's our last hello.
I can feel it in my shattered heart;
all through my weary bones.
You're the missing piece, the final scrap.
Someday we'll fit together;

someday I'll bring you back.'

The melody is light and hopeful, but there's a blue quality in his voice that makes my stomach twist.

'These pieces of you are promises,
whispering endless possibilities.
My pieces of you are haunted,
just echoes of shattered memories.'

He sings the chorus one more time before he starts the second verse. I know from the first line that this verse is about Abigail.

'I held your hand in mine,
Now the moment's gone
Felt the love in your tiny heart,
Never brought you home
You're my missing piece, a lovely dream,
Someday, I'll find you baby,
Someday, on me you'll lean.'

He concludes with a soft, diminishing melody that gives me chills and, amazingly, the tears have stopped.

'Chris?'

'Claire.'

'I need a little time to think. I'll call you before I go to sleep. I promise.'

'I love you more than this,' he says and I know he means that he loves me enough to forgive me.

'I don't deserve you, but I love you.'

'Don't say that. We've both hurt each other, babe, but we always get through it.'

I don't want to tell him that I don't think this is the

kind of hurt we will survive. We say our goodbyes and I'm reminded of the first line of the song he just sang: *This ain't our last goodbye, it's our last hello*.

I don't want to be without Chris. It's so selfish of me to put him through this when all he's done is forgive me and take care of me. He handed over his heart even though I've proven to be completely unworthy of it.

I have to call Senia, but she's probably in full party-mode right now. I don't want to ruin her night. There's only one other person I can call.

Jackie picks up on the first ring. 'Talk to me, hun.'

I launch into a long explanation of everything she's missed out on since Chris and I broke up last year. I want her to know everything, from the day we broke up to the conversation Chris and I just had. I want her to know the whole truth and the real me.

My biological mother wasn't strong enough to live for me. I can only hope Jackie's love for me is strong enough for her to forgive me.

When I'm done, there's a silence that I find both worrying and comforting. At least she's not screaming curses at me, but maybe that's because she's so appalled she can't form a sentence.

'Jackie?'

'Oh, honey. I wish I could tell you what to do. It kills me to know that you and Chris are hurting, but this is the kind of test that you two either face together or you move on. I don't have to tell you how much I love you both and how much I want you around. Claire,

316

you're my girl. I will always want whatever keeps you close to me. But more than that, I just want both of you to be happy. What would make you happy?'

This is a generous response from someone who has already been so generous with me. I've made one mistake after another trying to make Chris happy. I thought Chris would be happy not to have to worry about a baby just as his career was taking off. I never thought I could be making the biggest mistake of my life.

'I want to know what would make you happy,' I say. 'I think that what would make you happy is what would make me happy.'

She's sniffs loudly and I know she's crying now. When was the last time someone other than Chris cared about Jackie's happiness?

'Claire, it would make me very happy for you to do well in school and not worry so much about this stuff for a while, but you need to do what your heart tells you to do. Don't listen to an old spinster like me.'

'Jackie, you're not an old spinster.' I swallow the lump in my throat as I prepare to say the words I've wanted to say for fourteen years. 'You're my mom.'

She lets out a soft *oh* and I give her a minute to collect herself before I say goodbye. I look at the time on my phone before I tuck it into my back pocket and spin around on the barstool. Adam has been gone for over an hour. I'm worried, but also glad that he told me to stay instead of kicking me out. This is a sign that he might be willing to talk this out when he returns. I just wish I knew if that's what I want.

I slide off the barstool and walk slowly toward the drafting table in the corner of the living room. I slip a set of plans from the bottom of the three-inch stack on the table and lay them on top of the stack.

From my many conversations with Adam, I learned that Myles had two sisters, one older and one younger. His mother was a single parent after Myles' father left them for a woman twelve years his junior. His father was good at hiding his assets and hardly sent them any child support. His mother moved them into a tiny apartment near Carolina Beach so Myles could continue to surf. He won $800 in that first competition and Myles was so excited when he called his mom to tell her about it. Then hours later all their hope was lost.

If anyone understands the guilt I've lived with this past year, it's Adam. He's my lifeline and I'm pretty certain that I'm his. But we both gave up on each other. He broke up with me then I ran into Chris's arms instead of fighting for us. I should have driven the hundred miles to see what kind of surprise Adam left for me in his apartment. But I was afraid I would find something like the locket, something that would be too painful to accept.

I run my fingers over the cool paper of the blueprint and trace the pitched line of the roof. This is the home that Adam wants to build for Myles' family. He has it all planned out, from the concrete foundation to the flowers in the garden. He may never be able to build it now that he quit his job. Adam's father will probably empty out his trust fund just as Adam suspected he would. And he did it for me.

I trace my finger over the front door as I think of the first time Adam knocked on my door, the same night he almost ran me over. He brought me the purse I had left in his truck then asked if he could come inside. As much as Adam loves to plan his life, he's never afraid to take a risk.

I have to find whatever he left for me in his apartment while he was in Hawaii then I'll leave.

I skim through every page of the blueprints on his desk, thinking maybe he left a message for me hidden in the pages, but I find nothing. I move to the coffee table behind me and my heart drops when I see the tiny black dish no bigger than the palm of my hand with the glossy coconut-scented oil. As nice as Adam's apartment is, it always smelled a little briny because he likes to air-dry his wetsuit by hanging it over the shower curtain rod. I got him the scented oil so his apartment would smell nice whenever I visited. I thought he would surely get rid of it as soon as I left to UNC.

I dig through the sofa cushions and come up with nothing but a half-eaten Red Vine. He must have interrupted me mid-chew. I heave a deep sigh as I remember the sheer happiness I felt when we were together in this apartment.

After searching the bedroom and the bathroom, I move on to the kitchen. The only cupboard I haven't looked in is the cupboard above the refrigerator. I grab a chair from the tiny dining table he never uses and stand on top of it to reach the cupboard. As soon as I open the cupboard door, I know I've found it.

The cupboard is empty except for a single box of macaroni and cheese.

I grab the box and sit down in the chair, closing my eyes as I remember our first date.

'I have something I need to tell you,' I say as I climb onto the stool. 'I meditate.'

'Cool. So do I.'

'You do?'

He dumps the dry pasta into the pot before he answers. 'Well, sort of. Whenever I'm stressed or if I can't make it to the beach to surf, I'll chill out and do nothing for an hour or so, to clear my head.'

'You're not supposed to put the pasta in until the water's boiling.'

'Fuck the rules. How often do you meditate?'

I take a deep breath as I prepare to reveal my secret to this almost-stranger. 'A lot. Like, a few times a day.'

'A few times a day? Do the customers at the café stress you out that much?'

This conversation is not going in a safe direction, might as well push it all the way over the edge.

'Meditation is the way I cope . . . with the memories.'

320

He looks up from the steaming pot of water to look at me.
'Go on.'

'I'm not going to spill my guts to you,' I insist.

But I did spill my guts to him and he never judged me. In fact, I think my secrets made him love me more.

I slide my finger under the flap on the top of the macaroni box and discover that it's held in place by a small piece of double-sided tape that gives easily. I lift the second flap and see a folded piece of paper. I pull it out and it's not his handwriting. He must have had someone else write the note for him while he was in Hawaii.

If you're reading this it means you came looking for me. First of all, thank you. I look for you everywhere, and every day I find you in the smell of the ocean, the bright ray of light that sparks on the horizon a moment before sunrise, and the laughter of strangers. Memories I can't seem to grasp onto long enough. I'm coming back for you, but until then I wanted to give you something to show you that you still have my whole heart.

I look inside the box and see another folded piece of paper. When I pull it out, I realize it's a folded envelope and it's holding something much too heavy to be another note.

Chapter Forty-One

Claire

The sound of the door opening startles me and I drop the envelope back into the box. I look over my shoulder and Adam is looking straight at me. I stand from the chair as he walks into the kitchen. He glances at the box in my hand then looks me in the eye.

'Did you open it?'

'I opened the box.'

'And the envelope?'

'Not yet.'

He reaches for the box and I'm too stunned to stop him as he takes it from my hand and places it on the counter. 'You don't have to open it.'

'You don't want me to open it?'

He sees the note he had someone write for him clutched in my hand and he looks conflicted. 'I was so sure you'd come here. Now I'm not sure of anything.'

He stares at the box of macaroni on the counter for

a moment before he picks it up. He pulls the envelope out of the box and looks me in the eye.

'What I do know is that I've never met anyone like you. My mom told me what she said to you the day we visited my uncle's ranch.'

I think back to that day and remember how Adam's mother asked me to keep my heart open when Adam opened his heart to me. What she meant was, *Please don't judge him when he tells you what happened to Myles.* Once Adam confessed his secret to me, I got the feeling that other girls may not have been as understanding as I was. But how could I not be.

'What your mother said to me had nothing to do with the way I reacted to what you told me.'

'I know, but I want you to know that you're the first girl to know all my secrets. And you're the only girl I want to share my secrets with.'

He rips open the envelope and my heart races as I anticipate what is about to drop out of it.

'Thinking of you with Chris kills me. I drove for a long time before I ended up on Shell Island and I sat there on the sand for a while thinking of what I would do if I were you.' His eyes penetrate me and I hold my breath as I wait for his response. 'That was difficult. But then I forced myself to think of what I would do without you. And that was worse.'

He upends the envelope and a ring drops into the palm of his hand. It's a silver band with a princess-cut diamond. My heart is in my throat and I grab the back of the dining chair next to me to steady myself.

'This isn't an engagement ring,' he quickly clarifies as he places the empty envelope and the box of macaroni on the counter.

He holds the ring between his thumb and forefinger and I'm mesmerized by the way it sparkles in the harsh kitchen lighting.

'What is it?' I ask and he finally smiles.

'It's my promise to never leave you again.'

His smile fades a little as he waits for my response.

'I want that ring. I want to put it on and wrap my arms around you and never let go.' He closes his eyes because he knows what's coming. 'I'm sorry, Adam. I just can't trust myself to make a sound decision right now. I love you,' I say as I grab his face so he looks at me. 'I do love you. You believe me, don't you?'

The look in his eyes is pure heartbreak. I stand on my tiptoes and throw my arms around his neck, but he doesn't hug me back.

'Adam, please believe me. I have never met anyone like you, either. What you and I have is so different and so fucking amazing.'

I squeeze him tighter and he finally bends down a little to wrap his arms around my waist. He pulls me flush against him and I sigh as I breathe in the scent on his collar. He buries his face in my neck and takes a deep breath, then his lips are on my skin, warm and inviting. He opens his mouth to softly bite my neck and I moan.

'Adam.'

His lips graze the curve of my jaw until they land on my mouth. I know I should stop this, but I can't. I want the heat of his mouth on mine. I want to feel how much he needs me.

I clutch handfuls of his hair as our mouths move together, tasting each other for the first time in four weeks. He tightens his hold on my waist before he lifts me off the floor and sits me on the counter. The box of macaroni topples over onto the floor, but the clatter of dry pasta doesn't deter us. He spreads my legs and slides me forward on the counter as he kisses me firmly. Then suddenly he stops.

He shakes his head as he steps back. 'I'm gonna go to my room so I don't have to watch you leave,' he says as he takes my hand and places the ring in my palm. 'Just keep this and call me when you make up your mind.' He kisses my forehead, then my temple. 'I love you.'

I close my eyes as he walks away and wait a moment, until I'm sure he's in his room, before I slide off the counter. I look at the ring for a moment and notice the words engraved on the inner surface of the silver band: *Olive you forever.*

I feel numb inside and out as I tuck the ring into the pocket of my jacket. I leave the apartment and close the front door softly. Staring at the doorknob for a moment, I consider going back inside and asking him to put the ring on my finger.

But Jackie is right. I need to focus on school for a while.

I turn away from the door and begin the slow, painful descent down the stairs. I've only managed a few steps when a flash of headlights stops me. Then a black Porsche pulls into the parking lot and stops a few feet from the bottom of the stairs.

Through the driver's side window, I glimpse the back of Tristan's head. Then the passenger door flings open. Chris steps out of the car, grabbing the top of the door to pull himself up. I rush down the last few steps to help him out of the car. He slams the car door shut just as I make it to him.

'Where are your crutches?'

His eyes burn into me. 'You're my crutch.' He grabs my left hand, but his eyes never leave mine. 'You asked me why I told my mom we were engaged.' My heart hammers against my chest as he reaches into his back pocket and pulls out a small, black box. 'She found this a few months after we broke up and she threw a fit because she thought I had already moved on with someone else. I was too ashamed to admit to her that I bought the ring a month after we broke up. So I told her that we were engaged and you never wore the ring because you were afraid people would judge you for being engaged at nineteen.'

He opens the box and I have to blink a few times to believe what I'm seeing.

'Oh, my God,' I whisper as I shake my head.

He takes the ring out of the box and places the box on top of the car. 'You know I would get down on my knee if I could,' he says with a smile as he takes my hand again. 'I used to lie awake at night, when we were together, and I'd imagine this moment, but I never imagined it like this. Please forgive me for doing this here.'

'Chris, please—'

'Just hear me out,' he responds quickly as he rubs his thumb over the top of my hand. He's nervous. 'Since the day we met, when you insisted you weren't going to fuck me, you've captivated me.' I chuckle, but his smile disappears as he continues. 'The year we spent apart was the worst year of my life. The years we were together were the best. Your face and your words are entangled in every one of my happiest memories. You're a part of me that I can't let go. I refuse to let go. I'm not myself without you.' His eyes are full of such intensity and pain, but there's also a dim spark of hope. 'We don't have to get married anytime soon. We can wait until you graduate or longer, if that's what you want. I just want you to be mine and I want you to know that I'll always be here for you, to love you and to take care of you. I want to sing you to sleep every night and wake up with you in my arms every morning.' He pulls my hand up and lays a soft kiss on my ring finger. 'Claire Brooklyn Nixon, will you marry me?'

I close my eyes and draw in a long breath that smells like the ocean and Chris. He said my face and words are entangled in all his happiest memories, but my happiest memories are filled with everything from his face and words to his scent and the comforting sense of home. If this past week with Chris has taught me anything, it's that Chris and I have an unshakeable bond. Even if we break up, we will always share the kind of love that I'm not sure I'll ever find again without him.

I bite my lip as I open my eyes and the tears come again. 'You and I will always share something untouchable. And I'll never stop loving you and Jackie. You both gave me the greatest gifts I've ever received, a home and a family. I love you and I want you to be in my life forever, but I can't marry you. I can't be with anyone right now.'

The disappointment in his eyes kills me. I step forward and carefully wrap my arms around his shoulders so I don't put any more weight on his leg. He wraps his arms around me and squeezes me tightly. His heart beats against mine and I sigh as I realize this is my favorite thing about Chris: how relaxed I feel when I'm in his arms.

His hands slide over my back and under my jacket as he holds me, but he never attempts to kiss me. We hold onto each other for a while, though it's not long enough. It's never long enough. When I pull away, I'm surprised to see a hint of a smile on his face.

'Are you happy to be getting rid of me, or something?' I ask.

He shakes his head slightly. 'Are you spending the night with Cora or are you driving back?'

'I have to drive back. I can't be here.'

'Do you mind if I ride with you?'

'Of course I don't mind.'

He grabs the ring box on top of the car and opens the car door to tell Tristan he's going back with me. The two-hour drive back to Raleigh is spent mostly listening to Chris talk about music while I dodge questions about school. I tell him about the conversation I had with Jackie and he laughs.

'I'm not surprised,' he says. 'When I broke the news to her that you weren't coming for the weekend, she and Tristan had a good laugh pretending it was because of my gimpy leg. Then she told me very seriously that I need to give you some space.'

'And your idea of giving me space is asking me to marry you?'

'Hey, go easy on me. My high-school sweetheart just rejected my marriage proposal.'

'High-school sweetheart? You dropped out junior year. We went to the same high school for, like, three weeks.'

'Worst three weeks of my life. Why do you think I quit?'

I shove his arm and the car swerves a little to the right.

'Hey, watch the road,' he warns me. We ride together in silence for a while before he speaks again. 'I didn't want to tell you this earlier, but the open adoption is off. They don't want anything to do with us.'

My body floods with adrenaline and I grip the steering wheel as I try to formulate a response. 'When did you find out?'

'I found out yesterday, but I wanted to wait until we were together to tell you. I'm sorry. I feel like I failed you.'

My hands shake as I realize that the one thing I feared the most when Chris told me he was going to pursue an open adoption has come true. I never got to see or hold my daughter.

'You're not sorry. You got to hold her hand.'

'You think holding her hand was enough?'

'I didn't even get to touch her and now she's gone! Forever!'

'I tried my fucking best! I went so far as to offer them money just so you could have one more opportunity to see her before they made up their minds, but they want nothing to do with us.'

'You offered them money? No wonder they backed out, with you flashing your money all over the place. They don't want your money and they sure as hell don't want your fame. What do you think they pictured in their mind? What do you think they thought would happen years from now when Abigail figured out who you are? You scared them off. They can't compete with a fucking rock star.'

My heart is racing as I spit out these vile accusations that I only half believe, but I feel the need to hurt someone right now. I want him to feel just a fraction of the pain I'm feeling.

I yank the locket off my neck and roll down the window so I can toss it out. I look over my shoulder at the road behind us. The locket glints in the faint glow of my taillights and time seems to stop as I say a silent prayer for this heartache to end soon. I want to wake up in a time and place where my mother is still alive and she is perfectly healthy and happy. I want to live without the fear that every decision I make will hurt everyone I love. I want to be the person who believes that love and time are truly enough to heal a broken heart.

I want to die.

'Claire, watch out!'

Chapter Forty-Two

Claire

I turn forward to face the road just as Chris grabs the steering wheel. The car swerves to the right as he attempts to stop us from crashing into the center divider. I grab the wheel as I slam on the brakes.

The tires squeal as the car spins around one full revolution and comes to a stop in the middle of two lanes. My hands shake as I grip the steering wheel. The car is surrounded in smoke and Chris is saying something, but I can't hear him over the thump of my heartbeat.

I'm hyperventilating. Each breath comes shorter and more painful than the last. Chris yanks the keys out of the ignition and I finally hear him.

'Climb in the back. I'll drive. Claire, climb in the back.'

I scramble over the console and into the backseat. I'm on my hands and knees, my head hanging forward, as I attempt to catch my breath. I don't know what's going on, but suddenly Chris is in the driver's seat and the car is moving again. Then it stops again and I see the faint red of my hazard lights flashing.

'Do I need to call an ambulance?' he says.

I turn my head to the side to look at him. My chest is on fire, but I cough a few times and the air slowly returns to my lungs.

'No. I'm fine.' I collapse and I must appear as if I'm praying or meditating, with my face buried in my knees and my arms splayed out in front of me.

'Are you sure?'

'Yes.' I sit up on my knees and look out the window. Chris pulled the car onto the shoulder, with a broken leg. 'Get out of there. I'm driving.'

He stares at me, but he doesn't move. 'I'm sorry. I don't know what else to say. You're right. They probably would have agreed to an open adoption if it weren't for me.'

'It's not your fault. And none of this would have happened if it weren't for me keeping the pregnancy from you. My sins will always outweigh yours.'

'I can still try, if you want me to. You never know, they may change their minds if they see I'm not touring anymore.'

'No. And you have to go to L.A., Chris. Don't stay here for me.'

He looks annoyed by me telling him what to do. 'I'm not going to L.A.' He pauses for a moment, his mind obviously far away from the inside of this car. 'Thanks for thinking of me. Thank you for thinking of me last year when you pushed me to go to L.A. But I'm not doing it. I'll hate myself if I leave you again.'

I nod and he finally gets out of the car and back into the passenger seat. I pull up in front of the house an hour later and we sit in silence for a few minutes. I don't know what he's thinking, but I'm thinking of how lucky and cursed I am to have Chris and Adam competing for my heart. And what a truly crushed heart it is. I try not to think of Abigail so I don't cry again, but trying to not think of something is like trying to not fall after you've already jumped.

I wipe the tears on the sleeve of my jacket and Chris pulls off his T-shirt for me to use instead. 'Here,' he says as he stuffs it into my lap. 'You can give it back to me later.' He leans over and lays a soft kiss on my cheekbone. 'Goodnight, babe.'

By the time I get back to the dorm, Chris's shirt is pretty soaked and I'm extremely parched. When I get to the entrance at Spencer Hall, I reach into my jacket pocket to retrieve my cardkey and my fingers bump into the ring – but it feels strange.

I feel around a little and realize there are two rings in my pocket. I pull them out and shake my head. Chris must have slipped the ring into my pocket when we were hugging. That's why he was smiling when he pulled away. That sneaky little . . .

I sigh as I swipe my cardkey and make my way up

to the third floor. When I enter the dorm, Senia is sitting on her bed with her headphones on and her laptop open in front of her. She sees me and looks a bit confused, then frightened.

She tears the headphones out of her ears and sits up straight. 'Why are you back?'

'I can't believe you were in on it, tricking me into going to see Adam,' I say with a smile so she knows I'm not truly angry with her.

She grins sheepishly. 'I'm sorry, but I thought I was doing the right thing. You're not staying with Chris, are you?'

'Really? You used to *love* Chris. Now you're trying to sabotage our relationship?'

'I loved Chris until he left you.' She closes her laptop and pouts for a moment. 'Don't get me wrong, Chris is hot and he's got money coming out of his ears and he wants to take care of you and be there for you . . . *now*. Where was he when you needed him most?'

I take a seat at the desk and shrug. 'Yeah, well, the same could be said about Adam. He broke up with me the same day I had a meltdown in the hospital. I wouldn't exactly call that *being there for me*.'

'Yeah, but I'll bet Adam wasn't in Hawaii fucking a bunch of groupies. And he came back for you just a few weeks later. He didn't wait a whole fucking year.'

I pull the two rings out of my pocket and hold my hand out in front of me for Senia to see. Her eyes widen and she jumps off the bed.

'What the fuck is that? *Two* rings?'

She snatches the rings out of my hand and holds them both up between her thumb and index finger. She shakes the ring with the bigger diamond. 'Chris?' I nod and her jaw drops. 'You got two proposals in one night?'

'No. Adam didn't propose to me. He gave me a promise ring.'

Senia looks relieved. 'See? Adam is thinking of what's best for you. You can't get married.'

I glare at her. 'Chris doesn't expect me to get married anytime soon.'

She sighs as she hands the rings back. 'Whatever. I take it you have both rings because you still haven't chosen. And I know it's none of my business, but you know I'll support you whatever decision you make. I like Chris. I'm just a little pissed at him.'

I place the rings on top of the desk and notice an envelope addressed to me sitting on top of a pile of mail. My name and address are spelled out in precise handwriting with a return address sticker from Phillip E. Lungren in Petaluma, California.

'What's this?' I ask, holding up the envelope.

Senia shrugs as she goes back to bed. 'It came in the mail today.'

I slide my finger under the flap and slide out a folded piece of lined paper. Inside, I find the same neat handwriting and a short letter.

Claire,

You may not recognize my name. Your mother did a good job of protecting you from her past. Henry Wilkins at Northstar Bank contacted me recently. He informed me that you refused the trust fund your mother set up for you before her death. I hope you will reconsider your position on this, as that money is rightfully yours.

I also hope you can find it in your heart to forgive me for my transgressions and that you won't hold my past against your half-sister. Nichelle just turned seventeen last week and she's very eager to meet you.

I hope this letter finds you well.

Your father,

Phil

Read on for exclusive, never-seen-before material from Cassia Leo and more information about the *New York Times'* bestselling author's irresistible books . . .

Deleted Scene

Chris Knight's POV

I end the call with Claire then lean my guitar against the wall and set my phone on the concrete step next to me. I'm so angry I could flip over the fucking Porsche in this garage. If it weren't for this damn broken leg.

'Fuck!' I shout, grabbing the phone off the step and hurling it at the empty space where my motorcycle once stood. The phone hits the far wall of the garage and explodes into a million shards of plastic and silicone. 'Fuck this fucking leg.'

I stand up on my cast and grit my teeth against the pain as I enter the house. The adrenaline flooding my veins provides a slight buffer for the pain as I half-climb and half-hop up the stairs to retrieve a small blue box from the top drawer of my dresser. I tuck it into my pocket then head back downstairs. Tristan sits in the living room looking perplexed as he watches me gritting my teeth and struggling not to limp across the

339

wood floor then disappearing into the kitchen without my crutches. In the kitchen, I yank my car keys off the hook and swiftly turn around.

'What the fuck are you doing?' he asks as I walk back toward the door leading into the garage.

'I can't let this stop me. I have to do something.' I push the door open and take the first step down.

I glance at the one crutch I left propped against the steps and, reluctantly, take it under my arm so I can make my way to the Porsche. Tristan bursts into the garage and laughs when he sees me approaching the driver's side door.

'Are you fucking kidding me? You're not driving with a broken leg. Give me the fucking keys.'

I really don't want to ask Tristan to help me with this; he never understands the lengths I go to for Claire. But he's right. I can't risk crashing my Porsche. I don't have time for a car accident.

I slap the keys into the palm of his hand and make my way around the back of the car to the passenger side. Once we're inside, Tristan hits the button on the remote to open the garage door and we're out on the main road in seconds.

'Where the fuck are we going?'

'To see Claire.'

'I know that, but where the fuck is she?'

I clench my jaw as I imagine Claire in *his* apartment doing God knows what because she's too fucking confused to know better. And this piece of shit is taking advantage of her confusion instead of leaving her alone. She was so fucking happy when she called me between classes this afternoon. Now she's a fucking wreck again. I knew it was a bad idea for her to go back to that apartment building so soon.

'Just drive and I'll tell you how to get there.'

Tristan is quiet until he pulls the car onto the highway and increases his speed beyond what any reasonable person would allow. 'Why are you doing this? Just let her go. She's obviously moved on or too fucked up to know what she wants.'

'Don't talk about her like that or I'll throw you out of this fucking car.'

Tristan has never really gotten along with Claire. And she made no secret of the fact that she only tolerated him because she loved me. Tristan probably feels the same way about Claire, though he's never really talked about her other than to accuse me of being whipped or to tell me I need to get over her. He's the one who pressured me into getting the tattoo of her name on my back covered up when I was too drunk and heartbroken to refuse. I can't imagine what he'd think of Claire if he knew the things she did while we were on tour. He doesn't know about Abigail yet.

And Claire doesn't know about the news I got about Abigail today. I need to get to her.

Tristan lets out a huge sigh. 'Are you going there to talk some sense into her or what?'

My chest tightens with anxiety as I contemplate

this question. 'I'm . . . I'm gonna propose to her.'

'Are you serious?'

'Dead fucking serious. I should have done it years ago, then none of this shit would have happened.'

'You really think that's what you need to do, right now?' he insists. 'I mean, come on. She's fucking some other guy and—'

'She's not fucking another guy! She's – she got blindsided, okay? I left her alone then she got pregnant and—'

'She's *pregnant*?'

'No, she's not pregnant. She's . . .' I stare out the passenger window so I don't have to look at Tristan. I may put on a carefree attitude, but I do care what my best friend thinks about my first and only love. I don't know if Claire and Tristan will ever be friends. All I know is that, if it came down to it and I had to choose, Tristan knows I'll always choose Claire. And that's probably one of the main reasons he doesn't support my getting back together with her. 'She's not pregnant, but she was . . . while we were on tour. She found out after I left for L.A. Anyway, I don't want to get into it, but she made some tough decisions that we're both paying for right now. I need to go to her. So, for fuck's sake, just drive.'

With Tristan behind the wheel, and the power of my Porsche humming around us, we're able to cut the two-hour drive to Wrightsville Beach down to ninety minutes. I spend the entire ride there going over all the things I could have done or should have done differently with Claire. Then it finally dawns on me: Claire came back to me. She was just caught off-guard today. She'll come back to me again. I'm more certain of that than I am of my own existence.

By the time we pull into the parking lot of the tiny apartment building on Lumina, I'm a little more relaxed and ready to speak the words I've wanted to say to Claire ever since I bought this ring shortly after we broke up last year. Tristan pulls the car as close as he can get to the apartment and the headlights illuminate Claire as she descends the steps. The warm white glow of the headlights makes her squint her eyes and I move swiftly to exit the car.

'Good luck, man,' Tristan blurts out, and I nod as I throw the door open and grab the top of the car door to pull myself up.

Claire's eyes widen when she sees me and she rushes to my side. 'Where are your crutches?'

I gaze into her eyes and my confidence ebbs a little as I anticipate her reaction to my proposal. I just have to keep reminding myself: *She's still mine. She's still mine.*

I keep my eyes locked on hers as I grab her hand. 'You're my crutch.'

The Story behind the Playlist

Chapter 3
Clarity

I think this might be the perfect song for the entire *Shattered Hearts* series. It perfectly sums up Claire's feelings about multiple people in this series.

Chapter 4
Pieces

The mood and lyrics of this song are such a great representation of Chris's feelings while he's in London.

Chapter 6
Forget Me

This captures the anxiety and sadness Claire feels when she comes home to Jackie's house for the first time in so many months. It also shows her struggle with the need to be both remembered and forgotten by the Knights.

Chapter 7

Break Even

This song perfectly portrays Chris's feelings about Claire and her new relationship with Adam.

Chapter 8

Dazed and Confused

This song totally suits Adam in this chapter. In *Relentless*, Adam wants to leave Claire 'dazed and confused'. In this song, it's the other way around. He finds everything about her intoxicating.

Chapter 11

Stay

The angst and resistance in Claire's goodbye to Adam is perfectly captured in this song.

Chapter 12

Featherstone

This is a great depiction of Chris's feelings about Claire. He feels she left home and got lost. 'You live like your love wasn't meant for mine.'

Chapter 13

Comfortable

This song is just a great representation of an awesome guitarist playing a song live, which happens to be about losing his first love. I think it's a great song to capture Chris's feelings about Claire being on the side of the stage with him at his jam session.

Gimme Shelter

Chris and his idol, Neil Hardaway, play this to get warmed up for the show.

Chapter 14

Arms

This reflects how Claire feels about Chris after she admits the extent of her despair after giving birth to Abigail and she and Chris embrace.

Chapter 18

Hiding My Heart

Claire's feelings about Adam and his absence are beautifully depicted in this remake of one of my favorite Brandi Carlile songs.

Chapter 21

Love Like This

This is also one of my favorite songs of all time. It is gut-wrenching and so perfectly describes Adam's feelings when he lets Claire go. 'Was it my mistake? / Or maybe it was just as simple as a change in your heart.'

Chapter 22

Ghost

Claire's feelings about losing both Chris and Adam are depicted so well in this track. This is a low point for her in the series and she feels as if she may be losing herself, too.

Chapter 32

Ho Hey

This is one of those infectious tunes, which are so difficult to get out of your head once you've listened to them. The lyrics just happen to be a near-perfect depiction of Chris's feeling that he and Claire belong together.

Chapter 33

Bloom

This is the song Chris sings to Claire when they make love for the first time since the day they broke up.

Chapter 37

Warning Sign

This song depicts Adam's sentiment when he invites Claire into his apartment after surprising her at Cora's. He's laying his soul bare and the lyrics and tone of this song feel so appropriate.

Chapter 39

More Than This

'I love you more than this' is something Chris says to Claire when they encounter something that seems insurmountable. This song totally fits with the moment Chris realizes Claire has strayed.

Chapter 41

Turning Page

This is such a beautiful song, which flawlessly portrays Chris's realization that he wants to spend the rest of his life with Claire. It's perfect for when he proposes to her. 'Nothing makes me stronger than your fragile heart.'

Chapter 42

The Light

This is how Claire feels at the end of the novel, though it's not clear whether it's Adam or Chris who makes her feel this way.

Listen to the *Pieces of You* playlist – just visit Cassia's website and follow the links to YouTube.

In Conversation with Cassia Leo

Who is your favorite character in the Shattered Hearts series?
Ooh, this is a tough one. I don't like to play favorites, but I'm going to have to say Chris. He was so utterly betrayed yet he still found it in his heart to forgive, and I admire that. I don't know if I could have done the same thing in his place. But I believe his confidence and his determination were huge factors in his ability to forgive. He knew what he wanted (Claire) and he knew that the only way to get her back was to forgive her. I admire his tenacity and compassion. Also, being a songwriter, he has a way with words that I find charming. And he's pretty darn sexy, too.

Where do the ideas for your characters come from?
My characters are inspired mostly by real people I've encountered in my life. Bits and pieces of real life always make it into my books. I believe strongly in the old adage 'write what you know.'

Sweet or savoury – what's your snack of choice?
I have a thing for sour candy. Sour gummy worms and Sour Patch Kids are some of my favorites.

If you could live anywhere in the world where would it be and why?

Northern California. I don't think there is any place better to live in than California, but Northern California has better weather than Southern California, in my opinion. I like sunny weather, but I don't like having to run my air conditioning all year round.

If a film was to be made of your books, who would you cast in the lead roles?

I'm a fan of Teresa Palmer for Claire and Alex Pettyfer for Adam. I've had trouble finding the perfect person to play Chris, though. Suggestions are welcome.

How long does it take you to write a novel?

It depends on what I have going on at the moment. If I'm traveling a lot, it takes me longer than when I'm not traveling. I wrote and edited *Relentless* in four weeks. *Abandon* is the same length as *Relentless*, but it took about ten weeks to write because I was traveling all over the country for book signings.

Who is your role model?

Markus Zusak. I'd love to one day write as beautifully as he does. I'd love to write a story as heartbreaking and uplifting as *The Book Thief*.

What was your favorite subject at school/college?

Besides literature and writing, I'd have to say biology. My obsession with books as a child was not limited to fiction. I also read various medical encyclopedias as a child. I know, it's weird. But the human body fascinates me.